COMING HOME

WENDY SMITH

Edited by LAUREN MCKELLAR

Cover design by SPRINKLES ON TOP STUDIOS

Photography by CJC PHOTOGRAPHY

BOOK ONE IN THE COPPER CREEK SERIES

❊ Created with Vellum

FOREWORD

I originally intended to publish this book in 2015. Instead, I got distracted by another story that urgently wanted to be written (In a Lifetime as Ariadne Wayne) and Coming Home was delayed until 2016.

My father died in March of this year.

It's to my eternal regret that he didn't live to see this book in print, but I think the delay has also meant that this is a better book than it would have been a year ago.

My dad was a Vietnam Veteran who had a lifetime of illness as a direct result of war. I knew at the start that Adam would be a veteran and have issues. They might not be so evident in this first book as I wanted this to be primarily about his return to town, but as the series continues, his road will continue to be rocky and his years away will be revealed.

As always, love prevails. Lily has her own demons to conquer. Together they're stronger.

This isn't a military romance, but I'm so grateful for my

cover designer, Sarah, who picked up on what I wanted and added those little dog tags to the book title.

Those are for you, Dad. B27928 Staff Sergeant Arthur G Frederikson of the 161st Battery, Royal New Zealand Artillery. Lest we forget.

I also want to say a huge thank you to my amazing editor, Lauren McKellar. This is our 10th book together and I would not be able to do this without her.

And to Christopher John and BT Urruela, the photo fits the cover in so many ways. Thank you so much for being amazing.

GLOSSARY

There are a few Kiwi words in this book, so I thought it worthwhile including a glossary

Chilly Bin - Insulated box to keep food or drink cool
Number eight wire mentality - The ability to improvise to solve a problem.
Kia ora - Māori for 'hello'
Ka pai - Māori for 'good'
Boot - Trunk of car
Bonnet - Hood of car
Morepork - Also known as Ruru. Small brown owl.
Wheel Brace - Tyre Lever
Torch - Flashlight
Togs - Swimwear
Cordial - fruit flavoured drink
Mobile - Cell Phone

Swanndri - Wool bush shirt
Ute - Utility vehicle

Please note: if there are any other words you stumble on, don't hesitate to track me down online and ask.

1

LILY

Today is going to be the happiest day of my life. My wedding day.

I wake and smile to myself, but something's not quite right. The air is chilly and this doesn't smell like my bedroom. My eyes are heavy, and I struggle to open them. I blink, Mum's built in work desks coming into focus. *Mum's sewing room?*

I turn my head. I'm on a mattress on the floor, and her sewing gear is gone. There are still the cupboards she stored her fabric in, emptied with the doors wide open, and the table and machine have been moved.

A sharp pain tears through my left leg, and my back aches from the awkward angle I've been lying. I try and push myself up on my elbows to take a look, but my head swims and the whole thing is way too much effort. What the hell is going on?

It takes a lot of effort, but I manage to get myself up a

little. Enough to push back the blanket and spot the large bruise coming up on my calf. What happened last night, and why don't I know how I ended up down here? I have no idea what the time is, but I'm marrying Adam today.

Panic rises in me as I struggle to stay upright, and I let myself sink down into the mattress again.

The answers come in the form of my mother. The handle rattles as she opens the door, and her heels click as she walks down the wooden stairs.

"You're awake, sleepyhead," she says.

"What the hell is going on?"

She gets onto her knees beside the mattress and leans over, kissing me on the forehead. "I'm taking care of you. I brought you breakfast."

"Why am I down here?"

Mum sighs. "I told you. I'm taking care of you."

"I'm not sick. I've got to get ready. What's the time? I have to be at the courthouse by ten."

As she shakes her head, her eyes so sad, I know I'm in big trouble. "Shhh."

"Mum?"

"I have to protect you Lily. That boy's just going to break your heart."

A sob breaks from me, hot tears spilling down my cheeks. "What have you done?"

She smiles, and I know she truly believes the words that come out of her mouth next. "I'm keeping you safe. I won't have you go through what I did. He'll get you pregnant and then he'll leave, and you'll struggle the rest of your life. Or, you stay here with me."

"Adam's not like that." I'm so weak, I can barely protest.

What did she give me? She's been on so many different drugs over the years, it could be anything.

Bile rises in my throat. I push to stand up, but I'm so weak my hand barely moves me. Inside, I rage to escape but my body fails and my fury only grows. Everything's foggy and so many thoughts pass through my mind as I'm unable to act on them.

Mum ... no ...

Adam.

———

I START COUNTING THE DAYS, but it's hard when you have no way of keeping record.

When the power gets cut, I know it's been at least six weeks. In the past, Mum's missed a couple of bills before it's got to that stage.

The lighting's usually pretty good in the basement. Mum had this place refitted several years ago when she turned it into her sewing room. And I'm thankful there's a toilet with handbasin in the corner.

Now there's nothing, and I lie in the dark and listen to my heart beating for company.

A handful of times a day I get to the bathroom and back, but I always end up back in the same place. There's nothing else to sit on.

Adam knows I'm gone—he must. Does he not wonder where I am? Did he come looking for me? Or has he deserted me just like Mum said he would?

The odds had always been against us. His mother took an instant dislike to me, no doubt buying into the rumours about Mum. For Mum's part, she hasn't done too badly these past years until now. Apart from the mending work she does, she's kept to herself. It helped a lot when she started getting a few jobs from that weird commune place up on McKenzie's Mountain.

It isn't really a mountain, more like a hilly area up in the bush. Commune or cult, I don't know, but it's somewhere where they all dress the same and act weird. Whatever. It's funny the random things that pop into your mind when you have nowhere to go and no way to get anywhere.

It's Adam that weighs on my mind the most. A few weeks ago he loved me more than anything else on the planet. At least that was what he said. Where is he now?

Instead of being Mrs Adam Campbell, I'm sitting or lying around, and no one's found me. I thought this would be the first place anyone would come looking, that Mum's reputation would be enough for someone to check. She has a history of being a little eccentric, and thanks to the open-mouth policy that some people in Copper Creek practice, people know she's on a variety of medications … and yet, nothing. No knocks on the door. Only the occasional sound of her heels on the stairs as she brings me food.

Adam …

When I get out of here, I'll ask him for answers, ask why he's abandoned me. My mind twists everything, including the love I bore him. My heart still belongs to him, but did his ever belong to me?

Doubt is demoralising.

Being demoralised is scary.

It's the kind of thing that can kill you in this situation. That overwhelming feeling that there is no hope.

I close my eyes and think about the dark house above.

Mum wouldn't disconnect the power deliberately. Without fail she watches her soap operas, and how's she going to catch her daily dose of drama with no power?

I pray she gets it back before she decides to light the house with candles. No one knows I'm here if anything goes wrong. So simple and yet so deadly.

This is a nightmare I can't wake up from.

It's the dark that haunts my dreams.

2

ADAM

Twelve years later

I slug back another mouthful of whiskey.

Maybe the silky amber liquid will help me forget the expression on Jenna's face as I tore her heart to shreds. All because I couldn't let go of the past. Deep down, I knew I could never love her the way I'd loved Lily.

Her name was a curse on my lips, the one who got away. Twelve years ago, I'd left the town where she'd broken my heart. I'd gone back to the US, stayed with family friends before joining the military and travelling the world. I'd seen things I'll spend the rest of my life trying to forget.

For such a short while, I'd seen Jenna as the way forward. My safe harbour. She'd been the one who stood by me when I left the army, broken and tired, wanting to drink myself into oblivion. Jenna had brought me back from the brink.

I'm such an arsehole.

It wasn't until I stood in the jeweller's store choosing an engagement ring that I realised I didn't want this. I can't give her all of my heart, give her all she deserves. She needs a man who will love her completely and unconditionally. I can give her neither.

Instead of proposing, I came home and told her it was over.

Two days later, I'm still drinking my sorrows away.

The key to avoiding the inevitable hangover that will follow this binge is to keep drinking. Drink until the pain that consumes me fades away. Even when it isn't at the forefront of my thoughts, there is still some small part of me that nags, feeding the darkness inside.

Buried deep is the distant memory of true happiness, but sometimes I have doubts about whether that's a memory, or an illusion.

My eyes heavy, I lie down on the couch and drop the empty bottle to the floor.

That's the last thing I remember as sleep claims me. The phone rings in the distance, but it's too far away to care about. My head will be pounding in the morning, but I don't care about that either. All that matters is killing the pain.

I don't know if it will ever go away.

———

I WAKE, my head thumping in a rhythm that's hard to cope with and unwanted. I groan as I open my eyes, only to slam them shut again as the morning sun streams through the window.

It's the last thing anyone with a hangover needs.

I sit up with my eyes still closed and stand, opening them a tiny amount as I make my way to the blinds. I've stumbled around this apartment in the dark before; I know every inch of it. This has been my retreat these past few years, the place that comes closest to being called home. I never thought of myself as someone who would be a homeowner, but when it came up cheap, I leapt at the chance with help from Mum and Dad. It's only gone up in value the last few years, one of the few constants in my life. Although, that's been by my choice.

As I pull the blinds closed, I sigh. *Should have had that glass of water. Must be coffee time again.*

Coffee, a shower, and some more sleep. That'll help.

Remnants of Jenna are everywhere. She hadn't moved in that long ago. Half her things were still in boxes, so it hadn't taken long for her to pack and leave.

I tug open the dishwasher to find a clean cup. Jenna's tea mug sits in the top shelf, a reminder of her with that stupid horoscope stuff on the side. She would read that crap every morning out of the newspaper, sometimes planning her day around it. I'd thought that was a little nuts, but I had no doubt there were things she didn't like about me either.

The tea that she drank still sits in the cupboard. It's no favourite of mine, and I throw the box of tea bags and her mug in the bin and go back to the dishwasher for another cup. A clean break has to be exactly that. No reminders of her can exist.

I flick on the kettle and wait for the water to boil.

This whole thing is stupid, pining after Lily, a girl who'd made her feelings clear a long time ago. One day she was so in love with me, and I was planning out our life together.

The next day she'd run, not showing up for our wedding and leaving me broken and humiliated. Maybe it was for the best that I hadn't seen her again, but I still had a million questions about why she'd changed her mind.

The kettle switches off as it hits the right temperature, and as I lift it to add the hot water to my coffee, the blinking red light on the answering machine catches my eye. I pour the water and place the kettle back down before pressing the button.

"Adam, it's James. I hope this is the right number. There are a quite a few Adam S Campbells in the phone directory. If you're the Adam Campbell from Copper Creek, please call me on this number. Don't call home. Mum'll just get upset."

I stare at the phone as he leaves the number. That has to be my baby brother James. I haven't seen him since he was six. The only person I've spoken to in years has been my mother. Cutting contact had meant just that. I'd left and never looked back. For a heartbroken eighteen-year-old, it had seemed the safest thing to do.

But right now, I still need coffee, and then I'll replay the message to get the number James left.

What the hell can be so important?

————

"James?"

The guy on the other end of the phone exhales loudly. Is it relief? "Adam. Is that my brother Adam?"

"How many people did you call trying to find me?" For the first time in days, I smile. If James had to resort to the phone book, it couldn't have been that easy to track me down.

"Thirty maybe? That was after I tried stalking you on Facebook."

I laugh, picturing him dialling person after person. How many Adam Campbells now have random voicemails? "I'm not on Facebook. Fuck that. Why didn't you just ask Mum?"

James sighs, and I hear the exasperation in his voice. "I did that ages ago. She says she doesn't have a current number for you and that you don't want to hear from any of us anyway. I managed to find out what town you were in by eavesdropping. Otherwise I'd have been dialling for months."

I grimace. I guess that's the price you pay for becoming the black sheep of the family. To be there one day and gone the next. My last face-to-face contact with my brothers was the night after I'd been jilted by Lily, and most of that I'd spent in my bedroom, hiding from the world.

Once I started running, I didn't stop. It's easier to avoid finding answers than face the past. Once I lost the girl I loved, there was no point in sticking around.

"So, why track me down now?"

"Mum has cancer."

The words hit me like a bucket of cold water. Mum is frustrating—shit, she is *the* most frustrating person I know, and that's huge considering all the guys I've served with in the military. Because of that, my contact with her has always been sporadic at best as I hid from the pain of the past. When was the last time I spoke to her?

"What?" It's not that I haven't heard him, just can't believe it.

"Breast cancer."

Shit. This was one of the few things I thought serious enough to take me home. All other personal feelings would have to be put aside to focus on her. She might have bugged the hell out of all of us with her heavy-handed parenting, but she was always the driving force behind the family. I'd go so far as to call her a force of nature. She'd ruled her roost with an iron fist, or at least she had until Corey and I grew old enough to rebel.

Corey was the start of it, getting in trouble, running with the wrong crowd. In an attempt to remove him from the bad influences, Dad had changed jobs and we'd moved to Copper Creek. Dad took over management of the nearby hydroelectric power station, and we'd ended up in a place Corey nicknamed 'Bumfuck, Nowhere'.

The closest major city was a hundred and fifty kilometres away, but for us, it might as well have been a million. I had hated it, but forgot my resentment as soon as I spotted Lily in school. Even at fourteen I knew I wanted to spend my life with her. What a mess that had turned out to be.

Lost in thought, I almost forget that James is on the other end of the line, and I swallow. "I … I'm sorry to hear that."

"I thought you should know."

I close my eyes. I've been away for twelve long years. Is this a sign to lead me home?

"Mum doesn't want any fuss. She's had surgery, and she's resting up at the moment. Well, when I say resting up, you know what she's like."

"Being a pain in the butt?"

"She doesn't have to be sick to be that."

Despite myself, I laugh. James's got the same sense of humour as the rest of us, and for the first time in forever I have pangs of homesickness. Not just because of the always lingering feeling that I have unresolved business in Copper Creek, but because I miss my family. I haven't spoken to most of them for years. At first I was travelling, then busy after I enlisted, and by then my younger brothers—except for James—had left home.

"Thanks for letting me know."

There's silence for a moment before he says, "Um, so will you come home?"

I'm already debating the answer in my head. "I'll have to see what I can work out."

Truth is, there's nothing to keep me here.

Maybe it's time to go.

3

ADAM

Three weeks later

It's been a long time since I traversed this road. When I left, Dad drove me all the way to Auckland Airport, and the flight that took me to the States. I've long since left the main highway, and now the road twists and winds on its way to Copper Creek. I take it slow, the corners unfamiliar after all this time.

Nothing much has changed. Trees line the road, and in between them I spot sheep in the paddocks, with the occasional cow thrown in for good measure.

The radio hisses with static. I lost the signal a while ago, and I press random buttons to find the one that searches for another station.

As the sound of "The Green, Green Grass of Home" fills the car, I laugh. I can guess the source—the crackle of the vinyl album gives it away. The local radio station's run out of

13

the caravan park near the cove by George Matheson. The old guy must be in his seventies by now at least. Some things never change.

It's easy to get lost in memories, but I shake it off as I draw closer.

I wonder how much has changed.

Closing in on the town, my homesickness grows. I've never completely forgotten, but I've managed to get on with my life to a certain extent.

Deep down, I've never been able to bear the thought of Lily being with anyone else, but that is a stupid, unrealistic way to think. Especially when she is the reason for me leaving in the first place.

Now it is time to face that fear. If I want to regain my relationship with my family, this is what I have to go through —the possibility of seeing the woman I once thought of as the love of my life with another man.

———

THE FOLIAGE around the old house has grown substantially in the years I've been gone. It's beautiful, as if the house is hiding in the bush with just the lawns and garden around it immaculate. This really is heaven on earth, and I feel home for the first time in what feels like forever looking at the house where I'd spent four short years.

Bellbirds and Tuis are everywhere, singing songs I haven't heard in so long. I slow to take in the scenery as I make my way down the long driveway.

Stopping outside the gate, I get out of the car and push through into the yard until I reach the back door. It's been so long. Do I knock, or just enter? I close my eyes at the memory of all the times I've run in and out of this door. Usually on my way to Lily's.

Bang.

Even the distant sound of a shotgun makes me freeze. When I first decided to leave the army, Jenna was there, teaching me what I thought were her crackpot calming techniques. They turned out to be more useful than I imagined. I take deep breaths, breathing out through my mouth to get through the moment.

I open my eyes, twist the door handle, and enter.

"Hello?" I call, walking through the kitchen and into the living room.

Nothing's changed. The polished wooden china cabinets are still along one wall, full of trophies, ornaments, and all the precious things Mum's collected over the years.

The carpet and wallpaper still match, the dull beige colour that never seems to fade. The lounge suite's new, but everything else looks as it did when I left.

Mum lies on the couch, her eyes closed. I smile watching her, even though I'm still pained over why she didn't call me herself. Dad didn't call either. The last time I spoke to her was only a few months ago, when I was thinking of proposing to Jenna. This isn't a small thing—it's huge. I've stayed away for birthdays, Christmases, and other events over the years, but this is different. She has a life-threatening illness and never said a word.

I sit on a chair opposite the couch, cracking a grin as James walks in the door. His jaw drops at the sight of me, and I stand again, embracing him when he makes his way to me. He's a sight for sore eyes. Last time I saw him, he was six, with the same cheeky grin we all had as kids. Seeing him is so good.

"I didn't know if you'd come," he whispers.

"Try to keep me away. Look at you, all grown up."

He laughs, his smile vanishing as he looks down at our sleeping mother.

"Let's go out to the deck, catch up there."

He nods. I can't get over him. He must be six-foot-some-thing-or-other, just like the rest of us. Pride leaps from my chest as I follow him.

James grabs a bottle of juice and a couple of glasses on the way out, and we take a seat on resin deck chairs sheltered from the blazing sun by a big umbrella.

"This is the life," I say, leaning back in my chair.

He laughs. "I have so many questions I want to ask. We barely know each other. It's good to see you."

"I can't believe Mum and Dad didn't tell me themselves. Sometimes I get the feeling they don't want me coming back."

James twists his mouth and shrugs. "Sometimes they act weird. Maybe it's this whole cancer thing. Even though you've never come back for anything else, I thought you would at least want to know."

"I appreciate it more than I can tell you. Your timing was perfect."

My little brother cocks his head and looks at me curiously.

"James, can you go to the store and get some milk? We're about to run out." Mum's voice comes from the house, and I stand, turning towards the sound. She pushes open the screen door, the flush in her cheeks draining as she looks at me. "Adam?"

She chokes down a sob, taking a step toward me, but I make up the distance, pulling her into my arms. Her eyes shine as she takes me in, raising her fingers to my beard.

"It's so good to see you, but what are you doing here? Aren't you supposed to be in some foreign country doing something important?"

I grin. "I am doing something important. I came to see you."

She frowns. "Why?"

"Why do you think? James tracked me down. He thought you might have something to tell me."

She shakes her head. "It's nothing. Not worth you coming all the way here for. I know you have a busy life."

I let her go. "I'm beginning to think you don't want me here."

"I'm just surprised you came. I thought after all these years there wasn't anything in Copper Creek for you. I'm fine now. You don't have to worry about me."

This is weird. Even though she hadn't been the one to let me know, I thought she'd be happy to have me home. "I'll be here as long as I need to be. In the meantime, you can tell me what's going on."

I follow her back inside, shooting a confused glance at James. James shrugs, and I wrinkle my nose.

"Nothing's been going on. I was sick, had surgery and treatment."

On the kitchen counter is a steaming cup of coffee. The smell is divine. I know it's only instant, but after my long flight and drive, a coffee would be amazing around now.

Mum stops at the kitchen counter to pick up the cup. "Do you want a coffee?"

"What I want is to understand why it took James to track me down and tell me what was going on. Why you didn't call me? Didn't you think I'd want to know my mother had cancer?"

She turns toward the living room, returning to the couch and sitting down, cradling her coffee. "I'm fine, Adam. No need to interrupt your life."

Five minutes back and already I want to throttle her.

My memories are full of her and her quest to rule our lives. She liked to be in control while Dad had just faded into the background

"Well, I'm back and you just have to deal."

She fixes her gaze on me. When I was a kid that look would fill me with fear, but I'm not a kid anymore.

I shrug. "At least James is happy to see me."

If that's all I get from coming home, it's worth it.

4

LILY

The knocking on the door makes me sigh. It's a little after two in the morning and what little sleep I've managed to get has been disrupted by a noise I dare not move for.

Soft light from the hallway illuminates my room, and I lie, staring at the cream paint peeling off the ceiling.

The pounding on the door grows louder, and I roll over, my head encased in my pillow in a vain attempt to drown it out.

"Lily, let me in." Eric sounds mournful, as always. The sound of his tyres over the loose stones in the yard gave him away about fifteen minutes ago. He's drunk again and has driven home from the pub when the last thing he should have been doing was getting in a car. My house is the turnoff before his, and somehow he always finds his way here. He might legally own the property, but this is my home until such time I choose for it not to be. Doesn't give him the right to turn up whenever he likes.

I sigh, and pull the pillow tight as he groans loudly, slapping the door in a pathetic attempt to convince me to open it.

Smiling at the sound of footsteps, I laugh quietly as there's a bounce on the bed and Max joins me, hiding under the other pillow. He grins in the dimly lit room, but I can see him. His smile lights up the darkest of spaces.

"Mum, Eric's at the door," he whispers.

"I know, sweetie. Just get some sleep." I keep my voice low. If Eric gets any sign that I'm awake he'll make more noise. If we keep quiet, he'll probably fall asleep on the doorstep. He'll be gone by morning.

"I just pretend it's *zombies*." He growls the last word, raising one hand in the shape of a claw. I stifle a giggle, far too amused to even ask him where he's learned that. Maybe one of the kids from school.

I claw the air alongside him, and we end up laughing into our pillows. Max snuggles up against me, and I breathe him in. He's growing way too fast.

"Night, Mum," he whispers.

"Night night, baby," I whisper back, kissing his forehead. I love him more than I can ever say. Even though he's eleven, he'll always be my baby.

The banging stops, and I close my eyes and wait for sleep. Tomorrow, Eric will show up and give me a grovelling apology. He's never managed to get inside the house in one of these moods. I don't know what he'd do if he did.

Max wriggles. I swear he never stays still, at least not when he's awake.

If only I had as much energy as he does.

———

I WALK DOWN the stairs and open the front door to greet the morning. The yard is empty, the tyre tracks in the dirt the only indication Eric was even here.

If I know him, he's at home licking his wounds, working out how to face me again. He's such a creature of habit I know he'll be here later to apologise.

He'd never given me the time of day until I'd started going out with Adam. No one had wanted to know me before then. Mum's reputation had always been in front of me, the other kids thinking I was as crazy as she was. Before Adam, I'd had no one.

Everything good in my life came back to him. That is, until the point when he'd left town and I'd never seen him again. By the time I got away from Mum, all my focus was on Max. It's always been so hard to talk about that period of my life. It's not like anyone I know has been though anything remotely similar. I went through counselling, but I still shake off thoughts about that time.

By the time Max and I were settled into our new life, the barriers to finding out where Adam was were too hard to break through. I had to move on. Now, Max is my life.

"Mum, the zombies are gone." Max walks out to join me and growls, clawing the air again and I shake my head at him, tousling his hair.

"That's right, Max. No zombies. Not at the moment anyway." I sigh and reach for his hand, turning back inside. The kitchen beckons as my stomach grumbles. After a night of interrupted sleep, I can't wait for a cup of coffee and some toast.

He gives me a look that sends a shock through my system. His nose wrinkles as he narrows his eyes at me. So much like his father. My mind wanders to Adam. Why, I'll never know. It's not like he's ever coming back. Yet, there are days when I can think of nothing else. Maybe because I still have so much that has never been resolved with him.

I reach the door only for Max to pull me back out. When I look down, a plain brown box is right beside the door, tucked into the corner of the deck. We both walked straight past it as we came out.

"Mum, there's a parcel out here."

Another one? Since we moved in, some mysterious bene-factor has been leaving packages on the doorstep every so often. It's not Eric—I know that much. If it were, he'd be announcing to the world that he was helping to support me. Corey Campbell sometimes brings me meat; Owen brings me bread and cookies; Drew sometimes pops in with pastries or books for Max. Even James visits from time to time and plays with Max, giving me a much-needed break. All the Campbell boys but the one who started a new life without any of us.

The one who still occupies my thoughts.

Usually these packages contain clothing for Max. He's already ripped the top of the box open by the time I get there, and is foraging through it. Sure enough, there are T-shirts for him. Some are a little big, but there's nothing he can't grow into. Whoever it is doesn't know him well enough to get his size right. The whole thing's weird, but I'm grate-ful. The clothing he's received over the years has meant I've been able to spend money I would have needed for clothes on things like food instead.

Something pink and floral catches my eye, and I bend to pick it up from the bottom of the box. It's a dress, simple with short sleeves and a scoop neckline. I've lost so much weight it might be a little baggy, but it'll be comfortable and it's new. I haven't had new clothing in forever.

Tears prick my eyes at the thought of how kind this person is, and for the millionth time I rack my brain to work out who it could be. *No idea.*

"Mum. Check this out."

I turn my attention to Max. He holds up a T-shirt, grey in colour with what looks like a rapidly disintegrating man depicted in the centre. The image is cartoony in appearance, not scary at all, and only one word graces the front of it —*Brains.*

I chuckle. Maybe there are people out there who won't find it appropriate, but after last night ...

"Zombies, Mum. Zombies."

Pulling him into a bear hug, I plant a kiss in Max's soft, dark hair. "Zombies, Max."

"Get off. I want to put my shirt on."

I let go, and he races inside the front door and upstairs. It makes him happy, and that's everything. I look down at the dress in my hand, smiling at it. It's been forever since I wore a dress. Today will have to be an exception.

Following him into the house, box in hand, I climb the stairs and make my way to my bedroom. Placing the box of clothes on the bed, I slip off my T-shirt, frowning at the sight of myself in the mirror. This morning when I first got dressed, I was wearing the same old clothes. Now, with the thought of a new dress, I pick at the frays on my bra straps. It's going to need replacing soon.

What I need is new underwear, among other things. I don't notice sometimes how much I neglect myself until it's staring me in the face. Max comes first, and that's how it should be. *At least my old underwear will be hidden by the dress.*

I unzip and push my jeans down, tugging at the hems to get them over my feet. When they're discarded, I slide the dress on over my head.

It's not anything expensive or flashy, but the microfibre fabric feels smooth and soft against my skin. It might as well be the most expensive silk, and I twirl in front of the mirror, feeling like a girl again. Most of the time I wear a T-shirt and jeans. They're cheap and last a long time, which, given the nature of some of the work around the property, I'm grateful for.

"Mum, you look pretty." Max stands in the doorway, wearing his zombie T-shirt. It's a little large, and he holds the hem, swaying from side to side as he shows it off.

"You look very pretty too, Max."

He rolls his eyes. "Muuum," he groans. "Only girls look pretty."

I laugh. "Then you must be very handsome."

He rolls his eyes again and that squeeze on my heart is back.

"You look so much like ..." The words escape, but I leave the thought unfinished. There are days when he looks so much like his father, and it's a punch to the gut knowing he'll never come back.

"Do I look like my dad?"

I swear my heart stops.

"A little. You have my eyes, though. I see me when I look at you." It's not quite the truth, but it's close enough. "Let's get you to school."

One day, I'll tell him everything. He'll know that his mother and father loved one another above all else and made plans to spend forever together.

Until his father left.

5

ADAM

Twelve years away and the main street hasn't changed a bit. Sure, some of the stores might be different, but the buildings remain the same. This is still the same town I left behind.

I've travelled the world, been in so many different cities and towns, but they don't compare to this. I spent four years of my life in Copper Creek, and this is home.

School's just finished, and this is probably the worst time to venture out and explore. There are children all over the place, walking home past the shops, just as I'd done with my brothers. If we were lucky, the owner of the local supermarket, Mr Flannegan, would be standing outside, handing out lollipops. Didn't matter how big a kid you were, he was always happy to oblige. He's gone, but the Four Square supermarket he founded is still around. I doubt there are any lollipops now though.

Back when I was at school, Copper Creek was a busier

town than it is today. Dad tells me that a lot of the forestry projects that fed business into the place closed down. It's bounced back a little, but it's still very much a community that struggles.

A group of boys catch my attention as they run toward me. Their target is obvious—a small dark-haired boy whose leaner and faster than any of them. And yet they keep chasing.

He looks back over his shoulder as he runs, and I step sideways to let him through, but he still slams into me. His lithe frame doesn't make a dent, and I look down. Big blue eyes look back at me, not quite hidden by the dark mop of hair covering the boy's head.

"Hi," I say.

The boy keeps staring at me. At the sound of footsteps, I shift my gaze back over his head to the larger boys closing in on their target. They slow down as they take me in.

"Lucky," one of them says.

They walk past, giving the boy filthy looks. One even has the nerve to spit at his feet and I give him a dirty look in return, taking in every detail I can.

When they're gone, I kneel in front of the boy who's still silent, still staring.

"Max! I thought I'd never catch up. Those damn kids. Please don't run—let me deal with them." A female voice comes from the same direction the boy has run from.

The owner of the voice draws close. "Thank you. Thank you so much. They bully him all the time, and he just ran, and I couldn't stop him." The words tumble from her mouth, and her tone suggests stress and agitation.

I stand, finding myself looking into the same blue eyes

the kid has. My heart stops. These are the same blue eyes I once fell in love with.

"Adam?" Lily's chest rises sharply as she tries to catch her breath, and it's distracting. This is too much, but I drink her in.

She's a lot thinner than she was when we were together. Hell, there wasn't that much of her to start with. But she's just as alluring. The dress she's wearing shows off her significant cleavage, and I know I linger on her breasts a little longer than I should before taking in the rest of her. The girl I wanted to spend forever with. The girl who left me at the altar.

"Lily?" I look back at the boy. That big grin and blue eyes are so much like hers. His hair's dark instead of blonde, but there's no doubt they're related. "This your boy?"

A little part of me dies inside. The part that knows she's moved on, but doesn't want to face it.

She frowns, a crease forming between her eyebrows, and her gaze tells me she's wounded. "Yes. There's a group that picks on him when they think they can get away with it. I don't think they realised I was there. Max didn't help things when he took off." She bends, turning him toward her. "Baby, Mummy lost you. Please don't do that again."

He flings his arms around her, not saying a word. His actions speak louder than anything.

"Okay?" She pushes him away far enough to see his face.

He nods, hugging her again, and she closes her eyes. Whatever fear she had for him hasn't passed, but his hug heals whatever is going on with her as her face relaxes.

"Does he talk?" I ask. Those big blue eyes shift toward me again.

"Only when he gets to know someone. He has to be really confident you're his friend." She smiles a little.

I smile at the boy. "Are we friends now?"

His eyes light up. "Thank you," he says.

The effect on Lily is immediate; she takes on a radiance that's hard to look away from. Even after all this time she affects me like no one else ever has, and right now my heart is in my throat over how beautiful she is. I was so sure that even though my thoughts still lingered in the past that this trip would put an end to that. Clearly not.

"I like your shirt." I point at the zombie on Max's T-shirt and his grin grows bigger, if that's possible.

"I got it today. And Mum got her dress." He points at Lily and the knee-length dress with the distracting neckline.

"Well, you both look very nice." I meet Lily's eyes, and whatever emotion she had in them is gone as she blanks her face.

"Come on, Max. Let's get these groceries and get home." She stands, giving me a small smile. "Thanks again."

I cast my gaze over her and note the thin gold band on her left ring finger. My stomach clenches at the sight and the realisation that she's someone else's. Why on earth do I still feel this way?

"Sure. No problem. I really didn't do much."

"You stopped him in his tracks. That's enough."

She takes Max by the hand, leading him toward the Four Square. As they walk away, Lily looks back over her shoulder, shooting me that shy expression that got me into trouble sixteen years ago. I bet she still doesn't know she's doing it. She never did. All of a sudden, I am that fourteen-year-old, sullen and already counting the days until I could leave home —until I laid eyes on *her*.

How old is the boy? He looks maybe nine or ten. The thought of her moving on after I left bothers me way too much. But of course she did. Over the years the anger has faded, but I still have unanswered questions about why she jilted me, why she changed her mind. Will I ever get answers?

Lily and Max disappear into the distance, and I wake up to the fact that I'm still standing there, staring after them.

Damn it.

Despite my mother not seeming to want me here, I'm not going anywhere. I came home wanting to check on her, but there's so much more now. Seeing Lily with Max has aroused my curiosity further. Mum never told me Lily had a child.

Across the road and down a bit is the sign that says *Copper Creek Bakery*, unchanged from years before when we'd arrived here. James told me Owen bought the bakery a few years ago, having completed his apprenticeship working there.

My head is filled with a million thoughts including Lily and my upcoming reunion with another brother as I cross the road. I'm nervous, but excited.

From outside the bakery, nothing's changed, but as I push open the door, the bell tinkling above me, everything inside looks bright and sparkly. New.

Owen stands behind the counter, serving an elderly woman with a blue rinse. Slowly, she points at the different things she wants. *He has to have the patience of a saint. I'd be hopeless at this.* As he gathers the pastries, his gaze locks with mine and recognition flashes on Owen's face.

I grin. He blanks.

I wait for him to finish serving and step closer.

"How much for the gingerbread man?" I ask.

"Eight dollars fifty."

Laughing, I shake my head. "That's one expensive gingerbread man."

"Includes the asshole tax." He doesn't even hesitate to roll out that line.

"I missed you too."

Owen says nothing, just narrows his eyes.

"Owen ...?"

"Do you want the gingerbread man or not?"

He's not budging. I guess he's pissed that I haven't been in touch for all these years. But I can't pursue it further, not now the door has just tinkled again, indicating someone new has joined us.

I pause, not sure what to say next, but he's already moved on. "What can I do for you, Mrs Jenkins?"

For a moment I stand there, watching Owen serve her before I turn and leave. What's the point in staying where I'm clearly not wanted?

I have some big bridges to mend.

———

"Where's James?" I ask over dinner. Mum serves the meal in silence, having refused all help to prepare it. My plate is piled high with mashed potato, peas, carrots, and a slab of unrecognisable meat.

"He went to Ashley's for dinner." Mum says as she sits.

"Who's Ashley?" When I left, James was six. His life has changed a bit.

"His best friend. She went through school with him."

"Just his friend?" I put on the biggest grin I can muster.

She glares at me. "Apparently so. Leave your brother alone."

I chuckle. "I didn't mean anything by it. It's hard to have a conversation with you sometimes."

Out of the corner of my eye, I just catch Dad nod.

"I'm not in the mood for laughing, Adam. There's no reason for you to be hanging around here; I'm fine. You have your career and girlfriend to get back to. Weren't you going to propose to her? What's happening with that?"

I swirl the food around the plate with my fork until the carrots and peas are mushed up with the potato. It's hard to look her in the eye when she's in that kind of mood. "Actually, we broke up instead."

When I meet her gaze, she twists her mouth, but says nothing. She takes a bite of food, her eyes never leaving mine. This is what makes it so hard. We used to joke about that scary look—now all I see is a bitter woman who's not getting what she wants. Why's she so keen to get rid of me?

"I'm sorry to hear that, Son," Dad speaks. He's been under the thumb for as many years as I can remember. Mum was always the one in charge.

Mum's gaze breaks from me as she turns her attention to Dad, who shrugs and takes a bite of food. *Good on you, Dad.*

"It's a shame," Mum says. "She sounded so pleasant when we talked on the phone."

"She's not the right one."

At that, she drops her fork on the plate, the sound echoing through the dining room. "Weren't you happy?"

"I thought I was. Then I realised that she wasn't who I wanted to spend my life with. She's great—pretty, smart, and I really care about her. But not enough to make a family with her."

Until I'd arrived in town, I'd thought Lily to be the impossible dream. The first call I made when I'd received phone privileges during basic training was to my mother, who had told me Lily had taken up with Eric Murphy as soon as I left. The thought that Lily had found it that easy to move on haunted me for so long afterward, I don't know if I truly got over it.

"Oh, Adam." There it is, the disappointed tone. "She sounded like a lovely girl. Nothing in life is perfect. Sometimes you just have to settle." She looks down her nose at me in that oh-so-condescending way she does. I haven't missed that.

"Is that what you did, Mum? Did you settle?" The words are out before I can stop them.

Mum grimaces and I glance at Dad, expecting to see him irritated. Instead, he snickers, shaking his head and going back to his meal. He knows better than to get in the middle of our sniping. He always did.

"I thought you might have regained some of your accent while you were away. Not sound so ... Kiwi," she says. Changing subjects abruptly has always been her speciality.

"Actually, I think the opposite happened. I was pretty unique. Surrounded by Americans who sound American, I made my own little place among them. Besides, Mum, after all these years, you sound really Kiwi yourself."

33

She lets out an eye roll. *I win.*

Mum's the only one in the family left with a hint of an accent, as far as I know. Even before I went overseas, we boys had all dropped it given that we'd spent most of our lives in New Zealand. Having a New Zealand father had been a huge influence. Over time, enough of the accent had rubbed off on her, slowly eroding the way she spoke, the words she used, no doubt without her even thinking.

She lifts her fork to take the next bite.

"I saw Lily in town today."

The fork goes back down and the glare returns. I always did know how to push her buttons.

"How is she?" Dad asks.

I shrug. "I didn't see her for long. She was with her boy. He was being chased by some kids. Little shits."

We return to eating, but in my peripheral vision I see Dad pause and stare. I can't make out his expression, and I don't want to turn my head and get Mum's attention. Is it sympathy?

"Where do kids get off bullying someone that way?" I put my own fork down. "They were all bigger than him."

No reaction. Mum continues to eat, not bothering to look up. Dad's focus has switched to his food. Funny how the conversation dies now.

You're so frustrating.

I take a deep breath. "I might track her down and visit. He looks like he's a lot of work. Maybe she just needs some help."

"There's something wrong with that boy," Mum says without looking up.

"Surely that means it's more likely that Lily needs help."

Mum sighs. "She has plenty of help. She's had Eric Murphy running around after her for years."

Did that mean ...?

"Running around after her?"

"Just leave it, Adam. She has her life—you have yours. The past is the past."

What if I don't want it to be the past? I open my mouth to continue, but Mum's lips are clamped together. Dad has his head down, completely focused on his dinner. *Shit.* No point in even arguing this.

Wait. She hasn't exactly said Lily and Eric are together. Just that Eric runs around after her.

I lean back in my chair, scooping a fork piled high with potato, relishing each bite as a tiny glimmer of hope grows.

Maybe there's a chance.

6

LILY

The one thing I inherited of any value was my mother's car. Although describing it as having value is scraping the barrel. It's a 1984 Toyota Corolla, and I needed to replace it a long time ago. Needing to do something and actually being able to do it are two very different things in my world.

One of the few reasons I'm glad I live in a small town is that I don't have to travel far for anything, and there's nowhere to go, so this pile of crap only has to go short distances. I don't think it'd survive anything beyond that.

I park outside the school and wait for the bell. I'm as close as I can get to the gate to avoid a repeat of yesterday when Max went flying past me and I had to run to catch him, only for him to bump into Adam, if only until I could think of a logical escape plan. We didn't really need any groceries, but I'd spent five dollars on bread and milk to waste some time.

Seeing him again had scared me. I think of him sometimes, but I never expected to see him in the flesh. Not after all this time. My body had reacted like the teenage girl I was when I last saw him. Sweaty palms, erratic heartbeat, the lot. I'd just had to get away from him to gather my thoughts, although they've always been muddled as far as he's concerned.

The bell rings, and I get out of the car and walk into the school grounds. Heading for Max's classroom, I spot my son throwing his bag over his shoulder and striding toward me. It's funny—there are days when he's so reticent and shy, and then there are days when his confidence shines. Today's a good day for Max.

"Mum," he calls, and I smile as he approaches me. He won't hug me in public except on his own terms, but he will hook his pinkie with mine as we walk back toward the gate.

"How was your day?" I ask.

"I got one hundred per cent in my maths test."

I stop and grin at my proud boy. "Really?"

"Yep. I beat Karl."

Karl was one of the older, bigger kids who picked on Max from time to time. I swallow down my concern over that for the moment as my son basks in his success. Max scoring big on the test is brilliant. He's come a long way the last couple of months. Even a year ago this wouldn't have happened—he'd be somewhere in the middle, scraping through. It speaks volumes for the amount of determination he has.

He doesn't even care if he's the top of the class—he just wants to do better than the boys who treat him like he's second best.

"I'm kicking arse, Mum."

Despite him using a word I don't like him saying, all I can

do is smile. His teacher, Ginny Robinson, is brilliant. It's always been a struggle to find people who understand Max, but she's so good with him. He's thrived the last two years he's been in her class.

"Want to grab an ice cream before we get home?" I ask. "I think we need to celebrate."

"Can we get a tub?"

I grin. "I think so. We'll get some waffle cones and sprinkles too."

"Yum." His enthusiasm is infectious, and he always makes me smile no matter how sad or tired I am.

We drive back toward home until we reach the supermarket and park outside. He's bouncing as we walk inside, and he picks vanilla ice cream while I grab the cones and sprinkles.

"*Kia ora*, Lily, Max."

Mary Cuthbert has worked in this place forever, taking over the store when Mr Flannegan passed away. She always has a smile on her face for Max, which is more than some others have.

"Hi Mary, how are you?" I ask

She nods. "*Ka pai.*"

"Glad to hear it." I place the items on the counter.

"Celebrating something?"

Max beams. "I got all the answers right in my maths test today."

She grins. "Good boy. I wish I could have some ice cream."

"You can come over and share ours," Max says so earnestly that I grin too.

"I think I'll let you and your mum enjoy it." She fixes her

gaze on me. "How are you going, Lily?"

I nod. "Not bad."

"Adam's back, I hear."

I nod again. "I know."

"Doesn't seem that long ago you two were in here buying treats after school."

Laughing, I shake my head. "It was a long time ago."

"James came in to pick up some milk for his mum. She's sick, you know."

A mixture of irritation and concern flashes through me. None of the boys had told me. I had no idea. "She is?"

Mary bites down on her bottom lip. The gossip is about to spill and although she no doubt has had enough to say about me in the past, I can't help but like her anyway.

"Being treated for breast cancer. I don't think it's good."

My stomach lurches even though Joanna Campbell has been no friend to me. Despite my dislike of her, I wouldn't wish cancer on anyone.

"I'm sorry to hear that. I guess it's why Adam's back." Makes sense, even though he clashed with his mother a lot before he left town. Maybe he's come to say goodbye.

She nods. "No doubt."

I pay and leave the shop with Max in tow. My heart pounds as I buckle in. I held this dream for so long that Adam would come back. I endured so much after he was gone. After all this time, he's returned for his mother. I can't resent her, not when she's ill, but a tiny part of me hates that he did it for her and not me.

"Come on, Mum." Max is impatient, as he often is with me. He gets frustrated when I stop and daydream as I do sometimes, but then he's the biggest dreamer of them all. It's something I adore about him.

"Okay." I turn the key in the ignition and we set off toward home. When we move from the tar-seal road to the unsealed one, it gets bumpy. The shock absorbers in this car are almost non-existent, and it makes for a bumpy ride.

But not so bumpy I don't notice the sensation of one tyre not being quite right.

We're still a distance from home, and I would rather check and be wrong than drive home and make things worse. Indicating, I pull over.

"Mum?"

"I just have to check something."

Unbuckling my seat belt, I check to make sure there are no cars coming and get out. Sure enough, as I walk around the car, the rear tyre on the passenger side is flat.

I slam my palm against the side of the white car. Of all the dumb things to happen. Knowing my luck, Eric will come down the road and see me, another reason for him to make noise about how I need to move in with him and not have to worry about anything anymore. *Over my dead body.*

"What's wrong?" Max asks.

"We've got a flat tyre."

"Do we have another one?"

I open the boot of the car. "We sure do. I've only changed a tyre once before though. Better hope I know what I'm doing."

"I bet Adam knows how to fix a tyre."

I'm glad I'm standing behind the car so Max can't see my eyes roll. I can't blame him. As far as Max is concerned, Adam saved him from the bullies by just standing there.

"I'm sure he does. But he's not here and I am. So you're stuck with me." I lower the boot and poke my tongue out so he can see me, before opening it again and pulling out the spare.

"Just as well you're clever, Mum."

I chuckle. "That's high praise from you, sweetheart."

Leaving the tyre leaning against the car, I pull the jack and the wheel brace out, placing them on the ground. I could limp home, but I'd still have to change it.

Max opens the door and steps out. "I reckon the car will be too heavy with me in it."

Biting down my laughter, I nod. "Good thinking."

As I pull the jack around the side of the car, Max points behind me. "There's a car."

A black car with a loud, throaty engine slows as it approaches and pulls up behind me. At least it's not Eric. I stand and turn my head, catching the gaze coming from familiar eyes.

"Adam," Max exclaims, recognising him in the same moment.

Adam opens the driver's door and steps out. "Need a hand?"

"No, I'm fine. Thanks for asking."

His lips twitch. Maybe I make him as nervous as he makes me. "I can help if you like. I was just on my way out to the cove. Thought I'd take a look to see if it's changed."

I laugh. "I'll save you the trip. It hasn't."

He grins, and my heart aches as we slip into easy conversation. "I thought I recognised the car. Can't believe you still have this pile of crap."

Adam doesn't mean to hurt me with his comment, I

know that much. While I think it myself, it stings coming from someone else. This is what I have with no hope for anything more modern. There are ways, but not without making sacrifices I'm unwilling to make.

"It does the job."

I slot the jack into position.

"Let me do that."

"I don't need your help." I frown.

His dark eyes are so intense I have to look away. "Have you called Eric for help?"

What in the world? "No. Why would I do that?"

Adam licks his lips. "Mum seemed to think you two were a thing."

"Your mother seems to talk a lot about things that aren't any of her business." I spit the words as I twist the handle of the jack, slowly raising the car.

"Eric's a zombie." Max laughs.

"Is that right?" Adam asks, a bemused tone in his voice.

"Mum, you should get Adam to do that. You look tired."

My face is turned toward the car and I bite down on my bottom lip. I haven't needed help so far. "I'm fine, Max."

When I stand straight, Adam moves around me, squatting as he removes the wheel nuts.

"You don't have to do that."

"I know I don't." He doesn't look up from his work, and I can do nothing but watch. What else am I going to do—snatch the wheel brace from him and act like I'm twelve? Maybe I should be grateful for him helping, and I guess it's better than Eric showing up. Adam won't hold it over me.

Although why do I even think that? I haven't seen him in so long, and last time I saw him he was promising me undying love. That didn't turn out to be true.

I chew on my bottom lip. He *is* helping me. "Thanks."

Max hooks his arms around my waist. "See? Told you Adam could fix a tyre."

Adam grins as he shoots a glance at us, and pulls the flat tyre from the car. "You did?"

"I told Mum, and she said I was stuck with her." Sometimes Max clams up and won't talk. Today he's doing a spectacular job of dropping me in it.

"I'm sure she does a great job. Your mum's a very smart lady."

"I'm smart too. I got one hundred per cent in my maths test today."

Adam stands as he picks up the spare tyre. "Really? That's awesome. You should celebrate that." He frowns as he looks at the tyre. "The tread on this isn't that great, Lily. You need a new one."

"It's on the list." I fight back tears as my eyes meet his. My list is a mile long, but he doesn't need to know that.

"Might pay to bump it up a bit." There's nothing but concern in his eyes, and I hate this feeling, hate not being able to open up to him, hate that he still brings this out in me after all this time. I should hate him, but I could never do that. Not with Adam. "Just make sure you get this fixed so you've got a spare."

I bite my tongue as he replaces the tyre and starts screwing on the wheel nuts. He means well.

"The last thing I want is either of you getting hurt."

Oh, it's way too late for that. My heart lurches at his words, and I squeeze Max tight, kissing the top of his head.

"Mum," he whispers, irritable. I've broken the cardinal rule of kissing him in public. He has to make the first move.

"It's okay. No one saw," I whisper back.

"Still not cool." He sounds grumpy, but the smile on his face says otherwise. I thought I knew what love was before Max came along—now I realise I had no clue. He's my everything. I've felt guilt at times over keeping his father from him, but I'd decided to tell him everything when he was ready to ask. That time is swiftly approaching.

"Sorry."

Adam stands, dusting off his hands. "There you go. I'll chuck the other tyre in the back."

"I'll take it to get fixed tomorrow."

He frowns. "Is there anywhere left around here that does that sort of thing?"

"It's a bit of a drive, but it's important. I'll get it sorted." It's an expense I don't need, but a necessary one. Especially with the roads around this place.

"I can take it for you if you want."

His words touch me. He's concerned about our welfare. But it's too late for that. "No, I can do it. We'll go for a Saturday drive, right, Max?"

Max squeezes my waist. "Yep."

"Okay. If you need any help, just give me a call. I'm staying at Mum's."

Anywhere else, and maybe I'd consider it. But the chances of me ever calling that house are so remote they're in the negative per cent.

I don't want to speak ill of her while she's sick, so I swallow down any nasty words. "Sure."

"I'll leave you to it. Might not bother with that trip to the cove today, then." The look in his eyes is confusing—caring and a touch of longing. Longing for what? I think I know the answer. I feel it, too. "Take care, you two."

"We will." I shift my gaze to Max. "Say goodbye to Adam."

"Bye, Adam."

I nod. "Thanks for everything. Bye, Adam."

Adam turns to get in that big flash motor, turns around, and drives back in the direction he came from. I'm left standing beside my rundown old car, watching as he leaves, my heart heavy when it should be over all this.

At least this time I got to say goodbye.

7

ADAM

Twelve years ago

My heart is empty.

I followed through with our plans after Lily jilted me. The apprenticeship I had lined up in Hamilton lasted a month before I needed out. I either had to return home and face the fact she no longer wanted me, or I had to shake up my life and stop moping.

There had been no word from Lily, but there had been reports of a blonde girl hitchhiking out of town around the same time as Lily took off. She was gone. I'd been all kinds of mixed up, hurt and angry that she couldn't just speak to me.

Now I'm staying with old friends of Mum on their farm in Iowa. Working on the farm keeps me busy and brings me some income, and it makes for a cheap place to stay. I miss home, but at the same time I know I'd struggle to be there.

It takes me a while to call home. I know Jacqui, Mum's

old school friend, called her when I arrived to say I'd got there safely. I'm just scared of what I'll find out if I call. *Has Lily moved on?*

"Hello?" To my relief, Corey answers.

"Corey, it's Adam."

"Hey, man. How's it going?" Corey's tone suggests a mix of concern and relief to talk to me. I guess he's worried. We've always been close, being the oldest two.

"I'm doing alright."

"Are you coming home?"

I look at my shoes, even though he can't see what must be a pained expression on my face. "I don't think so. I've made some decisions the last few weeks."

"What kind of decisions?"

Shifting my gaze to the ceiling, I bite my cheek. "I'm enlisting in the army."

He snorts. "When did you ever want to join the army? I thought you didn't like guns."

"I can train as a mechanic and see the world all at the same time."

Corey sighs. "Pretty sure you can do that back here."

"Maybe I could. But I think there are more opportunities if I stay. Besides, it means I don't have to think about what happened back home."

For a moment, there's silence.

"Corey?"

"Dude, maybe you need to come home until you find out where Lily went. She owes you an explanation."

Out of frustration, I kick the cupboard under the bench. Bella, Steph's Pug, leaps out of her basket as if I'm indicating that we're going for walk. Going for a walk isn't a stupid idea. "I just can't deal. You have no idea what it's like to hurt so much you want to just curl up and die. I love her more than anything, but she didn't even talk to me before she left."

There's silence for a few moments. "Maybe she didn't think she could talk to you."

"What's that supposed to mean?"

"Maybe she knew you'd be a big baby about it if she wanted to postpone the wedding. Given how you're sulking right now, I think she was right to leave you."

Prickly heat fills my chest and arms. Deep down I know I am being more than a little selfish, but Lily and I had been open about everything. She's the one I shared my hopes and dreams with. I'm at least entitled to an explanation. "You know what? Screw you. I thought out of everybody you'd understand."

I slam the phone down, and if I thought my heart was broken before, it's shattered now. Of everyone in my life, Corey should be on my side. I always backed him, even when I knew he was up to no good.

Turning, I head out the door and into the backyard. The warm sun soothes me, and I close my eyes as I raise my face. Rehashing everything isn't going to help. Lily left me and I have to move on.

"Adam?"

At the sound of Steph's voice I turn. It doesn't help that she has more sympathy in those doe eyes than I just got in that phone call. Despite the nagging feeling that I'm about to make the worst mistake of my life, I give in to the four months' worth of those soulful eyes telling me what she wants.

The knot in my stomach lets go as I walk toward her, and

cupping her face, I brush lips with only the second girl I've ever kissed in my life. She doesn't smell right; she doesn't feel right; but she's the best thing in my life right now.

"It's just us here," she whispers.

Her parents aren't due back for another two hours, and I can't think of a better way to spend the time than losing myself with someone who wants me.

Someone who cares.

————

HALF AN HOUR LATER, I lie staring at the ceiling. I'm either the biggest arsehole alive or I've just made the best move I could have to get on with my life. Steph is all kinds of sweet and she deserves better than me, but we could make this work. I'm not being fair to her, I already know that, but I can give her part of my heart. Even if the rest still belongs to Lily.

"What are you thinking about?" She runs her hand across my chest and snuggles into my side.

"You're going to hate me if I tell you." I'm not about to lie to her; that won't help either of us.

"Try me?"

"I'm not sure if this is going to go anywhere."

"Because of Lily?"

I swallow and close my eyes. "Yes."

"She broke your heart. You're allowed to start again. She has."

Turning my head, I give her a small smile. Her brow's all wrinkled from frowning and I would give anything to lose myself in those curves and puffy lips again. I need to change the topic. This isn't anything I want to speak about.

"Your parents will be home any minute."

"Stop trying to change the subject."

I bury my face in her dark hair and chuckle. "I'm not keen on getting you into trouble. I'll be gone soon enough."

She sighs. "I don't want you to go."

"I have to admit, I thought your brother was nuts for suggesting enlisting at first. It's not something I ever considered. But it opens up a whole world of opportunities."

Steph pulls back a little and raises her gaze to meet mine. "I know. I'm just glad this happened before you left. Now I know what I'm waiting for."

It's so unfair on her, but my heart loves the idea of her being there for me when I need her. She soothes my fears and eases the pain.

I'm sorry, Lily.

———

LEAVING for basic training was difficult. I didn't love Steph the way I loved Lily, but I cared about her.

The first phone call I am able to make is home, though. I didn't get a chance to speak to Corey again after our argument, and I want to smooth things over. I close my eyes as the ringing fills my ear.

"Hello?"

I grin at the sound of James's voice. The baby of the family, he's six, and I love that he's brave enough to answer the phone. "Hey, bud, it's Adam. Is Corey there?"

"No."

"Oh. Is Mum there?"

He doesn't quite pull the phone away enough. "Mum," he shrieks.

"Bro, you'll deafen me. What are you up to?" It's just so good to hear a familiar voice.

"We went and saw the baby."

The baby? "What was that, bud?"

There's a clatter on the line, and Mum's voice comes down the receiver. "Hi, who is it?"

"Mum, it's Adam."

She lets out a contented sigh. "Adam. It's so good to hear from you. Do you have long to talk?"

"Not long. I was hoping I could talk to Corey."

"Corey moved out." Her tone is clipped, suggesting she's not too happy about it. But I guess it was par for the course. He was always the most independent one out of all of us.

I bite my lip before asking the next question. "Has anyone heard from Lily?"

There's a moment of silence. "Mum?"

"Lily's back. She's living with Eric Murphy."

If I thought in any capacity that I'd moved on, that all falls away in this moment. I'd thought my heart had begun to heal, but Mum's words just twist the knife even further.

"I have to go. My time's up," I whisper.

"I wish we had longer. Take care of yourself, Adam."

Nausea sweeps me, and my legs crumple under me. A reassuring hand lands on my shoulder and I look up to see Ben, Steph's brother. He's the one who gave me the idea to enlist, and over the past few months has become like a brother.

"What's wrong?"

I lick my lips because I don't want to put my foot in my mouth. After all, I am dating his sister.

"I won't tell Steph if it's about your ex."

"Lily's moved in with someone else."

He frowns. "Well, screw her. Let's get back to the barracks. There's a card game going on I don't want to miss."

"Why do I have the feeling we're about to get into trouble?"

Ben chuckles. "Because we probably are."

I shrug. "What have I got to lose?"

My heart still aches as he walks beside me. I'll work with these men here, some longer than others. But it reminds me so much in a way of my family and the closeness I've shared with my brothers all my life. This is my new home.

I really have lost her.

8

ADAM

Now

Saturday afternoon and I can't stop thinking about her.
Somehow I always knew if I came home that one
flutter of those long eyelashes would pull me back under her
spell. Except she doesn't flutter eyelashes at me—she frowns.

Why am I left feeling that I owe her some kind of explanation when she's the one who owes me? Maybe I should be
angry but whenever I close my eyes I see her, standing beside
the car as I approach, that bead of sweat sitting right above
the cleft of her breasts.

This is not the girl that walked away from me. She's more
confident, not to mention stubborn. I would have helped her
get that tyre fixed in a heartbeat, although what she really
needs are new ones.

The thought of her and Max driving around in that car

with the balding tyres drives me crazy. It's funny—for years I haven't been here, and while I might have thought about her, I never worried about her. Now, I do. I've only seen her twice.

This house makes me a little stir-crazy.

James hasn't reappeared for me to get any more information out of. Mum's not about to spill any beans. Dad just follows what Mum tells him to, same as he always has.

I grab my car keys and head outside. Mum and Dad probably assume it's a rental, but the first place I went when I hit Auckland was to pick this baby up. Twelve years of having no one else to provide for and being able to save my pennies had left me with a nice nest egg. It was good to spend some of it. My apartment is on the market too. With prices having risen a lot since I bought it, my nest egg will only grow.

So, I'd bought a car online and picked it up, heading straight for Copper Creek. The sleek, black, brand new Holden Commodore V8 roars as I hit the accelerator. It's comforting and luxurious, and it's mine. There's nothing keeping me in the US, and while I'm undecided as to how long I'll be here, having one of these cars was something I always dreamed of.

Now, I take off toward the exit to town, diverting down the back road that leads to the cove. After running into Lily yesterday, I aborted my visit. I didn't want to make things more awkward, following her down the road. The cove used to be one of my favourite places, and I've spent hours walking along the sand there with Lily, holding hands and finding quiet moments against the background of the watering hole.

The road has never been sealed, probably never will be. As kids we skidded down here on our bikes, kicking up the dirt and making each other cough. Houses are few and far between, and I have some vague memory of Eric living this way. If I can avoid seeing him I will, but maybe Lily ... Even if I see no one, it's good to spin the wheels and get some dirt and gravel under them. The car will be caked in dust by the time I get home, but it feels so good to be alive.

A flash of white, and a rabbit ducks out from under the fence and onto the road. The tyres squeal as I hit the brakes hard.

"Well, the brakes work," I mutter.

Out of nowhere, a small boy in jeans and a grey shirt streaks across the road after the rabbit. A hard lump forms in my throat. If I had swerved or been just a few seconds earlier, I could have easily hit him. I know this boy.

"Max," I cry as I unbuckle my seat belt and open the door.

Max stops dead in his tracks, as if oblivious to the danger. His eyes grow big at the sight of me.

I step out of the car and run, throwing myself to my knees in front of him. My heart hurts at the thought of anything happening to Max.

"What on earth were you doing?"

Max lifts his hand, pointing at the rabbit. It's quite happily nibbling weeds in the next paddock. "I saw that," he says.

"Where's your mother?"

His lower lip wobbles. "She's asleep. I'm s'posed to be, but I woke up and saw the rabbit."

I let out a long breath. This kid. I've never been one for

children, always thought about them in a distant sense, but Max tugs on my heartstrings, and I have to admit I'm drawn to him. The more I look at him, the more I see his mother. "How about we get you back to her?"

Max looks around, and his expression changes to confusion as if he's just realised how far he is from the house.

"Come on. I'll give you a lift."

Yesterday, he didn't stop talking. Today, he says nothing, and I have a lightbulb moment of what's causing his hesitation. *Stranger danger.* I lick my lips. "Hey, Max. We're friends, right? You know your mum knows me. I was on my way to see her when I found you. Maybe you can show me where she is?"

At the mention of Lily, he beams, and I take his hand in mine, leading him around the car to the passenger side. He lets me buckle him in and as I sit in the driver's side, he points at a house off the road. The houses are few and far between down this road, it makes sense. "Over there."

"Where's the driveway, buddy?"

He points straight ahead. "Up there."

I start out slowly to avoid missing the turn. Not that there's much chance of that. Max nearly hyperventilates pointing out the gate. It's hard not to smile around him; his enthusiasm is infectious.

Lily stands on the decking, and as I draw closer, I hear her calling for her son. I pull up outside the house, flashing her a smile as I round the car and let Max out.

"Max. What are you doing?" she yells, her eyebrows furrowed in concern. She barely looks at me as she runs, stumbling in the dirt.

"There was a rabbit. Just like in the book you read me."

"Oh, Max." The exhaustion in her voice is obvious, and she hugs him tight as she cries.

I shift my gaze to the house. It's an old rustic house. Small, but enough for a family. It's rundown and in need of maintenance—the red tin roof needs painting and the guttering is failing in one corner. My blood boils at the thought of her living in a house like this. *I wonder if she's as neglected as this place.*

"And then you go and get in a car with someone you don't really know." She's telling Max off now, tears still falling, irritation in her voice.

"To be fair, I did have to talk him into it. We're not exactly strangers." I place my hand on her shoulder.

Wrong move. She turns as she stands and brushes my hand away. "You might have met him a couple of times, but you don't know him. If he gets in your car, he could get in anyone's."

In comparison to the day before she looks so tired, with purple smudges under her eyes indicating just how sleep-deprived she is.

"Okay, okay. I'm sorry. I didn't want him running out on the road again."

She closes her eyes. "I'm sorry for yelling. It's just one thing after another right now, and if anything had happened to him I don't know what I would have done."

Max's expression falls as she breaks down again. She's so frail, thin, as if she'd snap if a strong wind came up. After all this time, after everything, I ache to hold her in my arms.

"Lily," I whisper, moving closer to her. She opens her eyes, and my heart hurts to see how broken she is. Someone's done a real number on her. "Hey, if you want some help with anything, I'm back."

She shakes her head. "I don't need your help."

"Really? You look exhausted, this place is falling down, and Max is out of control." I don't mean it, but the words are out of my mouth before I can stop them. Lily scowls, grabbing Max's arm.

"Come on, Max. Let's go get a drink and a cookie." She raises her face and looks down her nose at me, that precious nose I used to love, right above the lips I kissed more often than I can count. "Thanks, Adam, but no thanks."

"Whatever you have stuck up your butt about me, it's been there a while. Can't you just accept help at face value?"

She pushes Max toward the house. "Go and get a cookie. I'll be in to make a drink in a moment."

Without so much as a backward glance, Max takes off, running into the house. Lily sighs and moves her gaze back to me. "You don't get to come back after all this time and tell me what to do."

"I'm not. I just want to help." I can't remember her being so frustrating. We just used to get along.

"Then go back to wherever the hell you ran away to and leave me alone. Leave us alone. The last person I need parenting advice from is you." She spits the words at me, so unlike the Lily I knew. *What happened to you?*

"I ran away because you didn't want me."

The silence is uncomfortable as we stare at each other. Slowly, her lips turn down and she sighs as if struggling to know what to say next. "I never stopped wanting you, Adam, but you never looked back, and you never rescued me from any of it. I was so dumb. Eighteen, thinking I was going to get to marry my knight in shining armour, but you were never that. You said all the right things, but when it came down to it, you walked away."

She might as well have stabbed me over and over in the heart. It's so far from the truth.

She turns toward the house, taking two steps before I grab her arm. "What the hell are you talking about? You walked away from me."

The pink in her cheeks disappears. "Go away. We don't need you."

"Like hell I will. I want to know what you mean. I didn't come here for a fight; I wanted to see you."

She moans as if in pain, and her eyes are so sad I want to hold her again and reassure her everything is okay. "Why? After all this time? Why would you suddenly care?"

I don't know what else to do but watch as she walks away, running when the scream comes from the house.

"Max," she cries.

Letting out a sigh, I shake my head and follow. He's so much work for her. And what's she doing, living in the middle of nowhere by herself?

I push though the screen door, following the sound to the back of the building. Max stands in the middle of the kitchen. Cookies are everywhere. Lily scrambles around on her hands and knees, franticly picking them up and placing them back into a container.

"What the ..."

"Help me find the last cookie. Max is freaking out because he counted them and now he's lost one."

Holy shit. I stand here, one eyebrow cocked. Lily looks

back over her shoulder. "Please, Adam. If you're serious about helping, look for the damn cookie with me."

I drop to the floor and crawl under the big old dining table, bumping into her as she comes the other way. "Here it is." I reach under a chair and grab it, backing out and standing. I hand Max the cookie. "There you go, big fella. Take good care of it."

He beams, and takes a big bite. I take the moment to look around. The outside of the house might be rundown, but the inside is spotless. Anything fragile is up and I guess out of Max's reach, though it won't be long before that becomes an issue. It must be so much work for her.

Everything I see makes me hurt just a little more for Lily. If she's alone, it doesn't explain the ring. If she's with someone, why the hell isn't he taking better care of her?

"Thanks," Lily says.

I watch Max wolf down that cookie and count the ones still in the container. "There are sixteen left, Mum."

Shifting my gaze back to Lily, I smile. "Why don't you go back to your sleep and I'll stay with Max for the afternoon?"

Max nods, a grin spreading across his face. "Adam can play with me, Mum."

Uncertainty crosses her face.

"Lily. Go and have a lie down. I've got this."

Her eyes soften as she looks between Max and I. "I can't expect … you can't."

"Mum, we're good. Go and sleep. I won't get in any cars again. Not even Adam's."

I flick a smile at Max. At least he understands how much his mother needs a rest.

Lily sucks in her bottom lip, looking between the two of

us. She sighs. "Fine. Max. Be good for Adam." Running her fingers through his hair, she bends and kisses his cheek. He rolls his eyes, but leans into her. They're clearly very close.

If she weren't so tired, I'm guessing she'd never let this ride, but she does, and as she walks to the kitchen door, she turns and meets my eyes, a grateful smile on her face. My heart's in my throat all over again. She's still so beautiful.

What happened?

9

LILY

I feel as if I've been sleeping forever when I open my eyes. The clock beside the bed tells me it's 5.16 p.m., and the scent of spaghetti and meatballs floats through the air. It's not unusual. It's Max's favourite dish, and he could eat it for every meal. No doubt he's told Adam all about it.

Adam. I don't know why I trust him; I've got no cause to, but he brought Max home, even if it made my blood boil to see Max in his car. Max is my whole heart, but he could well be the death of me and himself one day. It's a fine line we walk. As he gets older, he understands more, but I'm less likely to be able to control him.

Every day gets simultaneously easier and harder somehow.

For twelve years, I've managed to eke out an existence here. We lost the house to the bank when Mum died. Selling the contents has given me bits of income I supplement with the small flock of sheep Mrs Murphy left me and a top-up I get from welfare. It's not much, but we get by.

I sit up and throw my legs over the side of the bed. My jeans are on the floor where I dropped them, and I pull them up, noting they're no longer getting stuck on my ankles or hips. Feeding a pre-teen means sacrifices.

Making my way down the narrow stairs, I turn the corner and enter the kitchen. Max sits quietly at the table, reading a book, while Adam stands at the stove. The sight makes me want to cry. This was what I dreamed of for so long. The impossible dream.

"Hey." My voice cracks as I speak. "That smells amazing."

Max looks up, that cheeky grin of his lighting up the room. "Mum, Adam's making my favourite."

"I could smell that from upstairs." My gaze locks with Adam's.

"I hope you don't mind. I raided the freezer."

My heart sinks. Of course he has.

Walking across the kitchen, I open the freezer door. He's used two freezer bags of meat. I portion it out to last. I hold my breath and stop myself from sighing. It's not his fault. He wasn't to know.

We'll make it work. We always do.

"Food's nearly ready," Adam says. "Take a seat, Lily. I'll serve it up."

I grab a jug of orange cordial from the fridge and throw in some ice cubes from the freezer. As I take it to the table, I grab a stack of plastic cups along the way.

Pouring Max a drink, I sit next to him.

"I made enough for more than just the three of us. I guess though maybe you have a husband to feed too?"

I lift my head slowly until our gazes lock. Is that him digging for information, or is he just being polite? It's so weird him being here, uncomfortable, and yet the way it's meant to be. Maybe that's just wishful thinking.

"No, just us. Whatever's left we'll eat tomorrow."

He licks his lips and pauses before turning back to the stove. "Of course how much is left depends on how much Max eats."

I laugh. Max can eat seconds and has been known to eat thirds. The more he eats, the less I do. It's worth it, though, to see my boy growing up happy and healthy.

Adam places plates of spaghetti in front of us, and the smell of tomato and meat is divine. My mouth waters as he passes me a fork.

"This looks amazing," I say.

"I aim to please." He waggles his eyebrows, and my stomach somersaults in direct defiance to how I want to feel. Because I don't want to feel anything.

Max stabs a meatball, and twirls his pasta around his fork over and over. He's eaten this so many times he's an expert in it. Watching him enjoy it is an eternal delight. He takes a big bite, swallowing a chunk of food.

"Is it good?" I ask.

Max nods enthusiastically. "Soooo good, Mum."

"Did you doubt my cooking ability?" At the sound of Adam's voice, I turn my head. He sits opposite us, and my heart pounds just looking at him. How is he doing this to me after all this time? There had been no chance to say goodbye twelve years ago.

"Lily?" He frowns, and I realise I haven't answered his question. He shouldn't be here. I should have left him outside and dealt with Max myself. I've had enough loss and heartache in the past to last a lifetime. Him being here increases my chances of there being more.

"I'm sorry. I'll give it a try." I scoop up a meatball and load my fork with spaghetti. The meat just melts in my mouth, and I swallow my bite and nod. "It's very nice. When did you learn to cook?" The boy I'd known could barely boil water.

"I've picked up a few things over the years. Seem to remember you being pretty good at it."

I shrug. "Someone had to. It wasn't like my mother was capable all the time."

He opens his mouth and then closes it again. Maybe he doesn't want to dig up the past any more than I do. I have no idea why he's here, but I've heard more than enough stories from his mother to know he hasn't spent the last twelve years alone. At first I tried so hard to be nice to Joanna Campbell, hoping she would help me, but all she did was break my heart over and over again, telling me about Adam's conquests.

"I remember you being good at a lot of things," he says quietly.

A shiver goes through me. He doesn't have to resort to innuendo to make me blush as my face burns red. Before I met him, I was the shy girl who sat at the back of the class, the girl who was shunned by her peers. Meeting him changed my life; being with him ended in heartbreak.

I can't continue any conversation, so I focus on the food, picking at it in case Max wants more. I'm so entrenched in that habit I don't even notice at first the expression on Adam's face.

"Are you sure you like it?" he asks.

"It's good. I'm just not a big eater."

He frowns at my response. Adam might think he knows me better than that, but that was a lifetime ago—before everything changed.

"It's so good, Mum. I want more." Max licks his plate clean and holds it up. I laugh, handing him mine.

I can't bear to look at Adam's reaction.

"I'll make a start on the dishes." I stand, carrying Max's plate to the bench. Keeping my back turned to the table, I run the hot water and squirt detergent into the sink. I don't have to turn to know Adam's got his eyes on my back. I can feel it.

When Max finishes, he joins me at the bench and hands me his fork and plate. "Can I go and get some more of my toys to show Adam?" he asks.

"Sure." I want this over, but Max enjoys Adam's company, and I can't deny I've warmed to it. When his eyes aren't boring through me.

Adam's breath is hot on the back of my neck as he stands behind me, and I close my eyes as he reaches around and places his plate in the sink. "You didn't eat a lot."

"I told you I'm not a big eater."

"I know that's not true."

At one point in my life Adam knew me better than anyone, but that was so long ago and everything has changed. "It might not have been then, but it is now." I scrub his plate clean and stack it with the others to dry.

"Lily, we really need to talk."

For a moment, I close my eyes and focus. I have so many questions for him and yet there are a lot of things I just don't want to know.

"I don't know if we do."

His hand on my shoulder sends shivers through me. I want to hate him so much, but I can't. I've always been way too forgiving—my feelings over my long-dead mother are testament to that.

"Lily ..."

"Adam, come and look at these. I put some of my toys in the living room." Max comes in, and I turn and smile as he grabs Adam's hand and leads him out the door.

My past and present are becoming friends.

———

ADAM AND MAX sit on the floor playing board games. Max, who's so full of energy and good at wearing me out, has behaved the whole time as if a spell has been cast over him. He's not one for new people, or being out of routine, but he and Adam just fit. It's wonderful and scary.

We turn on the television and watch *Finding Nemo*. It's Max's favourite movie, and we've watched it more times than I can count. And yet, every single time that moment when Nemo is taken by the diver and calls for his father breaks my heart. I bite my lip and blink so the tears can't start. The last thing I want to do is break down in front of Adam.

"Are you okay?" he whispers.

Crap.

"I'm fine."

"Mum always cries at this bit."

I grit my teeth at Max's words. It's not his fault. I just

don't want to show any vulnerabilities in front of Adam. Not in my own house.

"Still a softy, then." His tone isn't teasing, and he's right. I think I know more about loss than most people. I didn't grow up with my father, don't even remember him, so the scene cuts me to the core.

"I don't know. Not as much, I don't think." I've had to be tough, especially with Max. By now I should be used to people looking, people talking about me, but I've always done my best to protect Max from it.

Max yawns, and shifts from the floor up to the couch beside me. With Adam on the other side, I have to shuffle over a little, and I'm a lot closer to him than I'd planned to be.

"You okay, bud?" Adam asks.

"He's tired. It's been a big day. We got up early to get to the garage. It gets busy there on Saturday mornings." I ruffle Max's hair, and he yawns again, leaning up against me.

"So you got your tyre fixed?"

"Sure did."

"Did you check out a replacement?"

I know he's asking because he's concerned, but it's still none of his business. "Not yet. There's still some life in that one."

"Not much. It's not safe, Lil." He hasn't called me that in years. He hasn't been here to, and no one else has ever called me that. It reeks of familiarity, familiarity he's not entitled to.

"It'll do."

"Lily ..."

"Can you two be quiet?" Max is grumpy now. He can't be far off falling asleep.

"Sorry, sweetheart." I kiss the top of his head and squeeze him against me. He doesn't protest—he's so tired.

Now he's had his hug, he moves back to the floor, lying on his stomach and propping himself up on his elbows. I know this move. It's the sign of a boy who's fighting sleep and is trying every position he can to keep awake.

It doesn't work, and I smile as his head flops to rest on the ground a few moments later.

"Is he asleep?"

I nod. "I'll wake him and get him off to bed."

"Don't."

My eyes prick with tears as I watch Adam scoop Max from the floor and into his arms. He's so gentle, and I guide him up the narrow staircase as he carries Max to his room and places him on the bed. I sit, and pull a blanket over my son, kissing his forehead. He doesn't even stir.

For a moment, we both watch over Max before Adam follows me out to the hallway and back down the stairs.

"I should go," he says softly, his gaze penetrating me.

I lower my eyes, unable to take his intensity. "Thanks for taking care of Max. He really loved it."

He nods. "I'm sorry about what I said before, that was out of line. He's a good kid. Those other children don't know what they're missing out on."

I bite down on my lower lip to stop it wobbling, tears forming. "He's the best," I manage to whisper.

Adam reaches out, touching his palm to my cheek and running his thumb across my lower lip. I have an over-whelming urge to kiss it—perhaps the contact would still my pounding heart. Instead I meet his eyes, still focused on my own.

"Lock the door behind me. Be safe, Lily."

He withdraws his hand and cool air fills the gap between us. All this time and everything keeping us apart, and I just want him to take me in his arms, kiss me, and make me forget all the time in between exists.

Instead, I nod, unable to speak for fear of telling him what I think. He's been to my home, satisfying his curiosity. When he leaves town again I'll have this tiny moment to remember him by. It's better than the way he left last time.

"Goodnight," I whisper, the words sounding wholly inadequate for the emotions overwhelming me. The past doesn't matter; right here and now, I want to be with him.

You're being stupid.

I follow him to the front door, watching as he makes his way to the car.

"Close the door."

I tear myself away from looking at him, closing it and flipping the key in the lock before turning to lean my back against the entrance. How, after all this time, is he so perfect?

The car starts up, and some deep urge grabs me, trying to convince me to open the door and call out to him. I hold it in. Max can't get close to Adam. I've already let things slip too far allowing him to stay so long. There was a reason he left the first time—why should now be any different?

As I climb the stairs, I touch my fingers to my lip where Adam's thumb grazed my skin. His touch still burns, the feeling of his flesh on mine lingering.

My bedroom seems empty and cold, but my body is warm from the rush that Adam gave me. I doubt the feeling is returned—judging by what his mother said, he's had enough women in his life. What's one more?

I drop my pants and pull my T-shirt over my head. As I unclip my bra and let it fall to the floor, tiredness overwhelms me. This sensation is nothing new. Between the work I do around the property and keeping up with Max, exhaustion is the standard. I tug my nightgown over my head. Sinking into my bed, I'm lonely for the first time in twelve years.

Damn you, Adam.

He looks better than ever. When I last saw him all those years ago, he was tall and lean, still a boy. Now he's a man, still with those dark eyes, but with a beard that I never imagined he'd have, and yet it suits him. He's filled out with those big strong arms of his that look so welcoming. And that chest ... I hold my hand out, curling my fingers as if stroking his skin.

I can't think that way. Not after everything.

I roll over and tug at the top drawer of the bedside cabinet. Feeling around until I find what I'm after, I pull out an old photo from the base. It's of Adam and I. The last formal dance at school. We were young and so in love. The feeling leaps from the photograph. All we had were eyes for each other.

What happened?

I stroke his face with my thumb, closing my eyes, remembering. When the dance was over, we'd made our way to his car before driving up the old road behind my house to a place where no one would ever find us. In the back seat of the car, we'd had sex for the first time and I still remember every kiss, every touch.

Stop it. This isn't helping.

I sigh, rolling onto my back and holding the picture up to look at. A year later we were torn apart by circumstances beyond our control.

Tears stream down my face, dropping on the pillow as I roll back onto my side and reach for the light. None of it had been fair, and now I find myself in conflict all over again. In my head, Adam had always been the one who had deserted me, leaving town and never looking back.

In my heart, he never left.

———

"Mum, Mum."

I wake to Max on the other side of my bed, staring at me, his head cocked to the point of almost looking upside down from the position I slept in.

"What's this?" In his hand is my photo, and he's gently cradling it as if it's the most precious thing he's ever found.

"It's an old photo of me."

"You and Adam."

I smile as best I can. So much for starting fresh this morning. Last night's thoughts echo through my head. It'll be a while before I can get rid of them. "That's right, sweetie. Want some breakfast?"

He stares at the photo, moving around as if he's trying to look at it from a different angle.

"Max?" All I want is to get it back into the drawer where it's sat since I moved in.

"Can I have it?" He's pleading with his eyes, and I always struggle to say no when it gets to that point.

"How about we get a nice frame for it, and we'll put it on your bedside cabinet? It'll be safe, and you can look at it whenever you want." It's been tucked away safe all this time, I'd rather it stay safe.

He nods, handing the precious photo back to me.

"Can I tell Adam?"

I hold my breath. By now, Adam must have satisfied his curiosity about us. We probably won't even see him again. What's the harm?

"Sure, sweetie. If he comes by again, you can tell him."

Max smiles and leans over, kissing me on the cheek before climbing off the bed. "See you in the kitchen, Mum. Don't be late."

I laugh. "I'll get dressed and be there in a minute."

Max rolls his eyes. "Girls always take forever to get ready. Hurry up."

"Yes, boss."

I shake my head as he skips off, heading downstairs. He's coming out of his shell more these days, although I've always seen a side of him that no one else has. Where they see a child with learning difficulties, struggling with even basic social skills, all I see is the sun.

He's my universe.

10

ADAM

It's still early when I arrive home, but the house is dark and quiet. Mum goes to bed by eight these days, and usually Dad is awake, but it looks like this time he's turned in too. I assume James is out.

I open the fridge and grab a can of lemonade, cursing myself that I didn't stop and grab some beer. That would have hit the spot.

When I hit the living room light, all the memories in this room hit me. It's happened every time I've entered it during the last few days. So many happy childhood memories, even for the short time I was here. Photos cover one wall, and for the first time in so long I feel pangs of regret over not being here. I haven't stopped to look at them, but I do now.

There are all the images that were there when I was a child, the ones of us boys at school. Now there are more. Drew graduating university, Owen at the bakery, Corey with some epic number of possum pelts. Mum said he's living a distance away, up McKenzie's Mountain, clearing pests from farmers' properties. I'll have to work out where he is too. Will he greet me the same way James did, or will he be more like Owen?

I sit on the couch and flick on the television. Not recognising the show, I cast my eyes around the room again. I don't even know where my brothers live, or have their numbers. That's how much I've cut myself off from this world. I'll have to ask James.

Simultaneously, I feel ashamed and angry at myself. What happened was between Lily and I, and yet I clearly hurt other people in my life who meant so much to me. But when it happened I was a teenager, not the man I am today. The man who feels the sudden urge to make amends with everyone.

I'm not leaving this place until I have more answers.

The back door opens and closes, and James appears in the doorway.

"Hey, stranger. I arrive home and you disappear. What's up with that?" I ask.

He grins. "Ashley's off to university soon. We're trying to get as much time together as we can before she goes."

"She your girlfriend?" I know Mum's answer to this, but as James's brother, I want to hear it from him.

James shakes his head and sighs. "Nah, we're just friends."

I know that look. "You want more?"

That does it. He frowns as he moves toward a chair opposite me and plonks himself down. "It wouldn't be fair."

"Are you going to uni, too?"

Sadness crosses his face, and he looks down at the floor. "Maybe in a year or two."

"Is that because of Mum?"

Being the baby of the family, it always seemed James was more spoiled than the rest of us. Maybe it was just a perception thing and he got everything we did, but when you're a teenager, a much younger sibling means the loss of affection from your parents. That's how it felt at the time.

He nods. "I don't know how long she's got. She says she's okay, but she's still got to have follow-up treatments."

I exhale loudly. "Dude, she's got the constitution of a goat. She could live another ten years."

"I don't think so." He says the words slowly, as if he's not quite convinced of what he says.

"Drew's in the same boat as you, and he's not here if anything happens. Hell, she didn't even tell me anything was wrong. You can't put your life on hold because of something that's out of your control."

And then it hits me. That's exactly what I did—put my life on hold ever since Lily stood me up. Everything I've done since leaving is superficial. Not the job—that was real enough—but the life I've led since leaving was exactly that. I drowned myself in meaningless hook-ups and moved around, leaving my real life on hold. This is it—this is the real thing. Being here is right, whether my mother is sick or not.

"Adam, I don't know."

I lean forward and catch his gaze. "Don't hold back. Go for what you want. When you get it, hold on for all it's worth and don't let go."

For a moment, he stares, his face contorting in confusion. Dad should be doing this. Dad should be making James see that he doesn't need to sit and wait here for Mum to die. Of all the times for him to hold back, this shouldn't be one of them.

Dad wasn't always like this. I remember him when I was younger being more vocal. At some point, he stepped into Mum's shadow and never emerged. Sometimes I wonder if that was for real, or if I just imagined it. What happened to him?

"I just feel bad thinking about myself when this is going on."

"What does Ashley think?"

He blinks rapidly and looks away. "She wants me to go."

"Have you got time to apply?"

He nods. "Late admissions is open, but not for long."

"Then get your arse on it. What's the worst thing that can happen? They accept and then you decide later on to delay it?"

James shrugs, and a wistful smile crosses his face. "I guess you're right."

"Have you got somewhere to stay? There's all that kind of thing to organise."

He gulps, and I have to stop myself laughing at the deer-in-the-headlights expression that now graces his face.

"You don't have to say another word." I chuckle.

"There's room at Ashley's apartment if I want it."

"Ashley's room?"

My little brother goes a brilliant shade of red and I laugh so loudly he waves his hands in the air. "Shhh."

"Do it, James. Don't live with any regrets." *Not like me.*

"I'll go and apply," he says, giving me a small smile of surrender.

"Like I said, what's the worst thing that can happen?"

I smile as he stands and walks away, up the hallway toward his bedroom. Even if he doesn't go through with it, I've tried.

Maybe he'll get the happy ending I didn't.

———

IN THE MORNING he's shut up in his room, and I raise my hand to knock on the door, about to ask him if he applied. Instead, I drop it. There's plenty of time to catch up with him later. Finding Lily with her flat tyre has given me an idea, one that might help a whole lot of people.

Including me.

I did some research of my own last night on the family computer in the living room. It's time to make a call on my future.

Mum and Dad sit at the table, having coffee and eating toast. I get as far as the phone on the end of the kitchen counter and pick it up, turning to leave again.

"Did you want breakfast?" Mum asks.

"In a bit. I'll grab my own. I've just got a call to make." What I need to do is go somewhere I can buy a mobile. Using roaming on my US one comes at a stupid price, and it makes sense to get a local number.

Back in my bedroom, I dial the number I wrote down the night before. An older man answers.

"Hi, is that Jack Kirby?" I say.

"That would be me. What can I do for you?"

"Mr Kirby, it's Adam Campbell."

"Adam." The warmth in his voice is unmistakable. If he'd been able to take on another employee back when I left school, I might have been able to complete an apprenticeship with him. Instead, he'd found me a job in the city. Where I'd planned to take Lily all those years ago.

"I just came back to town, and I wanted to ask you a few things …"

It doesn't take long to make an appointment to see him.

Now I just need to make one more call. The one to my agent to see how selling the apartment is going. The sale that'll give me the money to pull off my plan.

Maybe.

11

LILY

I can't stop thinking about him. Despite the overwhelming feeling we've seen the last of Adam.

I've had days before where he's been on my mind, but after the way he was with Max, there's new hope growing in my heart that shouldn't be there. Today's Thursday, so it's been nearly a week since we saw him.

There's no point in getting wound up about him when he was in town to see his sick mother. He might already have left.

After all this time I should be over it. I know what's important in my life.

I look at the clock. It's 2.37 p.m., and Max gets out of school at three. Time to go and get him. It's been a quiet day. The sheep are close to needing shearing, and selling the wool will help me fill the freezer. Maybe then I can squeeze in getting that new tyre.

Throwing my bag in the car, I start it up. It makes a weird

screech, and I smack my head against the headrest in irritation. The last thing I need is more issues with the car. It's made that noise off and on for a little while, and I need to get someone to take a look at it. Maybe I should have done it when I had the tyre fixed, but then it's not like I have the money to fix anything. I try to focus as I set off down the road. There's a lot to plan for in the coming years. Max will eventually go to high school, which is farther away. The other local kids catch the bus. Will he manage that, or am I overthinking it? Every cent I manage to squirrel away is for him.

I get to the end of our road and turn left toward town. The car splutters a bit, and I check the fuel gauge. There's half a tank left, so it can't be the gas.

Then I notice the temperature gauge rising. I once had a radiator problem, and the local garage gave me a payment plan to pay it off. There's no option for that now.

What the hell am I going to do?

Panic grips me, and I have no choice but to pull over.

Ironically, I'm across the road and down a little from the old garage. What I wouldn't give for that to still be open. It closed about a year ago. With it being time for Jack to retire, and no one to take it over, he'd reluctantly closed the doors. Now he lives closer to the cove, enjoying a quiet life, with the unfortunate consequence for the rest of the townspeople that it was now around fifty kilometres to the nearest garage.

I walk to the front of the car, a large black Holden parked up beside the garage coming into view. Hopefully that means signs of life in the old building, but I suspect I know who that car belongs to. I sigh and lift the bonnet. Steam comes out, but what I'm looking for I have no idea, and I curse Jack

Kirby for retiring. It's a good twenty-minute walk to the school and by the time I get there, it'll be well after three. I was cutting it fine enough as it is.

I've never been late before. How will Max react?

There are times when I wish he wasn't special, when he wasn't the impulsive, obsessive boy he is. It's exhausting keeping up with him. But Max is Max, and he's my whole heart regardless.

"Lily?"

Jack Kirby crosses the road and walks toward my car. I could kiss him for being there. My stomach drops as I spot Adam right behind him. I knew he was there after seeing the car, but he just makes me so nervous.

"Hey, Jack."

"What's up?"

I run my fingers through my hair. "I don't know. Can you please take a look?"

The old man chuckles and keeps coming until he stands next to me. Bending over and poking around the engine for a moment, he sighs. "Looks like a broken belt. Damn, Lily, this car is getting on a bit; you're probably lucky it's lasted this long. I'm glad you stopped. You could have done a lot more damage."

Yeah, really what I need to hear. "Thanks for looking, that's what I was afraid of."

"Are you wearing pantyhose?" Adam asks, and I shoot a glare at him. His lips spread into a cheeky grin. "I might be able to get it going with them. Fashion a belt to get you to the garage. Though it's a bit of an ask if you've got a long drive ahead of you."

"I just need to get to Max right now. I'm already running

late." I grab my bag and close the driver's door, sliding the key into the lock.

Adam pushes the car bonnet down and frowns. "Shit. I didn't think of the time. I'll take you."

I bite my bottom lip. Now's not the time to push him away. My need to get to Max is greater than my desire to get over this nostalgia over our former relationship.

"Lily?" he says.

Shifting my gaze to Jack, all I get is a wink in return. "Go on. I'll go home and have a dig around, see if I have anything. I doubt it though. Chances are you'll have to get one from Callahans."

Great. I've just made the trip there and back for the tyre a week ago. Now, my transport is broken.

"Thanks, Jack." I try to stay bright.

"Let's go get Max," Adam says.

I nod and follow him back to his car. Sinking into the black leather passenger seat, I'll readily admit to being envious. This is the most beautiful car I've ever sat in.

Adam climbs into the driver's seat beside me, and turns the key in the ignition. The car roars to life, and my heart slows a little at the thought of being with my boy soon. All I can do is pray he's not been chased off the school grounds by those bigger boys.

"He'll be fine," Adam says, as if reading my mind. He indicates to pull out and we're off, the car handling the bumpy road with such ease I could almost fall asleep. Even the sealed roads out here need maintenance—everything just seems a bit neglected.

We drive past the bakery. "Have you seen Owen?" I ask. I don't know why I ask—just that our silence is uncomfortable, and I'm as curious about him as he seems to be about me.

He nods. "Sure have. I went into the store, but he wasn't too pleased to see me. I need to catch up with him and find out what's up his butt. Probably the same thing that was up yours."

Despite myself, I giggle. It's the wrong reaction and completely inappropriate for the situation, but if I know Owen, he was an arsehole to Adam. He's always been good to me and Max, and we are often able to make toasties dripping in cheese with the bread and other odd foods he brings us. He'd say they were leftover, or ingredients he needed to use before the use-by date, but the bread was always fresh and the non-baked goods always neatly packaged.

Adam flicks me a confused glance. "That's funny?"

"You boys haven't changed. Still at each other's throats after all these years." When we were kids, I don't think a moment went past when two of them hadn't fallen out with each other. With five boys in the family, that had been bound to happen. Especially when the first four were so close in age.

"I guess you're right."

The conversation ends like that as we pull up outside the school. My stomach twists at the empty car park. I'm only five minutes late, but the teachers have all left, and I fist my hands, scratching the inside of my palms. Has Max taken off? Did no one see him?

My heart is in my throat as I scramble out of the car door, and I run toward the playground with Adam right behind. *Please let Max be there, please let him be there, please let him ...*

Max stands in the centre of a group of boys. Nausea

sweeps me when I lay eyes on him. No need to guess what they're doing.

"My mum says your mum's crazy. That's why you're so stupid," the biggest boy says.

I burst with pride when my boy puffs up his chest and looks the boy straight in the eye. "My mum's awesome. Your mum is clueless."

Behind me, Adam chuckles before stepping past, taking big strides toward the boys. "I think that's enough," he says.

At the sight of his large frame, there are a lot of wide eyes and dropping jaws before the boys scatter.

"Adam!" Max exclaims, and runs straight for him, wrapping his arms around his waist. My heart is back to pounding like crazy as I watch him. In all the time we've had the Campbell boys visiting us, he's never latched on to any of them. Not like this. It's confusing for Max to act like that, but he can be unpredictable.

Max turns his head and pokes his tongue at the departing bullies.

"Max," I say, trying not to smile at his courage, but right now I want his arms around me, not Adam.

Max lets go of Adam and grins up at him. He takes the few steps toward me and flings his arms around my waist this time. "It's okay, Mum. Adam and I got rid of them."

"Yeah, you did. I'm sorry I'm late." I bend, and bury my face in his hair and take a deep breath. He's safe, and that's the only thing that matters.

"Do you want a lift home?" Adam breaks the moment, and I shift my focus to him.

"I guess. I've got to call a tow truck and get my ..."

"You don't have to do anything of the sort. I'll come and

get you and Max tomorrow and once we've dropped him at school, I'll take you to go and get a new drive belt if Jack hasn't got anything. Then I'll fix your car for you."

I stand in silence for a moment, not quite sure what to say. I've done everything for myself for so long, it's weird to have someone wanting to do so much. This might not seem like much to him, but it's a biggie for me. I've always been grateful for the help I've received, but it's not been anything like this.

"Is that okay?" His cautious tone shows he knows he's overstepped the mark, telling me instead of asking me.

I nod.

"Is the car broken, Mum?" Max asks.

I nod again. "Sure is. But Adam can fix it from the sounds of it."

"We need a new one." He's right, but that's not happening any time soon, so I pull him tighter to me until he wriggles and protests. "Mum."

I laugh, and my gaze meets Adam's. If it was just Max and I, when we got home I'd find something to distract him and crawl off to cry in self-pity, but I can't with this audience.

"Let's go," Adam says softly.

He's still confusing, being so sweet and gentle.

My heart battles with my head, which tells me he's not really being the kind man I used to know. It's not out of love that he's helping me. He feels sorry for me.

But in a town like Copper Creek, there's not much sympathy to be had.

I'll take it.

12

ADAM

W hat the hell is wrong with this town?

At its best, it pulled together to help people who needed it. Now it seems to be at its worst, with the people ignoring Lily's struggles.

Hearing that boy angered me. I wonder who his mother is? I'd give her a piece of my mind over what her son has picked up. Thinking back to when I was here last, Lily was the stable one who kept her mother on track as best she could. Sometimes it'd be harder than other times. Lily's mother had been on all kinds of anxiety meds, and I used to wonder if the medication messed with her as much as whatever her condition was.

None of it was Lily's problem.

Sure, she had to deal with living with that. There were days she'd come to school with no lunch because her mother had had a panic attack about something and was curled up in bed not moving instead of buying food. That was where I came in. She had teachers who would help her out, but once I got there, I shared my lunch every time she was missing hers. Because I loved her.

But there was never anything of Lily's mother in Lily. From what I can see now, there still isn't. She holds things together for Max, and watching him, he loves his mum more than anything.

I don't ask what happened to her mother. From the little she's said, it's clear she's died at some stage. The thought of that makes me sad. I'm sure Diane Parker would have adored Max; he'd bring life to any situation.

I'll drop Lily and Max at home, sort out her car tomorrow, and then go and see Owen. Drew lives in the city, and I didn't stop to see him on the way in—I wanted to see Mum. But there's still Owen and Corey to catch up with.

As we drive through town, I realise I've been past the place she grew up in several times already. Not that I would have recognised it. The garden was always overgrown, but now it's almost impossible to see the house.

I pull up outside, and Lily grabs hold of my arm. "What are you doing?"

"Checking out this old place."

"What's this house?" Max asks, almost throwing himself between the front seats.

"It's where your mum used to live."

"Really?" His eyes are as big as saucers.

"Adam ..." Lily says.

"I used to sneak out of my house and ride my bike over here," I say.

"Who lives here now?" Max asks.

"No one." Lily crosses her arms and leans back in her seat.

I'm not asking her about her mother in front of Max. That's a question for when he's not around. Instead, I hedge. "It's been empty a while from the looks of things."

She nods. "About eleven years. Can we just go? We need to get home."

"Better buckle in, mate," I say over my shoulder to Max.

"I want to look at that house." He sits down as he's told and puts his seat belt back on.

"Maybe another day," I say, glancing at Lily. She takes a deep breath and exhales loudly, and I just know I've pissed her off again.

I indicate and pull out, driving away from the house where I spent a chunk of my years. Lily's mother was a seamstress, and her workshop was in a basement room. She'd bury herself in there for hours churning out clothing while Lily and I had the run of the rest of the house. There was a lot we got up to in that place while she worked happily beneath us.

We hit the end of Lily's road, and Max bounces in the back seat.

"We're nearly there," I say, laughing.

"Our house is so boring. That house looked cool."

"It was, a long time ago. Now, not so much."

Lily stays silent in the front seat, looking out the passenger window. I can't but help feel that she's avoiding looking at me.

"It looks like a jungle outside." Max seems to have no intention of letting go of this, and regret kicks in that I ever started it.

"What about your house? It's pretty cool." At least this

time I know exactly where I'm going, and I pull slowly into the front yard of Lily's place.

"It's okay," Max says in a flat tone.

"Thank you," she says in a voice so soft it makes bits of me tingle that shouldn't.

"You're welcome."

"Want to come in for a drink and a cookie, Adam?" Max's voice spills from the back seat, and I hear the click of a seat belt as he shoots forward again, his head between the driver and passenger seats.

I swallow hard and look at Lily. She's got the smallest of smiles on her face, and I read her resistance. Then she nods and widens her smile a little. "You're lucky if Max wants to offer you a cookie. You should grab the invitation while it lasts."

"Are these the floor cookies?" I grin, shifting my gaze to Max.

He rolls his eyes to look at the ceiling. "No, silly. Mum made some more."

"Glad to hear it."

This kid is getting so far under my skin, just as much as his mother. It's crazy. Sure, he's a little quirky, but it all adds to his character.

Lily opens the passenger door, and Max clambers over the centre console and into the seat. His dusty sneakers leave dirt all over the leather seat, and as he scrambles out behind his mother, she turns and gapes at what he's done.

"Max! Adam, I'm so sorry." She leans in and brushes the seat, but I capture her hand in mine and stop her.

"It's okay. It'll come off."

Those eyes of hers suck me in, and her breath hitches as

we gaze at one another. She's struggling with this as much as I am. Why's she so abrasive?

Lily frowns and pulls her hand away. She doesn't have to say a word. There's something between us even after all this time, and instead of being easy, it's so hard I can't form coherent thoughts about it. It's so right, and yet somehow so wrong. I don't know why, and it's maddening.

I get out of the car and walk toward the house, following behind Lily and Max. Max is so full of energy, he practically skips to the front door. I give myself a little smile. Now I get more time with them.

"Coffee or cordial?" Lily asks as we enter the kitchen. She walks to the bench and flicks on the kettle.

"Coffee, please," I say.

"Cordial, Mum. I'm not allowed coffee." Max sits at the dining table and I join him, tousling his hair along the way.

"I bet you're not. And I bet we could both have a cookie."

"They're my favourite." He grins. "Mum makes the best cookies."

"Better than the ones at the bakery?"

Max nods. "Except for the gingerbread men. Those are awesome."

I smile. "Owen wouldn't let me have one last time I saw him. They're pretty precious."

Looking up, I see Lily's eyebrows raised and I shrug. She carries the biscuit container to the table and lifts the lid.

"How many am I allowed?" I ask Max, remembering how he freaked out last time he thought he lost one.

"We can have one each."

I nod and am rewarded with a smile from his mother. These kinds of things must keep her on edge, not knowing how Max will react. She pours the hot water into the cups and stirs.

"I'll tell you what. You can pick out which one I'm allowed so I don't choose the wrong one."

Max rolls his eyes. "It doesn't matter, duh."

"Hey. Be nice to Adam. He's just trying not to pick out the one you want." Lily places Max's cordial and my coffee in front of us.

"Sorry," Max says.

"No harm done," Max smiles when I grin at him.

Lily puts down the biscuit tin between us, and sits beside me with her coffee.

"Can we get a new car?" It's the second time Max has asked this, and Lily can't distract him this time.

"We can't yet, sweetheart." Her cheeks flush as if she's embarrassed.

"It sucks."

"Yeah, it does, but that's life."

I feel like an intruder watching their exchange. What I want to do is reach out and help, but I'm also acutely aware of Lily's pride.

"At least tomorrow's Friday." I offer up a change of subject instead. "Nearly the weekend, Max."

He grins, crumbs from his cookie sprinkling all over the tablecloth. "Will Mum's car be fixed by then?"

"I'll fix it tomorrow."

Max sits up straight, his eyes wide. "Can I watch?"

"It'll be sorted out while you're at school. Are you interested in cars?" I ask.

"He is now," Lily mutters. Max nods.

"I was probably about your age when I started getting

interested in them. If you want to, we could sort out a day where I show you what goes where."

His gaze shoots straight to his mother. "Can we, Mum?"

"We'll see."

At least she didn't say no.

After coffee and two cookies, I reach over and touch Lily's arm. "I think I should get going. See you tomorrow?"

She nods. "I'll walk you out."

As I stand, I lean over and ruffle Max's hair. I get a grin in return. "See you in the morning, bud. Want to come for another ride in my car?"

He looks at his mother first and then back at me. "Yes please."

Lily follows me to the door, and I stand there once I've opened it to say goodbye.

"Thank you again for today." She still seems to hold back, almost thanking me reluctantly.

"Any time you need help, just call the house. I'll grab a mobile tomorrow. I don't think there's anywhere here I can buy one."

Her expression softens, and I'm rewarded with the smallest of smiles. "Sure."

Her tone suggests she'll never do it, but I've put the offer out there.

That's all I can do.

13

ADAM

I'm on their doorstep early in the morning. Lily told me school still starts at nine, and I want to make sure I'm there in plenty of time.

I grin at the thud of footsteps running toward the door. It can only be Max with that much enthusiasm.

Sure enough, his cheeky face appears as the door is flung open, and following him is his mother, frowning and exasperated.

"How many times have I told you to check who it is before you open the door, Max?"

He slouches. From what I've seen, the last thing he wants is to disappoint his mother.

"He'll do it next time. Right, Max?" I'm trying to cheer the kid up, but all I do is piss off Lily as she glares at me.

"I'm sorry, Mum," Max says, leaning against her. He gazes up at her with all this adoration in his eyes, and her frown cracks as she looks back down at him. There's so much love there, I assume the result of them just having each other for a while. I wonder how long it's been since his father was out of the picture?

"I hope I'm early enough."

Lily checks her watch. "We're good. Max, do you want to grab our bags?"

He nods and shoots back into the house.

"I'm sorry if I overstepped the mark. He seems like a good kid."

Lily nods. "He is. He just forgets, so I have to drum things into him. Max had developmental delays and he struggles sometimes." Her smile lights up her face. "But that's what I'm here for."

"Got them, Mum." Max runs back, passing her a brown leather bag and flinging his own over his shoulder. "Let's go. Yay, I get to go in Adam's car again."

I catch Lily's eye roll as Max walks past me and out to the car. At least she's smiling now, even if it is small and strained. What I need is some time to talk to her alone, and we'll get plenty of that on the road to get the part.

"Come on," I say, holding out my hand.

She nods and walks straight past me toward the car, and I smile to myself and follow. I don't think she's trying to treat me badly—that's not Lily. I think she's trying to keep her distance, maybe for self-preservation, and with her having a child, I get it. She needs to protect him as much as herself.

"Car's unlocked," I say.

"Make sure you use the back door this time," Lily says.

Max tugs at the back door, pulling it open, and Lily makes sure he's buckled in before walking around the car and opening the passenger door. I sit in the driver's side and wait for her to do up her seat belt before starting the car.

"Ready for a good day at school, Max?" I ask.

"Yep," he yells, bouncing in the back seat.

"Max loves school," Lily says. "Nothing gets him down for long. Does it, Max?"

"Nope."

I start the car and slowly turn toward the driveway. Lily glares as I rev the engine, spinning the wheels and kicking up the gravel in her yard.

Max, on the other hand, squeals with delight and claps. "Do that again."

"Your mum won't be too happy if I do."

"It's not safe," she grumbles.

"I'd never do anything to hurt you. Or Max," I say.

As I speak, I just catch another eye roll before she turns her head to look out the window.

She's impossible. I'm so going to enjoy getting under her skin.

The fifteen-minute drive to school goes quietly, except for Max. Lily continues to look the other way, but Max is full of pure joy as we make our way down the main street of town. He's in his element, beaming with pride as he gets a ride in my car. I think it's true love.

"Your car is so fast, Adam," he says.

"Sometimes. I can't go too fast or the cops might chase me."

He laughs, and I sneak a glimpse at Lily. The corner of her mouth twitches up to smile.

"Mum never drives fast. Her car is a piece of crap. I wish she'd get one like this."

"Max." That magic moment seems to be gone for her and she twists a little further away, as if she's here out of obligation and doesn't really want to be.

"I think your mum does a great job with what she has. Those cars last forever if you treat them right." While I think she needs something a bit more modern and safe, I know now to hold my tongue while I'm around Max. The last thing I want is to piss Lily off even further.

"I guess."

In the rear-view mirror, I see Max sit up straight. I slow down and perform a U-turn to pull up outside the school. This kid is so proud in this moment—the whole school is going to know it.

"Thanks, Adam," he says, unbuckling his seat belt. Lily's already got her door open, and gets the door for Max. "Thanks, Mum."

"Want me to come in?" she asks

"Nope."

She still stands and watches as he disappears inside the gate, shifting slightly I assume to get a longer look.

After yesterday, I understand her concern. "I might just go to the gate and check he's got into his class okay."

Before she can say no, I'm out the driver's side and around the car. I press the remote to lock the car, and together, we walk the short distance to the gate. Her shoulders slump in relief as Max gets to the grey prefab classroom and gets in the door.

"You okay?" I ask, watching her face.

"Why wouldn't I be?"

"You're worried about him."

She sighs. "Any time he gets picked on I get nervous."

"Lily."

Lily turns at the sound of her name and I turn too. Coming up behind us is a statuesque dark-haired woman. As she draws closer, she looks more and more familiar. I narrow my eyes to take a closer look.

"Adam?" She knows me. I know this face.

"Sure is," I say.

I flick a glance at a frowning Lily. Clearly, she's not happy, whoever this woman is.

"It's me—Sasha."

The light dawns. Sasha was in school two years ahead of us, and my mother had not been impressed when my fifteen-year-old brother had started seeing sixteen-year-old Sasha. Corey had dated her on and off for a year, and during one of their off times, she'd become pregnant with another guy's child. Then that guy left. Her oldest must be in high school by now. She must have had another kid.

"Sasha."

She turns her attention to Lily. "Which is what I wanted to talk to you about. Karl tells me he had to look after your boy when you were late picking him up yesterday."

"Look after? You mean pick on. My car broke down and I was a little late, but your boy wasn't looking after Max. Not in the slightest."

Sasha's face goes red, and her nostrils flare. I know that look. Before they'd split for good, Corey had often been on the receiving end of it.

"What are you trying to say? Karl said Max said some nasty things about me, and he was sticking up for me."

"It was the other way around. He said something about me, and Max spoke up."

"Liar. There's something wrong with that kid of yours."

Lily fists her hands.

"Actually, Sasha, I saw the whole thing. Karl said some pretty nasty things about Lily. Max stood up for his mother." I'm not about to let this go without speaking up, and not just because of my unresolved and unreturned feelings for Max's mother.

She rolls her eyes. "I should have known you'd stand up for him."

"I'm just telling you what I saw. I'd be talking to your kid if I was you. Make sure he knows not to bully anyone, especially smaller kids."

She's not going to get any further with this and she knows it—I can see it in her eyes. Instead, she draws a deep breath and jerks her head into a stiff nod. "I think we both need to talk to our boys if that's the case."

If looks could kill, Lily would be dead twice over. No wonder Sasha's kid has a shitty attitude.

"Pretty sure Lily doesn't need to speak to Max." I can't help it. Beside me, I hear Lily let out a quiet laugh.

"At least if you're around he'll have some sort of father figure."

Now I remember why Sasha pissed Corey off so much. She may have been hot and put out, but she was mega bitchy. "I think he's done fine up until now. He'll be even better if bigger kids didn't try bullying him."

She opens her mouth again as if to say something, then closes it. Guess she's happy picking a fight with Lily, but not with me. Without any further words, she turns and walks away.

Lily's hand lands on my shoulder, and I turn my head to

see a smile on those lips, her eyes twinkling with laughter. "You didn't have to do that."

"I know, but it made me feel better. Some things never change, do they? Like how annoying she is?"

For a moment we gaze at one another, and I take in the sight of a happy Lily. She makes me think of better times, when all we had was laughter and love and nothing else mattered. It seems so long ago.

"We'll check in with Jack and then shall we go and get this part for your car?" I ask, aching to link my fingers in hers and cover her hand in kisses. It used to be our thing once, and she would tease me about what a gentleman I was. At least in public.

She nods. "Yes please. Sooner I can get back on the road, the better."

The moment's gone as she turns back toward my car, and I trail behind her. I wish I knew how to break through with her, to get past that barrier that's between us. Every time I see her, I feel as if I'm closer, but there's so much of herself she keeps hidden.

I should know.

———

JACK DOESN'T HAVE the part, but he loans me some tools to fix the car.

I had planned on trying to speak with Lily about our years apart on the way to Callahans, but instead we sit in an uncomfortable silence while I try to work out what to say. Every time I'm near her, my thoughts are confused, and it's hard to get them together.

"I haven't had too many problems with that car. It's usually well behaved." It's surprising, but Lily's the one who breaks the quiet, giving me a small smile. I think this is as awkward for her as it is for me.

"They don't make them like they used to. There's a reason those cars are still around. Not hard to fix either."

"Thank you."

I grin. "You're welcome. I'm happy to help."

"I do appreciate it."

She's throwing me a lifeline. Do I grab it and push my luck, or just work with it and take it at her pace? "To be honest, I'm glad it waited until I was in town to help out. Must be hard when you have to travel so far to get anything done."

Lily sighs. "It doesn't make life easy. The apprentice Jack had when you were here qualified and left, and he struggled to find someone else. It just ended up too much for him."

"Yeah, he was telling me. It's such a shame for the area to lose services like that."

"That's what happens in a small town." She looks down at her hands. "I still wouldn't live anywhere else."

"Why did you stay here?" The question slips from me before I can stop it.

Lily shrugs. "Despite everything, it's a good place to raise a child. I don't know how Max would handle the city. I think it'd be too noisy and distracting for him."

"I guess you're right."

"Did you miss this place?"

Callahans is coming up on the left-hand side of the road, and I indicate to pull into the driveway, not wanting this moment to end. Who knows how the trip back will go? "I missed it a lot. Though I think at first it was the who I missed rather than the where. Being back makes me realise just how much homesick I've been, even if I didn't realise it at the time."

She nods, and then she's first out of the car when I stop in the car park. I'm not sure if she's running from further conversation or just eager to get her car fixed. I suspect it's the conversation.

"You're keen." I laugh as I get out the car.

"Sorry. I just want to get it sorted. We're so dependent on that damn car." She gives me her first truly genuine smile, and as they always did, her eyes light up and her gratitude is plain to see. "I owe you for this."

"Do I get to choose how I get paid out?" I take a chance.

Her eyebrows creep up and her lips quirk like she's trying not to smile. "What did you have in mind?"

I round the car to stand in front of her. "To spend some time with you. Maybe a date?"

The strangest expression crosses her face, uncertainty with a tiny bit of want. Although that might be wishful thinking on my part.

"I don't date."

"Ever?"

"Ever."

I cock my head and eye her up. "Why not?"

Her shoulders slump. "I can't. I also don't know if the car park of the garage is the right place to be having this conversation." She walks past me and toward the door. As she reaches it, she pauses and looks back over her shoulder. "Are you going to tell me which belt I need, or do I have to guess? I bet there's a whole lot of variants."

I'm not sure if she's flirting with me, so I take the risk. "I could tell you what part I think you need, but you might slap me."

Lily rolls her eyes as I hold out my palms to show I'm not being serious. Is it wrong to want someone so much who doesn't seem to be interested in you? At times she's been so hostile and other times I see her soften, like she wants to let me in but isn't sure of me. But what's there to be unsure of?

We sit on a precipice, and I don't want to push her over by questioning her. I'm torn between wanting answers and trying for a fresh start. She seems stronger than ever, but broken.

I don't just want to fix her car. I want to fix us.

———

NOTHING IS EVER SIMPLE.

I tell the salesperson what part we need and without thinking, I hand over my credit card. Lily's busy looking at car accessories and doesn't realise I've paid for the belt until I'm heading back toward her with it in a plastic bag.

"You didn't pay for that, did you?"

"Sure did." I can't help the smile on my face, even though I know she could flip out.

"Adam." Her light-coloured eyebrows dip, and she frowns.

"I got a little carried away. See anything else you like?"

"Nothing you're paying for."

"Let me pay for lunch." I catch her off guard, and her eyes widen as she gazes at me.

"I thought we were coming here and then going back."

"That was the plan. Seeing as we're here, I thought we could take a walk and check out the shops. Maybe find somewhere to eat. What do you say?" I try that smile, the one that usually worked to reel in the ladies. It is cheesy, and this is *the* special girl, but I have to give it a go.

"I say we go back home and get my car fixed. I have things to do."

For all I know she does, but I'm taking a gamble on her being free for at least part of the day. "Like what?"

"I've got to check the sheep. They're not far off shearing, and that's where a chunk of my income comes from. Plus, I have vegetables to get ready for the farmers' market on Saturday."

"I'll help you do it later."

She sets her jaw, but I don't want to let up. How often does she get someone wanting to help her, take care of her, do things for her?

I place my hand on my heart. "I promise I won't buy anything else for you, but I do want to buy lunch. We'll just look."

Lily shakes her head and licks her lips in a move that sees me shuffling on the spot. "Fine. But we have to be back in time to pick Max up. I'm not leaving him at the mercy of that cow Sasha's kid."

"We will be. I promise."

Her face shuts down, and I can no longer see what she's thinking from her expression. She's in shut-out mode for some reason, and I need to know what triggers that.

"Lily?"

"Don't make me any promises. Just do it."

She's back to business with her tone, and it's like a switch just turned off.

"No problem. We'll be back with plenty of time to spare."

She nods. My much happier companion has gone and been replaced by this defensive woman who's put me back to where I started.

How do I get past that?

14

ADAM

She relaxes a little as we walk, and I see her looking wistfully in the fabric shop. Maybe she inherited the sewing skill from her mother. That woman could make anything out of nothing with her sewing machine.

"Want something?"

Lily shakes her head. "No."

"Are you sure?"

"Positive."

We move on, but it still bugs me. Since the day we met, I've had the overwhelming feeling of wanting to protect her. Despite the distance, that's not changed. She deserves so much more than she seems to have.

"If it's a money thing, you can always pay me back."

She comes to a halt on the footpath and turns to me. "I know you mean well, but I'm not putting myself further in debt to you."

"I didn't mean it like that."

Lily turns and keeps walking. I shake my head, irritated at myself for putting my foot in my mouth and scoot after her, pointing across the street at a restaurant. "That place looks good. How about we get lunch there?"

"Sure."

The more time I spend with this woman, the more I'm frustrated and interested. It's driving me crazy. She's so hard to talk to until she's not, and words flow from her mouth freely as if we were lovers again. I want to make the most of every moment we get together.

We cross the road and I read the sign above the door. "Pacific Gold. Best food around. We'll see about that." I grin, and Lily sighs. She's not going to make this easy in any way, shape or form.

It's not exactly busy. There are two other couples sitting at the round tables, trimmed with stark white tablecloths. The food had better be good. This place has zero appeal otherwise. It's so bland.

I pull a chair out for Lily and she sits stiffly, looking around.

A waitress is already approaching and hands us menus as I sit opposite Lily.

"Would you like any drinks before you order?" she asks.

"I'll just have a Coke. Lily, do you want anything?"

"The same. Thank you" She opens the menu and starts scanning it. I do the same.

"Food looks good," I say.

"Hmmm."

"I think I'm gonna have to have a steak. Mum's cooking is as bad as it always was, and I've missed New Zealand food."

She nods. "I think I'll have the Chicken Parmigiana."

"Excellent choice, Miss Parker." I shoot her a smile, and she gives me that shy look that leaves my heart palpitating.

The drinks appear quickly and give Lily an excuse not to talk to me. She sips at her Coke with a straw and looks at me from under those eyelashes. Anyone else and I would think she's flirting with me, but my brief time back here tells me that's not what's going on.

The food arrives soon after we order, and I take a bite of the most succulent steak I think I've ever eaten. I groan at the taste. "This is amazing."

Lily nods. "The chicken's good too. Thanks for bringing us here."

"You're thanking me for the delay?"

She smiles. "No, just for the food. The delay is a pain in the arse." Her smile widens. "You're a pain in the arse."

"Why change the habit of a lifetime?" I break through and make her laugh. There was a time when that happened a lot, when all we did was laugh and smile. Now everything's awkward and forced except for in moments like this when it feels so natural.

Taking a sip of my drink, I decide to bring the conversation a little closer to home. "What's up with Max? He's such a great kid, but he seems like he has his moments."

She licks her lips, and seems to struggle to put words together. "He's had his health issues, and he has learning disabilities. Although, I wonder about that sometimes. He seems smarter than the kids around him who don't."

I look down at my drink. "He does. I love seeing how close you two are. I guess he's been good company for you."

She leans back in her chair as if she's been slapped. "He's everything." Lily blinks as if she's trying to push back tears. I don't know what I've said to prompt that response—maybe it's just her thinking of her son.

"I'm sorry if I'm upsetting you."

"Why didn't you ever come home?"

Her question hits me straight in the chest. It almost sounds like a plea. "I thought about it. But you had your life to get on with and so did I."

Tears roll down both her cheeks. I've unlocked something. "Sometimes I'd see your mother in the street and she'd make sure to tell me how you were getting on with your life." She sniffs and wipes her cheeks with her sleeve. I want to round the table and hold her until the tears go away. After all this time, I never expected us to end up like this, sitting across the table from each other. She's so close and yet so far.

We're interrupted as the waitress appears again. "Any more drinks?"

I shake my head, but not before the waitress frowns when she catches sight of Lily's tears. She glares at me before turning and walking away.

My focus shifts back to Lily. "I did get on with my life. Only because I thought there was no hope back here."

The words hang over us, and her expression is one of disbelief. "No hope?" she whispers.

This is getting way too much over a table in a restaurant kilometres from home. We need to go somewhere private to discuss this, not be sitting in a public place. I hate seeing Lily so upset.

"How about we finish our lunch and I get you back home?" I say gently.

Lily nods, pushing around the food on her plate with her fork. I wish I knew what was going on in her head. My heart hurts for upsetting her, even though I don't know what it was that did. It doesn't sound like my mother has helped my cause.

"I'm sorry if my mum's upset you. You know how she is."

"The crazy control freak? Yeah, I know." She lets out an exasperated sigh. "I'm sorry. I know she's sick."

"You're still allowed to think that way. You know better than anyone how I always felt about her being so controlling."

Lily places her fork on her plate. "I think I've had enough to eat."

"You haven't had much. We could ask for a doggy bag. Max might like some of that chicken."

She gives me a wan smile. "Sounds like a great plan. He'd love it." The colour's faded in her cheeks, and her eyes seem heavy.

"You look tired."

There's a slight nod as she agrees. "I think I need to take a nap."

"Want me to pick up Max from school this afternoon?"

She sucks in her bottom lip, and I don't know if it's because it's tempting or I've overstepped the mark.

"Why are you doing this?" she asks after a few moments.

"Doing what?"

"Being so nice. Wanting to take care of Max." Her eyes reveal nothing and it's driving me a little nuts.

"I just want to help out. Does he play sports? I bet I can wear him out."

Lily's lips tremble, and her throat moves as she swallows hard. Are she and Max that short of anyone taking an interest in them? Are they really that alone?

"Adam, I can't expect you to …" she whispers.

To hell with scaring her. I reach across the table and place my hand on hers. Touching her brings a peace to my soul long since gone. In that sliver of a moment before she pulls her hand away, I know I'm where I need to be.

"No expectations. I like spending time with you two." Is it so wrong to want to rewind the clock and pick up where we left off? Before it fell apart? It's hard not to get my hopes up when the woman I always wanted sits across the table from me, even if the distance between us is massive.

"I just don't know if it's a good idea."

"Why not?"

She drops her head as she bends down to pick up her bag from the floor, ignoring my question.

"Lily?"

"Let's just get back. I've got things to do."

Despite my telling her I'd pay for lunch, she heads straight for the cash register and pulls out her purse. Exasperated, I run my fingers through my hair and shake my head. Every so often I feel as if nothing's changed, that we're close and she's open to me. We used to share everything. Then she turns her back and I'm lost, floating in a sea of uncertainty. It irritates the crap out of me, and only leaves me wanting more.

As she goes to hand over her card, I reach over her head and place my credit card in the cashier's hand. Lily's so close I can smell her perfume—another inch and I'd be pressed against her. The thought of that wakes an urge in me, and I have to focus on the transaction to push it out of my head. There's no denying I want her.

"Adam." I don't have to see her face to know she's pouting.

"I said I was going to pay for it. Stop being cranky."

The cashier hands me back my card, and I smile at Lily until the waitress brings out the doggy bag for Max.

"Happy?" I ask.

"You're infuriating." She's suppressing a smile as I hand her the container of food.

We walk back down the road toward Callahans and my waiting car. On the way we stop at a small electronics store so I can buy a phone. It's an older iPhone, but it's a decent price and it'll do the job. The whole time Lily keeps her distance and doesn't look at me.

"What's going on?" I ask as we draw close to the car.

"What do you mean?"

"Is it so bad that I want to spend time with you and Max?"

She stops and turns toward me. "I don't know. You've just been gone for so long. I know why you came home, but why you're taking such an interest is beyond me." She sighs. "It's confusing."

"I've been confused for years."

Lily reaches up and rests her palm on my cheek. The touch confuses and soothes me all at once. "So have I." Her eyes tell a story of her confusion and fear. They're still so dead compared to how she used to be.

"Then let's help each other work this out," I say softly.

She drops her hand. "I don't know. Maybe. It's a lot to take in."

Turning back, she sets off again, and I sigh before following.

Whatever happens, this is going to take some time.

———

THE DRIVE HOME is equally quiet, and Lily struggles to keep her eyes open as we weave down the last of the country roads before we reach the town. I smile as she closes her eyes and gets some of the rest she seems to so desperately need. It's not just that I'm still as attracted to her as I was all those years ago—I'm also enjoying these little things I can do for her. As much as I think that I came home for Mum, truth is I also came back for Lily. Can I win her heart again?

I head back to Lily's car. She gets out first once we get there, as if she's keen to get away from me. Her light floral scent lingers behind her, and I take a deep breath before exiting. I have to make the most of these moments when she lets me in.

"Thanks for this," she says for the millionth time as I reach the front of the car. I prop up the bonnet.

"You don't have to thank me. I'm happy to help. Just wish we could have spent more time talking."

She shrugs. "I don't know what else there is to say."

I still have so many questions, but it's clear she's not going to answer anything. I'll have to chip away at that veneer and get on the inside to get any answers. What happened to that warm, sweet girl who would do anything for anyone? She's put up walls, and while I catch glimpses of her behind them, it'll take a lot to smash through.

She fidgets behind me as I pull out the old, broken belt and rip open the packaging of the new one. Hopefully this hasn't caused too much other damage to the car. I think she might break if anything else goes wrong with this thing.

"Is there anything I can do?" she asks.

"It won't take long. I'm just checking to see if I can spot anything else. I want this car safe for you to drive." I look back over my shoulder and she raises her eyes to look at the sky. Anything but look at me. "Although, it'd be better if you got a new car," I murmur. *Shit.*

Pain spreads through my shin, and I yelp before turning back toward her. "Hey. What did you kick me for?"

"You don't think if I could get a new car, I would? I'm thankful for the help, Adam, but my life's not so easy I can just do whatever I want."

"I get that. I really do." I take a step toward her. "I'm just looking out for you and Max. Being back here has woken some old feelings, and meeting Max …" I smile. "Meeting Max has been an adventure."

"An adventure." She's not smiling. Whatever I say is wrong.

"He's such a great kid, Lily." I lick my lips and take another half step, drawing level with her. "Seeing you again makes me realise how much I miss you. I've thought about you a lot over the years."

She nearly breaks her resolve. I always could read her face, and it's so hard for her to keep her composure. We're at the side of the road where anyone could see us as they go past, but I want to grab her and kiss her, reacquaint myself with the taste of those pink lips.

"I used to miss you. But I moved on."

That's a stab to the chest. "When did you get to be so stubborn?"

Lily frowns.

"I want in those walls. You can't hold out on me forever."

She flicks a look from under her eyelashes that warms me from head to toe. I wanted her when we were teenagers— now that urge is even stronger. This girl I used to be with has transformed into an impressive woman. Strong, resilient.

I'm still in love with her.

15

ADAM

I've spent the last four days trying to contact my brothers, and Owen and Drew won't return my calls. Corey is apparently off hunting and unreachable. What I really want is to sit down, have a beer, and talk shit with them. The longer I'm here, the more things about them I miss.

Instead, I try to be the dutiful son and spend time with my mother. If I didn't know better, I'd think there was nothing wrong with her. When he's not working, Dad hovers around me like he's wanting to say something, but he never does. It's driving me mad.

We eat another dinner which my mother insisted on cooking without help. Her moods range from being slightly happy to miserable, but I'm never sure if it's her illness or just her personality behind it.

After dinner, Mum, Dad and I settle in to watch television. It's boring as all hell, but at least I'm with my family.

Mum grumbles as the phone rings. "Who is it at this hour?"

"It's only half past eight." I laugh.

She shakes her head and shifts her view back to the TV.

Dad gets up and disappears into the kitchen to answer. "Hello? Lily? Are you okay?" Dad's tone is panicked, and he pokes his head in the living room door. "Lily's on the phone for you?"

"The world must be ending," I mutter as I take the phone. It has to be pretty extreme for her to risk speaking with Mum to talk to me.

"Hey, Lily."

"Adam, it's Max. He's gone." The words tumble out in a rush in a high-pitched tone.

"What's going on?"

"We had dinner and I tucked him into bed, but he sneaked out. I went to check on him and I can't find him."

I swallowed. "Could he be hiding?"

"He never has before. I've got the police here, but I really need you too."

She needs me. "I'll be right there."

I hang up the phone and stare at it for a moment. This isn't the way I expected her to take me up on my offer.

"Adam?" Dad touches my shoulder.

"Max is missing. Lily's going out of her mind."

His eyebrows dip, and he lowers his voice. "We need to talk …"

"When I get back." Dad trails behind me as I head out the door and toward the car.

"Adam," he calls as I climb in the front seat.

"Later, Dad." I start the car and hit the accelerator, leaving him standing in the driveway. Whatever he has to talk to me about can wait. I've got more important places to be.

There's a police car in Lily's yard, and on either side of the house torches flash as they search for Max. My stomach churns. He's a smart kid, but if he's gotten into trouble ... it doesn't bear thinking about. Every light in Lily's house is on.

I pull up near the porch and step out of the car. Turning as I hear another car behind me, I raise an eyebrow at the sight of Eric Murphy getting out of it. Did she call him too?

She's had Eric Murphy running around after her for years. Mum's words echo in my ears.

Despite being anxious about Max, I can't help the jealousy running through my veins. Maybe she just called me for extra manpower to search for her son, but Eric? The sudden thought that Eric might be Max's father leaves me nauseous. The thought of Eric touching Lily makes it worse.

"Eric?" I say as he approaches.

"Holy shit. Talk about a blast from the past. Adam Campbell?"

"Yeah. I'm home. Did Lily call you too?"

He frowns. "No. I just saw all the lights and the police car from the road. Wondered if she needed help."

Stalking past me, he reaches the bottom of the steps as the front door swings open. Lily darts through the door, past Eric, and straight at me. I catch her just as she flings her arms around my neck, sobbing into my chest.

"Hey," I whisper, kissing the top of her head.

"I'm sorry for calling. I didn't know what else to do."

"You have nothing to be sorry for. I'm glad you called." She's shaking. It's not that cold, but it is chilly. Max will be fine for a while in this, but we really need to find him.

"What's going on?" Eric asked.

Lily raises her head, and from the surprised expression on her face, I can tell she had no idea Eric was there. "Max has run off somewhere. At least I think that's what happened. I tucked him into bed, went back down to watch TV for a while, and when I went to check on him he'd gone." She gasps as she speaks, taking big breaths of the night air.

"What are the cops doing?"

"There are a couple of them looking around. If they don't find anything, they'll form a search party."

Tears stream down her face and instinctively I wipe them away with my fingers. "We'll find him, Lily. I promise."

I'll move heaven and earth to keep that promise to her.

———

THE POLICE SEARCH turns up nothing but the discovery that Max's bicycle is missing. Now we know he's probably not on the property, but he's out there on the dark roads on a bike with no light.

"Can you think of anywhere he might have gone?" Lily's asked by the police for what feels like the hundredth time. We sit on the couch, her hands enveloped by mine. She seems to find my presence reassuring. I only wish I could do more.

She shakes her head. "The only place he spends any time at other than here is school."

"Do you think he'd go there?"

"I can't see why."

One of the cops has already gone, taking a slow drive toward the cove. Max being out on the road terrifies me, memories of the day I could have run him over still fresh in my mind.

"We'll find him," I say, slipping one arm around her shoulders. She leans her head against me, and I rest mine on hers.

"I'm going to check the creek," Eric says softly. He's stood near the doorway, watching us this whole time.

Lily pulls away. "You don't think?" She stiffens as her eyes fill with fear.

"Just in case. I know Max can swim, but we need to eliminate that."

Now's not the time to get irrational and jealous that he knows this and I don't. I'm the one who should have been here for them. I know that now more than ever.

He leans over and kisses the top of her head. "I'll come back as soon as I've checked. I'll take a look around the back paddocks too, just in case he's gone to hang out with the sheep or something. The cops didn't check very far."

Lily nods, grabbing hold of his hand. "Thanks, Eric."

At the door he pauses, looking back at her with an expression I know well. It's the look of a man who's loved and lost. It's the same expression that's looked back at me in the mirror all these years.

She leans against my chest, and I stroke her hair, kissing her forehead. "He's an explorer, Lil. He needs to know everything," I whisper.

"How could you possibly know that?"

"I was the same at his age. It wasn't until I found you that my heart settled."

Her chest rises and falls at the deep breaths she's forcing herself to take. The effort is obvious. With her in my arms I feel whole again. Even if there's still a wall between us, it's a lot thinner than it was.

"Thing is that Max is even more so. He doesn't always see the world like the rest of us, and I bet he's not even thinking about how scared you are right now. There's something out there he wants to see, and it's important enough for him to sneak out."

She nods and sniffs, raising her face to meet my gaze. "I'm glad you're here, and I'm glad that you're getting to know Max."

I palm her cheek. "I'm glad you're letting me in."

"What are we doing?" Her voice is a whisper.

"What do you mean?"

"This. You're back five minutes and I'm here, in your arms. You make me feel safe, the way you always did." Tears roll down her face and over the back of my hand where it rests.

I raise my thumb, running it under her eye. "I can't tell you how happy it makes me to hear that."

"All I need now is to know Max is safe."

"He will be. I just know it. We'll find him, Lily."

———

AN HOUR LATER, the residents of the caravan park are out searching the cove. We've not heard from Eric, and Lily's going out of her mind. She and I have sat on the couch, with her enveloped in my arms, just waiting. She's frozen with fear. It's radiating from her and it kills me I can't make it stop.

"I've had enough of sitting here. I'm going for a drive toward town," I say.

"There are already people out looking. I don't want to be alone," she whispers.

"You won't be." A voice comes from the door, and we look up to see Eric. Hope fills Lily's face. "There's no sign of him at the creek, or with the sheep. I'll sit with you if Adam wants to go for a drive."

He flops in a chair beside the couch. His jeans are covered in dried mud, and from his tired expression, it's clear how hard on him looking has been. Dad told me it's rained a lot these past few weeks, and the ground must be soft.

"I might go for a drive toward the school, go past the bakery."

Eric nods, handing me a torch. "Good idea. Take this."

"Thanks."

Lily grips my hand. "Please find him." Her eyes plead with me, and I'd do anything to reassure her.

"I'll do my best. I swear."

She nods.

"I'll be back soon." I bend and kiss her cheek. Her grip tightens, and I squeeze back before pulling my hand from hers.

I get to the door before turning. Eric looks up. "I'll make a coffee. Want one, Lily?" He gives me a look that tells me she's in good hands. It sucks to leave her, but I can't sit still. It's one of those moments where I miss my army mates, the ones I've spent countless hours with, the ones who would be out combing this place for Max if I asked. But I'm a long way from the military and my other family. Max needs me.

The time in the car alone brings me the ability to think.

It's been difficult to concentrate with Lily so strung out. I'm as worried about her as I am about him.

When I hit the main street, I slow, cruising past the shops and heading toward the school. He has to be out here somewhere. Where would I go if I was Max?

As I pass the shops and with not much farther to go to the school, my eyes pick up Lily's old house. *Shit. What if he's gone there?* It was a few days ago I mentioned it, but what if his curiosity got the better of him? It can't hurt to check.

There's no traffic as I do a U-turn and pull up outside the place. I grab the torch and exit the car. The only lighting around here is the dim glow of the streetlights. Not enough to guide my way.

The old metal gate creaks as I open it. The garden has taken over the path to the front door, and I push my way through it toward the house.

"Max," I cry. *Please let me find him.* "Max."

Growing closer, I reach the front of the garden. Lily said no one has lived here in eleven years, but it's clear no one's even visited for that long. Maybe now she's accepted my help and seems to want to lean on me for support, she'll open up and tell me everything about the past twelve years.

"Max." I shine the torch on the front door. It's slightly ajar, and I push it open farther.

There's a musty smell inside, the scent of a house that's been shut up for a very long time. This place has been long since abandoned. *What the hell happened here?*

"Max," I call again, shining the light around and surveying the inside.

It's obvious there's been someone here at some point after all, maybe squatters. Graffiti covers the walls, and there's old bedding lying around. Even in a small town like this there are people down on their luck and delinquents out of control.

A small face peeks around the corner, and I let out a relieved breath at the sight of Max. Tears stream down his cheeks as he runs toward me and I catch him, holding him tight and trying not to cry myself. I've never felt such a sense of relief in my entire life.

"Adam," he sobs, and I just hold on, closing my eyes as I hug him.

"What are you doing here?"

Between breaths, he spits out the words, "I just wanted to see it. Mum wouldn't let me so I did what you did."

I used to sneak out of my house and ride my bike over here. That's what I told him. *Shit.*

"You should have told her where you were going. She's been worried sick about you."

"I was going back. But my torch went flat, and it was dark. I couldn't see the way out."

I sigh and stroke his hair. "Let's get you home to Mum. Don't you ever do this to her again."

He pulls away. "I won't."

We make our way back through the garden, and just before we get to the gate, he pauses. "My bike's here somewhere."

I shine the torch and see it lying in a bush to the right of the path. I'd walked right past it and missed it.

Shaking my head, I hand the torch to him and pick up the bike, carrying it the short distance out to the car. I open the boot and it almost fits. I'll just have to leave it open.

"Get in the car." He hops in the back obediently.

I pick up my mobile as I get into the car before realising I don't have Lily's number. "Hey, bud. Do you know what your home number is?"

"Mum tried to get me to remember it, but I can't." He's in the back with his arms crossed.

"Okay. Let's get you home. She'll be so happy to see you."

It's a quiet ride back to Lily's. Max isn't stupid. He knows he's in for a whole world of hurt once he's home. Although, Lily will probably just be glad to see him safe.

"Mum's gonna be pissed," he says. I keep my eyes focused on the road, my head turned firmly away from Max so he can't see me laughing to myself.

"She's right to be. That wasn't cool. She called the police she was so worried."

This time I look in the rear-view mirror. Max's face falls, and I can see he hasn't thought that bit out.

"I didn't mean to scare her."

"Maybe not, but you did." We reach the driveway and I slow. "She's also going to be so pleased to see you. Better make the most of it, kiddo, and tell her how much you love her."

Max's head is down, and it's clear the full impact of what he's done has just hit him. I feel sorry for him, but at the same time it angers me that Lily's been so upset. She turned to me when Eric was right next door, and the thought of that fills me with more hope than it should. The way she flew out of that house and into my arms sends me a message.

"Okay." A little voice says from the back seat.

"Max, your mum loves you so much. That's why she's scared."

I pull into the yard. One of the cops has returned, and

Eric's standing by the house, talking to him. Maybe Eric's reporting what he didn't find in the creek. Lily appears in the doorway.

When I come to a stop, Max is out of the car before me, running toward his mother and flinging himself into her arms. "I'm so sorry, Mum."

"Where were you?" She wraps her arms around him tightly, planting her face in the top of his head.

"I wanted to look at the house." His voice is muffled, she's got hold of him so tight.

"What house? Oh …" She looks up at me and I nod.

"It's my fault, Lily. If we hadn't stopped …"

She shakes her head. "No. Max should know better than to do this kind of thing."

A hand slaps me on the back, and I turn to see a man in a blue uniform smiling at me. "Glad you found him. Where was he?"

"Abandoned house on Main Street. The house Lily grew up in."

His expression straightens, and he nods. "I know the one."

"Thank you for all your help," Lily says.

"You're welcome. I'm just happy he's home again. I'll call it in, let everyone know he's safe."

Eric's right behind him. "I'm glad Max is home okay, Lily."

She nods. "Thanks, Eric."

"Adam." He nods and walks back to his car. I shift my focus to Lily and Max. She's holding him tight, but he's not complaining, and her eyes are closed.

"How about we get back inside and turn all these lights

off? The power bill will be horrendous." I try to lighten the mood, but Lily stays right where she is.

"Come on." I wrap my arms around both of them, and she lets go enough for me to guide them inside. Closing the door behind us, I follow them into the living room. It's much warmer in here, and Max sits on the couch while Lily places a blanket around his shoulders.

"What were you thinking?" she asks. There's fear and hurt in her voice. The crisis is over, but she has every right to let him have it.

"I just wanted to see." He pouts, but I don't think his mother is angry. She's over that and into the upset. If she was angry, her tone would be way different to this.

"There's nothing *to* see."

"I know now." He's so sad, and the pain she has is shared by him. It's clear watching the interaction between them.

Lily sits and wraps her arms around him. "I'm just happy you're safe. If anything happened to you, I don't know what I'd do." She gives him a little smile. "How about I get you a hot chocolate and a cookie. When you're warmed up, you can get changed and brush your teeth."

"Okay, Mum."

She looks up at me with a smile. "Does Adam want a hot chocolate and cookie too?"

I laugh. "I'd love that."

"Done." Lily stands, and as she walks past me she pats me on the chest. "Take a seat."

Her touch sets off emotions I can't get a handle on. I walk to the couch and sit next to Max. "You okay, bud?"

He nods.

"Tired?"

Max yawns and lies down, his head on my lap. My heart's warmed to see him so comfortable with me, and I place my hand on his head. If things hadn't gone the way they had, maybe he would have been my boy—maybe he'd have siblings. We'd be living happily-ever-after with our children.

Lost in thought, I don't hear Lily come back into the room until a tray with three mugs and a plate with cookies is placed on the table.

"You still awake?" she asks Max, ruffling his hair.

"I am now." He pushes himself back up into a seated position. For a moment, Lily studies the two of us with this wistful look on her face. Could she be thinking what I just did?

"Drink up and have your cookie. Then it's time to brush your teeth and go to bed." She bends and kisses him on the head.

Max nods, and Lily lets out a tired breath, picking up a mug and settling into a chair to my left.

"Are you okay?" I ask her as I reach for my drink.

"Relieved. I'm glad you worked out where he was."

"To be honest, I was heading toward the school." I shake my head. "That place is such a mess."

"I can imagine. It's been abandoned for a long time."

"What happened?" Last time I was there, her mother had had a nice little sewing business, and while they weren't flush with money, they weren't starving. I can't remember Lily saying anything about her mother. But she's here alone which tells me something went wrong.

"The bank foreclosed. Then the house didn't sell. By then I was living here, so I just watched as it ended up the way it is now."

"I'm sorry." I took a sip of my hot chocolate.

"It is what it is. This place has been good to us. It's old, but the roof keeps the rain off and it's warm in the winter. That's all you can really ask for." She smiles and the whole room lights up. Lily always did see the cup as half full.

"It sucks to see it so bad. Looks like people have camped out there."

She shrugs. "Probably. It's very private from the street."

Max's head bobs, and I nudge his arm. "You still awake?"

He grins. "I just want one more cookie."

"Grab one before I change my mind," Lily says. Her voice has lost that shake, and she no longer sounds afraid.

The cookie's in his mouth in an instant, and he munches on it, that big smile on his face, crumbs flying as Lily shakes her head at him.

"Love you, Mum," he mumbles, more crumbs spilling onto the floor.

"Love you too." She's tearing up again. I stand as she does, and Max rises when she takes a few steps toward him. "Come on, you. Let's get you sorted and into bed. Say goodnight to Adam."

"Goodnight, Adam." Max throws his arms around my waist. I close my eyes as I hug him, resting my head on top of his.

"You have a good sleep, bud. I'm glad you're safe." I look up at Lily. "I guess I'll get going now."

"Let me get him into bed before you go?" She wants me to wait, and she shares a smile with me that makes my heart leap to my throat.

"Sure."

I sit back on the couch as she takes Max upstairs and gets

him into bed. Kid must be exhausted. It's a decent bike ride to Lily's old place from here.

On the wall is a photo I never noticed before, and I stand and walk across the room to take a look. It's Lily and Max, and from the looks of it not long after he was born. She's cradling him in her arms and has the biggest smile on her face. I recognise the living room. It's this place. This must be the place she came home to after he was born.

Who took the photo? Was it Eric?

Despite her earlier ignoring him to get to me, I can't help the pangs of jealousy. How did I stay away after Mum told me they were together? I should have come back home and fought.

I still need answers, but every time I'm with her something else gets in the way. Tonight is no exception. She's been through a lot, and for now I'm content to see her reunited with her son. This isn't over by a long shot.

"You waited." She stands in the door, and the smile across her face tells me she's happy about it.

I shrug. "You asked me to. Besides, I wanted to make sure you were okay."

Lily crosses the room until she reaches me. "I wasn't sure if you would. Thank you for everything."

"All you have to do is call." I'm lost in her eyes as we gaze at one another. There's no mistaking the longing I see this time, the reflection of my feelings. "All you ever had to do was call."

"I didn't know."

She lets out a little gasp as I cup her face and bring her in to kiss her. I taste her lips for the first time in years and yet I've never forgotten them. Her mouth opens a little and I slip in my tongue, caressing hers as I drop my arms to her waist, pulling her in tight.

To my delight she kisses me back, moaning softly as the kiss grows in intensity. I've thought about this moment so many times, and it's everything I ever hoped for.

Lily wants me.

I back off a little, ending the deep kiss and pecking her on her lips.

"Well?" I whisper. "What next?"

"Let me catch my breath." She chuckles, placing a hand on my chest.

I'd give anything right now to throw her over my shoulder and carry her off to bed, but we have all the time in the world, and she's had a big night already.

"I'm going home. Give you some space. I think you need it."

She nods, and I have to confess to a little disappointment even though I suggested it. But from what I've seen the last thing she needs is for me to rush her into anything.

"I need to spend some time with Max after this." Her eyes fill with tears. "If I ever lost him ..."

"You didn't. He's safe. We had a talk in the car, and I don't think he'll do this again."

Lily lets out a big breath. Her relief that this is over is obvious. "How long are you in town for?"

"I'm not going anywhere. I'll be around." I reach up with one hand and stroke her hair. "I meant it when I said I missed you."

"I missed you." She bounces on her heels and plants a kiss on my lips. "Just give me a few days to work this all out in my head."

"Deal."

I let go of her only to link my fingers in hers. "Walk me to the door?"

Lily nods, her cheeks flushed, looking more like the girl I used to know than the woman I've seen during the last couple of weeks. She leans her head on my shoulder as we walk toward the entranceway.

"This is like saying goodnight when we were teenagers." I laugh.

"Except as soon as we said goodnight then, you'd double back and sneak in to see me."

I bend my neck and kiss her hair. "It's a bit harder to do here if the bedrooms are upstairs."

Lily raises her face to smile at me. "One step at a time."

"One step at a time."

Before I throw all reserve out the window and ignore the nagging feeling that she needs room to breathe, I brush her lips with mine one more time and extract my fingers from her hand. "Remember to lock the door behind me. I need both of you to be safe."

She nods, and I make my way out the door and towards to the car, turning to see her in the doorway. "Get inside. It's cold."

The door closes and I climb into the Commodore, grinning to myself.

I feel better than I have done in years.

16

LILY

That kiss.

That kiss took my breath away and with it twelve years of feeling that no one else understood me. Adam does. Adam always did. There are still so many unanswered questions about why he left, but for now it's time for me to go to bed and sleep.

Max can stay home tomorrow. Tonight gave us both one hell of a fright, and I don't know if I can focus on anything else. We've been through enough.

As I climb the stairs, my mind is awhirl with thoughts of Adam. What does this all mean? Surely he'll be leaving again soon. Why would he kiss me like that?

I round the door to my room and smile as I spot the lump in the middle of the duvet.

"What are you doing in my bed?"

Max pops his head up. "I wanted a hug."

"Wriggle over." I drop my pants to the floor and slip my

top off while he nestles into the far side of the bed. Slipping my nightgown over my head, I slide into bed beside him.

"I'm sorry, Mum." He snuggles in against me as I slip my arm under his neck.

"I know. You can't do that again, Max. You scared me."

He leans his head against mine. "It's a scary house. Did you really live there?"

"I grew up in that house. It wasn't always scary." There was also a time when it was, but Max never needs to hear about that.

Max hugs me. "I don't want to go back there ever."

"You never have to. Neither do I."

I drift off with my son in my arms and dream of Max, Adam, and I being one big happy family.

What I always wanted.

————

WHEN I WAKE Max is already out of bed, and as I come down the stairs, I hear the television playing cartoons. I poke my head around the corner. He's sitting quietly with his backpack on.

"What are you doing?"

"It's nearly time to go to school."

I laugh. "Don't worry about that. We're having a day at home."

His eyes widen. "Really? You never let me stay home unless I'm sick."

"It's okay for today. I think after last night we need it."

He frowns. "I'm sorry, Mum."

"I know."

Max unhooks his bag from his shoulders, letting it drop on the couch. "Adam saved me."

I laugh as I pick up the phone. "I know he did. I hope you said thank you to him."

The phone rings twice, and the answering machine at the school picks up. I leave a message telling them Max won't be there today.

"There, that's done."

"Do you think we'll see Adam today?"

His words echo in my head. *Give you some space.* "I don't think so."

"I wanna see him."

I smile as I sit beside Max on the couch. "So do I. What are you watching?"

With Max distracted with cartoons, I go into the kitchen and start working on breakfast. As the bread toasts and the water boils, my mind wanders again.

I have to try and keep my head together. I've got to organise the shearing crew to sort out the sheep. That means dealing with Eric. We get a better deal if we combine the flocks. He can be so hard to talk to sometimes. This is the man who asked me to marry him, but there were conditions attached. He would pay for Max to go to a special school, but it meant Max not being with me. I couldn't handle that, neither would Max.

Eric turned up last night uninvited, but then again, he did me a huge favour checking out the creek.

Beside me the toast pops up and I jump at the sudden sound, even though it should have been expected. Last night's events still have me on edge, and I need a coffee and something to eat to start this day.

I make a hot chocolate and put some Coco Pops in a bowl. Max is laid out on the couch, sitting up as I place his breakfast on the coffee table.

"Are we really staying home today?" he asks.

"We sure are. You can watch cartoons if you want."

As I turn to go back into the kitchen he leaps up, wrapping his arms around my waist. "I'm sorry, Mum."

"I know. It's okay." I hold him tight and close my eyes. He and I have this connection that's unbreakable, and it goes deep. All we've ever had has been each other.

"It was so dark. Is that why you don't like the dark?"

That's such a loaded question. "A little bit. It wasn't so scary when I was your age. It was my home, just like this is our home."

That seems to placate him for the moment, but if I know Max, there'll be other questions later. He's so inquisitive. It's a trait he inherited from his father.

"I'm going to go and have my coffee. Eat your breakfast and maybe you can help me make some more cookies today."

Max smiles and releases me to sit back down. As he loses himself in television and breakfast, I make my escape to the kitchen. Coffee brings me to life and calms me all at once. I close my eyes as I sip it.

Draining the cup gives me the nerve to call Eric. I try to avoid it; it's hard to say what kind of mood he'll be in. But this is important to Max and I. I don't have the capacity to pay the shearing gang by myself. Eric will sort it out and give me the balance of what I'm owed. This is one of those times when I hate that I feel I owe him, but it's better than being homeless.

His mobile rings a couple of times before he answers. It

depends where he is on the property as to how good his reception will be.

"Lily," he says as he answers the phone. His voice is full of warmth, although it always is until our conversation takes a turn he doesn't like.

"Hi. I need to talk to you about organising the shearing."

"Sure thing. You at home today?"

"We're not going anywhere. Max and I both need to recover from last night."

He laughs. "Fair enough. I'll be over soon. Put the kettle on."

When he's not being a dick, I don't mind Eric. His mother was my saviour and the reason I have a roof over my head and Max with me. I'll be eternally grateful for that.

I make my way back into the kitchen and flick the kettle on. From the window, my flock of sheep come into view, the only thing enabling us to make it through the year in one piece. In comparison to other families, I know I'm lucky. But it still scares me at times.

As far as earning money, this is a time of the year I look forward to. It helps me catch up and get a little bit ahead.

It doesn't take long for Eric to turn up.

"Thanks for coming over," I say as I answer the door.

He grins. "You're welcome. I was thinking yesterday it's almost time to get things sorted for this year. Seems like five minutes since we organised last year's shearing."

"Tell me about it."

"I also wanted to make sure you were okay, that Max was okay."

"We're fine."

Eric trails in the door behind me, following until I reach

the kitchen. "So, you and Adam. What's going on there? I thought he'd be the last person welcome around here."

I roll my eyes. No beating around the bush with him. I turn and shrug. "I don't know yet."

"Lily, you can't let him back in your life. Not after the way he stayed away."

I shake my head at him. "It's not really any of your business."

Eric grabs my arm, and I shoot him a glare I'm sure could melt steel. "He's not the one who's been here supporting you."

I snatch my arm away. "No one has supported me. I've taken care of myself."

"Who was there for you when you were found? Who was there for you and Max when he was born?"

"I've never stopped appreciating that, but I'm here by myself raising *my* son."

"In the house *my* mother said you could live in for free."

Anger grows in me. Eric's not often thrown that in my face, and he knows he can't do a thing about it unless he argues his mother's will in court. The only thing that's greater than Eric's ego is the control he has on his wallet.

I keep my voice level. "Until the court kicks me out, I suggest you leave."

His face falls as he realises he's crossed a line. I'm not stupid. For years he's told me he'd wait for me, as long as it took. And yet he's banged every eligible woman who would say yes, and a few who were taken. Not that it really matters —there is only one man who will ever fit into my life.

And now I know that more than ever.

———

I'M SITTING in the living room in the afternoon, when I hear the crunch of gravel beneath car tyres.

"Can you see who that is, Max?" I ask. He's closer to the window.

He peeks over the back of the chair he's sitting in and out the window. "It's Owen." Max jumps up, his eyes huge. "Do you think he's got a gingerbread man for me?"

"You'll have to ask him." I laugh.

I follow him out to the door and grin as he flings it open. He loves it when Owen visits, and I have to admit I do, too. Not only does he bring us bread, but he usually has some sweet treats. Although, it's not like him to visit during the day when the bakery's open. He has an assistant, but he likes being in control.

"Owen." I shake my head at the bags that he's holding. At least you can freeze bread.

"I thought after Max's escapade last night you might be hungry."

"Have you got me a—"

"Gingerbread man? Somewhere in here. I've got something for your mother, too." Owen nods, and I step back to let him in the door.

"That's all he's after."

Owen grins as we follow him into the kitchen, and he places the bags on the bench. "Need some energy, little man?" He retrieves a smaller paper bag and hands it to him.

"Thanks, Owen."

"You got it. Just don't scare your mother like that again, huh?"

139

Max shakes his head. "I promise."

"Good boy."

I chuckle as Max disappears back into the living room and the sound of cartoons floats back through to the kitchen.

"I brought bread, but given that I haven't had lunch, I grabbed some pies too. Want one?"

I nod. "I haven't had one in ages."

"So, how's Mum doing?" He opens the cupboard and pulls out a couple of small plates.

I let out a loud sigh. "Apart from wanting him to never leave the house again?"

He laughs. "At least he's home now, Mama Bear. And at least you only have one of him to worry about. Mum and Dad had five of us."

"One's enough."

"There are more pies in the bag. Just chuck the leftovers in the freezer." He pulls out two and places them on the plates before opening the microwave door.

"The baker puts the pies in the microwave to get the pastry soggy?"

"Sue me. I'm hungry."

Moving to his other side, I pull open one of the bags and move the remainder of the pies to the fridge. These will fill a gap.

"What's this?" I take out another paper bag.

"Fresh cream donuts. I brought one each. Max likes his gingerbread—I thought you might like something a bit more grown-up."

"Donuts are more grown up?"

He laughs, opening the microwave door when it beeps. "I don't know. I just felt like one."

"How are you not the size of a house eating this stuff all the time?" I open the drawer and take out two knives and forks, following him to the dining table.

"It's all the running I do. Before I go to work, after work, running away when the husband of my latest conquest shows up."

I shake my head as I sit at the table. Owen's so down to earth, but he's only partly joking when he says that. I've never laughed so hard as when he got caught with Cara Mitchell, the butcher's wife. Well, I knew he'd been caught—thankfully Cara's husband didn't recognise that white arse disappearing into the distance.

"So, how did you know about Max's exploits?" I slide my knife into the pie and thick gravy and cheese oozes out onto the plate. My mouth waters at the thought of it.

"I heard it from the desperate housewives of Copper Creek," he says, taking a bite of his pie.

"The what?"

He laughs. "You know. The ones who turn up for morning tea and make eyes at the custard squares while choosing the feta and spinach rolls. Because flaky pastry is healthier when there are green vegetables involved."

Laughing, I roll my eyes. "What did you hear?"

"That Max went missing and the police were involved. You could have called me."

I nod. I should have. Owen cares about Max. "I'm sorry. I was running on adrenalin and called your brother."

His eyebrows knit in confusion. "Which one?"

"Adam."

Owen puts down his food and studies me intently. "Why would you call him?"

"It seemed the right thing to do. We've seen him a few times lately. He helped fix my car."

Owen leans back in his chair. "I'm surprised."

"He *is* a mechanic."

"You know what I'm talking about."

I let out a breath, sighing loudly. "Yeah, I do. He seems to want to make amends. He's been nothing but good to me, and he found Max."

"Where was he?"

I stand, taking my empty plate to the sink. "A few days ago when I was having trouble with the car, Adam helped me pick up Max from school. He stopped to take a look at Mum's house. Max wanted a closer look."

Owen slams his fist on the table. "So it's his fault for showing Max."

"No. It's not." I walk back to the table and sit. "Max's curiosity got the better of him. He could have talked to me, but instead he decided to sneak out."

"What if he does it again?"

"He won't. We spoke about it. He got a fright and got confused in the dark. Adam brought him home." I reach for Owen's arm and rub it. "All I care about is that I got my baby back."

"And Adam? Is he going to stick around this time?"

I shrug. "I don't know. But I do know that it's not taken long for him to bond with Max, and while it scares me a little, it's so good for Max."

"How about you?"

We might be like family, but telling Owen about the kiss crosses a boundary for me. "I wasn't sure at first, but he's not pushed me in any way. We'll either spend time together or we won't."

"I hope like hell you know what you're doing. The last thing I want to see is you or Max hurt again."

I nod. "I know. It's scares me, but Adam getting to know Max feels like the right thing to do."

"Just be careful." He smiles, but there's caution behind it.

"Maybe it's time Adam got to know his son."

17

ADAM

By Saturday I'm itching to see Lily. I said I'd give her space, and I know she'll be busy today as the farmers' market is on in town. Tomorrow will be quieter, and I'll go and see if she and Max want to spend some time together.

Now I watch out the window over the garden below. James is down there, tending to a row of tomato plants that are just taking off. Dad says he has the greenest thumb in the house, which is saying something. Dad is the king of making plant cuttings thrive. James apparently has the magic touch, and I wonder if it's because he seems to be stroking the leaves and talking to them.

It won't be long until he leaves home, either to university or out on his own. The last of the Campbell boys. He was just a child when I left, a boy I didn't really know. Maybe it's time to remedy that. We keep missing one another, so now's as good a time as any.

I push open the window. "Hey, James."

James turns and looks up, grinning. "What's up, big brother?"

"Want to take a trip to town? We'll get some beers for after dinner."

He nods. "Sounds great. I'll just clean up."

Pulling the window closed, I make my way back downstairs and toward the door to the backyard. Dad stands at the kitchen counter, looking out the window. Was he watching his youngest son too?

"James and I are just going up the road to get some things for tonight. Want anything?"

Dad turns, shaking his head. "Are you going to be back for dinner?"

"Sure am."

For a moment, his brows knit together and my eyes see the sadness, or is it something more in his? "What is it, Dad?"

"We need to talk at some point."

"Sure. What do you want to talk about?"

"About when you were away."

I lick my lips. My curiosity itches. "Like what?"

"Ready." James stands in the doorway, a big grin on his face.

"See you soon, Dad. And tonight, I promise."

He nods, his lips curling into a small smile. "Sounds good, Son."

I lead James out the back to my car, and he grins as I unlock it. "I bet this thing goes fast."

"Pretty fast. Want to drive?"

"Serious?" His eyes light up.

I nod toward the driver's door. "I'm assuming you have your license. Come on."

"I do."

"Is it good to be home?" James asks. The windows are all down, a light breeze blowing through the car. I lean on the open window, my elbow propping me up. It's not a long drive, but a scenic one, with trees either side of the road interrupted only by the odd driveway.

"It's already turned out better than I'd hoped," I say, glancing at him. He's sitting back and relaxed, and he seems happy in my company. Of all the brothers, he's the one I have the fewest memories of. I never got in any trouble with James.

"Mum told me off for calling you. I figured you'd want to know. It wasn't fun tracking you down."

I laugh as we reach the end of the road.

"When do you leave?"

We turn the corner. The store is right down near the end, toward the road to the cove. Toward Lily.

"Who said anything about leaving, little brother?" I laugh, and James raises an eyebrow at the answer.

"Don't you have an army to get back to or something?"

"Not anymore."

———

JAMES HOLDS his curiosity in until the beer is loaded in the car and we turn around, this time with me at the wheel. I wear the silence, knowing there are a bunch of loaded questions just hanging in the air, waiting to spill out.

We turn down the long road leading home.

"You left the army?"

I nod. "It's time for me to get my life back. Settle down or something."

James laughs, leaning back in the seat. "You came back for Lily."

"No. I mean, I thought about her. A lot. I didn't know if she was available, or if she'd want to see me."

"She has a hard time, you know. Max is so full of energy, and she has a lot of other things to deal with."

At that, I shoot my brother a curious look. "How do you know?"

James grins. When he does that I can see the physical similarity between us. He's so much like me.

"I've helped her out. Max just needs to burn it off sometimes. Whenever I go into the city to get things for Mum and Dad, I stop in and visit."

My heart thuds. All this time I haven't been here for Lily, but James has. I'm grateful, even if I don't know the full story of what happened after I left, where Lily had gone, why she'd fled. Maybe it'll come out. Maybe James will help fill me in.

"He's a good kid. You're right about him being a handful though. She does an incredible job with him." I swing into the backyard, parking on the concrete pad in front of the garage.

"I always guessed he just needed a dad. Someone to teach him all the boy things." He gives me this intense look, and I don't know what's behind it.

I shrug. "Maybe. He seems to be doing okay. I think he's a lot smarter than people give him credit for."

James lights up. "Yes. There's a lot going on in that head that he doesn't let people know about. He and Lily have such a close relationship."

My chest tightens. If I'd stayed, worked things out with her … If I'd stayed, she wouldn't have Max and they're so close it doesn't seem fair. But there's hope for the future. Hanging over me is the knowledge she's lived perfectly fine without me all this time.

"Have you told Mum and Dad you're not leaving?"

We get out of the car and I retrieve the box of beer from the back seat. "No, and I don't want you saying anything. The last thing I need is Mum telling me again I should be overseas doing something."

James grins. "You're really going to get a place and move here?"

I nod. "You know, when we first came here, I couldn't stand the thought of coming to this tiny little hick town. Things change, though. If I was going to settle anywhere, it'd be here."

I walk toward the house, and James follows me. Mum's in the kitchen, and she shakes her head as she watches me unload the beer into the fridge.

"Just a little something for after dinner, Mother." When I finish, I walk over and kiss her on the cheek.

"It's not you I'm worried about." She nods towards James, and I laugh at the thought of corrupting him.

"A couple of beers won't hurt. He's old enough. Corey had me drinking beer at a younger age." Corey was good at talking people into buying beer for him before he was old enough to buy it himself.

"Your brother wasn't exactly a good influence on you. Look at the trouble he convinced you to get into."

I don't even have to ask. It's not come up much since I first arrived here, but I just know she's talking about Lily, always about Lily. Somehow my quiet, introverted girl is the reason for everything that went wrong in my life. Corey was the one who backed me the most when I asked Lily to marry me.

"Whatever, Mum."

"Don't you whatever me," she snaps.

"I never did anything I didn't want to do." Out of the corner of my eye, I see James make a quick exit out the door.

"Anything *she* wanted you to do anyway."

I close my eyes and shake my head. I can't let her get to me. "All this time and you still can't let that go. Lily never did a thing to hurt you."

Mum turns to face the garden out the window. "The best thing you ever did was leave. You have a real job, travelling the world. You did so much better when you left. Obviously I would have preferred you stay, but you've achieved so much. I often wonder if we did the right thing bringing you here in the first place."

I swallow down the lump in my throat. I always suspected she felt that way, but she'd never said it out loud. Perhaps facing her own mortality has brought the words to the surface.

I have no ability to speak. I'm upset, angry, and I want to yell at her, but I can't. She's so stubborn, and nothing I say will change her mind about anything. It never has.

Instead I walk out to the deck, slamming the screen door behind me.

"You okay?" James asks from the other side of the door. He pushes it open and follows me.

"If there weren't a million other reasons for me to stay here, I'd go right now," I grumble, but it's not James's fault.

"I never told her I visit Lily."

I smile and slap him on the back. "Thanks, bud. I appreciate it more than you know. She's never been far from my thoughts."

"Yeah, figured as much. I know the old lady won't say it, but I'm glad you're home."

"Me too, James. Me too." I look back toward the house. I can't see her behind the curtain, but I know she's there. Bearing a grudge after twelve long years. She never wanted Lily and I together—always thought she'd end up taking after her mother.

I still don't believe that.

OVER DINNER, the silence is deafening. I don't want to speak to Mum or I'll say the wrong thing. James and Dad spend the time looking between us.

We eat quietly and quickly, and afterward James and I do the dishes before stacking our beer in an ice-filled bucket. Mum watches as we head onto the deck where we plant ourselves on the outdoor furniture.

"Now for the best part of the evening." I hold up my bottle. "To being home and getting to know my brother."

"Hear, hear," James says, clinking his bottle with mine. "So what's the big plan?"

"I've put in an offer on the garage. I put my apartment on the market before I left and it's already sold. With the way prices have gone up, I made a tidy profit." I smile. "There's a sleep out in the back yard, so enough space for you if Mum drives you too crazy. If you're not going to uni."

He grins. "Thanks for the offer. Never know when I might have to take you up on that."

I lean back in the chair. It's a warm night, and I breathe in the country air. I didn't give this place a fair go when I first arrived, but I love it more than I can say.

"When you called me and said Mum was sick, it gave me the best reason to come home. Finding out that place is for sale has been the final piece to the puzzle. Well, maybe penultimate."

James cocks his head. "You're talking about Lily, right?

"Maybe I'm an idiot thinking she'd want me after all this time. I wasn't going to go and throw myself at her, but when I ran into Max … she still feels so right. And spending time with her and Max is incredible."

"I'm surprised she let you anywhere near her." James takes a swig from his beer.

"What makes you think that? Anyone would think it was me who ran out on her."

James leans forward, flushing red. His eyes narrow. "Holy shit. How do you not know?"

"What do you mean?"

"I mean, big brother, you did run out on her. What I don't know is why Mum and Dad clearly didn't tell you what happened." He shakes his head before swallowing the rest of the bottle in one gulp. "Shit, Adam. The whole freaking town knows what happened."

Anger builds in me again, especially after Mum's sanctimony. Whatever it is has to be big to get this kind of reaction from James. He seems far too level-headed to kick off over nothing. "You have about thirty seconds to tell me."

He takes a deep breath and continues, "Shit. I feel awful.

If I'd known, I would have found some other way to tell you. I thought you knew and still didn't want to come back. That's what we were all told. I even thought long and hard about calling you over Mum, she was so insistent that no one contact you."

"James. You're not making any sense. Tell me what the hell you know that I don't."

He takes another bottle out of the chiller and hands it to me. "Load up. When I'm finished, you'll need it."

"What do you know about what happened here after you left?" he asks.

I shrug. "Not a lot. Mum told me Lily had come back and set up house with Eric Murphy. I stopped asking about her after that. It was too tempting to come back and punch him out for stealing my girl. Even if she wasn't mine by then."

There's so much pain in James's eyes, and he shakes his head. "She did a real number on you."

"Who? Lily?"

"No. Mum."

I frown as I gaze at him. "Lily didn't shack up with Eric? Why would Mum lie to me?"

James's eyes grow big. "Have you met our mother? She lied to you. She lied to all of us. I knew she was controlling, but this is beyond shitty."

I'd gone as far away as I could, stayed away as long as I could before I came home. I'd avoided my brothers, my friends, anyone who might tell me about Lily moving on. I hadn't wanted to hear it, and I'd been too young and stupid at the time to stay and see why she'd left me at the altar. Mum had been all too happy to encourage me to leave, even finding me a place to go.

"Damn it, Adam. I don't want to be the one to tell you this."

Anger grows in me the longer I wait. "James. I am going to beat the ever-loving shit out of you if you don't spit it out."

James drops his gaze, shifting it to the ground. "Lily didn't stand you up that day. Her mother locked her up."

I let out a sigh. "I went to her house. Nearly tore it apart looking for her. She wasn't there."

"Did you check her mother's sewing room? The basement?"

My stomach drops to my knees.

"Lily's mum flipped out the night before. Lily made amends with her, or so she thought. Her mother told her she'd forgive her for marrying you, but she wouldn't attend the wedding. Her dinner was laced with her mother's sedatives."

"What?" I hear my own voice crack.

"She took Lily down the stairs to that little space she'd converted into her sewing room. You remember how she used to take in repairs? Well, she shut up shop and kept her daughter down there. I doubt when you were in the house Lily even knew you were there. She was probably still unconscious." He sighs. "Jesus, Adam. It was in the papers when they found her. Although they gave Lily and her mother permanent name suppression to protect Lily."

I swallow hard, unable to process what I'm hearing. "In the papers?"

"She was terrified Lily would leave her, and she went off the rails. She kept her there for months and told everyone that Lily had run away."

I'm numb. "How long?" I whisper.

"Six months. She lived on what her mother fed her, making it stretch when she had to."

Nausea sweeps me, and I place my beer down and my head in my hands to steady myself. My girl, my delicate flower trapped inside a basement. No daylight, very little food.

My head's spinning. "What about the report of a blonde girl hitchhiking? I thought that was Lily leaving town."

He frowns. "Oh, that was Gina Parsons. I don't know if you remember her."

"I remember the name. Went out a couple of times with Drew. Or it could have been Owen?"

James shrugs. "I'm not completely sure. But her dad beat up her mum the night before Lily went missing. Gina ran away."

"How did they find Lily?" I don't care about anything else right now. Lily's house was in the centre of town. It was a little rundown back then, but it was the one thing that had given her security. A roof over her head. Every day people would have walked past it. I fume at the thought of them all going about their lives, not doing anything to help. I agonise that I was in that house while she was there and didn't find her.

"Her mother called an ambulance when Lily went into premature labour."

My head's swimming. Lily was pregnant. I've not asked how old Max was—just assumed with the boy being so small that he was ten or so, maybe younger. What if ... "The child. Was it Max?"

James nods slowly. "He never stood a chance. Lily was malnourished so Max didn't get all he needed. They managed to stop labour when she got to the hospital, but only for a few weeks. He was in hospital forever. I have vague memories of visiting him. I was only a kid, but that baby had tubes for Africa in him, he was so small."

We sit in silence as I take all this in. My eyelids are so heavy, the weight of this newfound knowledge slowly crushing me. "Why did you visit him?

James shrugs. "Mum took me."

I stare at him. Max is mine. That smart, crazy kid is mine. "So if Mum and Dad knew about him, knew all about this, why the hell didn't they say anything? And why does Lily have nothing, living on Eric Murphy's mother's property?"

James shakes his head. "I guess they want to protect you. I don't know. You rang one day and I told you we went to see the baby. It's vague, but I'm sure I can remember it. All we knew was that you went away, joined the army, and travelled a lot. Mum said you knew you were too young to be tied down so you weren't coming back. Hell, Corey was just relieved to not be the black sheep anymore."

We sit in silence. My pain is so great I don't even know what to say. "You tried to tell me. I can't ... What about the Eric Murphy thing?"

"His mother took Lily in. I don't know, I guess so many people freaked out at Lily's mother and what she did so they wouldn't go near. They were always afraid that she had too much of her mother in her."

I drop my head to my chest. The pain grows, stabs me right in the gut. We were kids, but if I'd stayed, I could have tried to protect her, taken care of her.

"I have a kid." I look up at James, picking up my beer and

taking another sip. "I have a kid." Letting go of the tension, I grin.

"What are you boys doing?" Dad stands in the doorway, smiling at us.

I stand, turning slowly to face the man behind me. "Getting the truth from someone who gives a damn enough to tell me."

Placing the beer on the table, I step off the porch and into the darkness. "Going to talk to the mother of my child. The one you didn't have the decency to tell me about." So much makes sense. Her anger at our first confrontation in her yard, telling me she didn't want parenting advice from me, the tears in the restaurant. She thought I knew.

"Adam." Dad's voice carries through the darkness. But it's too late. I climb into the car, start it up, and back down the driveway.

———

I DRIVE THROUGH TOWN, my anger growing the further I get from the house. All this time. I hadn't been the best at keeping in touch, but there had been phone calls home in the early days.

My agony hits me as I pass into the countryside and down the dusty road where Lily lives. The living room light is on, and I drive slowly, still painfully aware of the little boy I could have hit the last time I came down here. *My* little boy.

Out here it's quiet. There's no road noise, and apart from the crickets in the grass nothing else makes a sound.

Stumbling from the car, I reach the front door and hammer on it.

A curtain twitches in the corner of my eye and when I turn to look it's back in place.

"Lily, it's Adam. I need to see you. Please." I waited too long to come back, losing another minute with her is too much.

A gentle halo of light surrounds her as she pulls the door open. There she is, the girl I loved and left, thinking she'd turned her back on me.

"You're drunk," she says, fanning her hand across her face as if to get rid of the beer smell.

"I've just had a couple. I need to talk to you."

Lily frowns, looking me over as if deciding whether to let me in or not. "Well, be quiet. Max took ages to get to sleep, and I do not want him waking up." She turns and walks away from the door. I trail behind like the lovesick puppy I always was with her. All this time and nothing's changed. I could try and deny it, but she holds my heart, the same way she always did.

I sit on the couch as she takes the chair opposite, suddenly tongue-tied and feeling like that love-struck eighteen-year-old again. The one who had the prettiest girl in school on his arm, in his bed. The years haven't changed the feeling, not now I'm in front of her again.

"What do you want, Adam?" She sounds so tired.

"I didn't know."

"Didn't know what?"

I sigh. "Any of it. You were so frustrated with me not understanding, but I only found out what happened tonight."

Her eyes are full of bewilderment. All these roundabout conversations we've had where she probably assumed I knew.

"James told me. Not even Mum and Dad. All the years I was away and they never told me."

Tears form in her eyes, and I sit on my hands rather than give in to the temptation of trying to hold her. She's so on edge—I don't know if she'd let me.

"You left and never looked back. I heard all about it. How you were off to this country or that country. With this girl or that. Your mother made sure she told me." She waves her hands on the air, never meeting my eyes.

The nausea's back again, and I place my hands palms-down on the couch to steady myself. "What?"

"I was in hospital with a baby who survived despite the shitty hand we were dealt. All my focus was on him. All your mother worried about was that I'd wreck your life because you were going places." She lets out a sob. "My baby was eight weeks early, and my mother killed herself because *she* was stressed. That's what you left me to deal with." She crosses her arms, tears rolling down her cheeks.

"If I'd known, I would have been here in a second. I was doing everything to forget you because I thought you'd moved on. I might have left, but my heart stayed here." I move from the couch, crawling across the floor to her feet. "The memory of you has driven me crazy all these years." I look up at her.

She avoids my eyes, looking past me to the wall behind the couch. "Don't, Adam. Don't you dare. It's the drink talking."

I reach out, placing my hand on her knee. Strain is plastered all over her face as she looks down at me. "It's not the drink—it's my heart. When I saw that ring on your finger, it damn near broke me thinking of you with someone else. Even if I had no right to be upset about it."

She closes her eyes and takes deep breaths. For a moment it looks as if she's fallen asleep.

"You didn't recognise the ring," she whispers.

I reach for her hand, cradling it in mine. It seems so small, her wrist so thin it might snap, but my skin on hers feels good. *Perfect.*

"It's my wedding ring. I had it on a chain around my neck so I didn't lose it before the wedding. It brought me comfort during the worst times, and it helped me remember the good."

I roll the ring around her finger. It's a little loose now, but that's not surprising given how slim she is. It's thinner underneath than on top where the metal's worn. It's not even gold. Neither of us could afford anything like that way back then. "Lily." I let out a sob, resting my head on her hand, hearing her crying too.

She'd been broken, and I wasn't there when she needed me most. No wonder she'd been so weird about my return, ranting that they didn't need me. She thought I hadn't wanted to be there when that was the opposite to how I felt. It's amazing she ever let me near either of them.

"I don't even know how to deal with all this. It's so much to take in. I need to think. Maybe you should go." Her voice is so small.

I raise my head. Her lips tell me to go, but all I see in her eyes is love. "I'm not going anywhere. Not again. I'm right where I need to be." I slowly stand, grasping her arms in my hands and pulling her to her feet. I'm face to face with the girl I never forgot. The mother of my child.

"If you feel you're obligated to us, I don't expect anything from you. You're free," she whispers, and it damn near breaks my heart.

Pressing my forehead to hers, I close my eyes. "I was never free. All this time I wondered what I'd done. My heart ached so much. I can't believe my parents hid this from me." I open again to see the blue gazing back at me. "Like I said, I'm not going anywhere."

18

ADAM

She let me in.

I don't know if I deserve it after taking so long to find out the truth, but Lily lets me hold her trembling body against me as we stand in silence, absorbing what just happened.

"I never stopped loving you," she whispers.

My heart swells in response. "I never stopped loving you."

She nuzzles my chest, the contact sending my body into overdrive. I have to have her, be with her, show her just how much I love her. How much I've always loved her.

I grasp her chin, raising her face to meet mine. Her eyes widen as I bring her in close, and I ache with need to kiss her. All these years, places, women, and I'm finally back where I belong. The realisation that she's had to deal with everything without me all this time eats at me.

I start my kiss gentle, slow, before deepening it. She relaxes in my arms as I claim her mouth, my arms wrapping around her slight body. I want to treasure her, bring her back to health, and love her for the rest of my days.

When we finally break apart, the longing in her eyes is clear as she gazes at me. I take in every feature, unchanged in the years we've been apart. This is the girl I dreamed of for all this time, the woman I fantasised about. So much has changed, but looking at her now, my heart still feels as it did so long ago.

"Adam," she whispers.

The years melt away as I grin, scooping her into my arms and kissing her again. "Where?" There's only one thing I want now, and from the look in her eyes, she wants it too. No more sneaking around like we used to, sex in the back seat of my car, me climbing in her bedroom window.

"Up the stairs. I'll walk though, they're narrow."

I shake my head. "I carried Max fine. If I have to throw you over my shoulder and carry you like a sack of potatoes, I'll do it."

She laughs, burying her face in my neck. Her laughter is the most beautiful sound. When was the last time she laughed like this? "I want to get up to bed too, but in one piece."

We reach the foot of the stairs. "I can do anything when I'm with you," I say softly, taking it one step at a time when all I want to do is run, get her up there as fast as possible. She points at the door to indicate which room.

"We're here. See? Nothing to worry about," I murmur.

Warm drops run down my neck, and I rock her as we enter the room. "Shh, Lily. We're together now, and nothing is ever going to keep us apart again."

The bed's unmade, the duvet at the base of it. I lower her onto the sheet and kick off my shoes, lying down beside her.

She reaches over to stroke my face, her eyes searching mine. "I never thought this day would ever happen."

I turn my head to kiss her hand. "Neither did I. I was always so scared I'd come back and find you with someone else, making a life without me."

A sob breaks from her throat. "I can't imagine making a life with anyone else. Not with Max. No one understands him."

I lean over and kiss her long and deep, running my hand down her side as she shivers. "I do. No wonder I feel such a bond with him. I can't believe I have a son," I whisper.

Fresh tears roll down her cheeks as she smiles. "He's amazing. You were never truly gone when he was around."

I kiss her again, unbuttoning her blouse, slipping it back to reveal her bra. Lily blushes, moving her arm across her chest as if ashamed.

"It's okay."

"I've got old underwear. We don't have a lot of money. I can't afford new stuff all the time. It's embarrassing."

I grin, pushing her arm away and planting a kiss between her breasts. "Just as well I get to pamper you then. Give you everything you need. Oh, God, Lily, I have such a surprise for you."

She sits up, sliding her blouse down her arms and unclipping her bra. I love the sight of her—I always did, with those perky breasts that used to fit snugly in my hand. As she discards her bra, I reach for her, pulling her back down beside me, my hand covering one breast as I stroke the nipple.

"Adam," she whispers.

"I'm going to give you everything. I swear to you, things will be better for you and for Max."

I can't wait, and I unzip her jeans, slipping my hand down and pushing her underwear aside. Now I have her, the woman I've always loved. I'll do whatever it takes to give her what we both need. I have this fantasy of making her scream.

Closing my eyes, I remember the times we were together in the past. Two young people not knowing what to do, but finding our way together. Exploring each other's bodies with touch and taste. Now I know just how to touch her, what to do to make her feel good.

She's ready, hot and wet, and she tilts her hips toward me, my fingers working their magic. I'm worlds' away from that teenager with no clue; this time I'll bring her pleasure like she's never had.

Lily gasps as I bring her to the brink. Her body tenses before it tumbles over the edge, and she thrashes against my hand, pulling me down to kiss her as I lose myself in her smell, the way her skin feels. The urgency with which she nips at my bottom lip makes me harder than I'd ever thought imaginable.

"I love you," I whisper, tugging at her jeans, then her panties.

"Wait," she says. "You have to undress too.

I grin as she pulls at the bottom of my shirt, and I sit to bring it over my head, baring my chest. She sighs as she runs her hands over my chest, her touch nearly undoing me on the spot.

Lying back, I unzip my own jeans, pushing them down, laughing as they jam up on my ankles. Pulling her naked body into my arms, I stroke her soft skin, breathe her in, begin reacquainting myself with her body. Once, I knew every single inch, and so little of it has changed.

When I look back into her eyes, I see just how tired she is, how much rest she needs. I should let her sleep, but I'm so greedy. I don't just want her kisses—I want all of her.

Our bodies are entwined, and I can't wait any longer, and I roll her onto her back, planting kisses over her face and down her neck. I never, ever want to let go of this feeling.

"I'm on the pill," she whispers. "My body went a bit haywire after ..."

I know I'm clean, so taking it as an invitation, I move on top of her. As if we were just meant to be, I slide inside her. She feels every bit as good as I remember.

"Adam." She gasps as I thrust, slowly at first, kissing her lips, her neck, her breasts. Her nipples have hardened, and I run my tongue over them. She meets my hips with her own and nothing ever felt so good as Lily hooking her leg around my thigh and pulling me in deeper. Now we're joined there's no going back. So many nights my heart cried out for her, and now those cries are being answered by her heart calling just as loudly.

My head spins as my heart soars, my body fulfilling its need for her, and I cry her name as I come before stilling and rolling to her side.

When I pull her into my arms, her eyes fill with tears. I just keep on kissing her face, her shoulders, showing her the affection she seems to need.

"I'm sorry. I don't mean to get so emotional."

"Maybe I don't show as much, but I feel the same way." I kiss her temple, and she snuggles up to me.

"I never thought we'd find each other."

I close my eyes and hold her close. Considering proposing to Jenna seems like something I did forever ago. Now I cuddle up with the only woman whose finger I ever imagine being graced by a ring. That she's worn the ring I bought her all those years ago touches my heart more than I can say.

Lily's hand rests on my chest, and I stroke her fingers. Touching her overloads my senses—she smells sweet, just clean, and the scent is tantalising. Her skin might mostly be soft, but her hands are thin and the skin rough. She's clearly worked outside. Maybe now I can give her a break and let her rest.

"What are you thinking about?" I whisper.

"How good I feel." She looks up at me, her guilt evident by the way she chews on her lip.

"You're allowed to feel good."

Lily runs her fingers over my chest. "I like being here with you. Not cramped like we were in the back seat of your car. Not under pressure to get out of bed in a hurry because we had parents coming home." She lets go of me long enough to pull the duvet over us.

I laugh. "You mean you didn't enjoy those times?"

"I did. A bit too much."

Her hair smells like strawberry shampoo, and I kiss it. Everything about her is a turn-on and I want her so badly again, but at the same time, I know I need to let her get some sleep. "Tell me about Max."

She grazes my chest with her lips. "What do you want to know?"

"Everything."

"I don't even know where to start."

"James said something about you going into labour early. I feel awful that he knew and I didn't. I guess they all knew."

She detaches and rolls onto her back. "I didn't even know I was pregnant. My stomach was distorted, but I thought that was the lack of food. I thought I was dying."

I move to my side to face her, cupping one of her breasts. "I'm sorry. I know how hard this must be for you."

With a smirk, she catches my hand and raises it to her lips. "It's okay. It's only fair you should hear it." She takes a deep breath as she snuggles into my arms. "I didn't know what was happening. I'd been so sick. I knew Mum was drugging me—I thought she was poisoning me. So many times I tried to get up those stairs and out, but I was so sick and tired, I never got far. My stomach was so hard, but it wasn't that much bigger than normal. I thought I was dying."

Tears well in her eyes, and I brush her face to soothe her. "I was in agony, and then I started bleeding. Finally, Mum called for an ambulance, told them some bullshit story. I was out of it, too far gone to know, but I was free. Once I got to the hospital they worked out what was going on pretty quickly and managed to stop the labour with drugs. I got a month where they fed me and put me on a drip for nutrients to try to give Max as good a start as we could. He was born at thirty-two weeks, and the cord got caught around his neck. He never stood a chance."

Her shoulders relax. How many times has she told her story? Who's cared enough to listen?

"My baby was undersized and premature, and they couldn't tell me how much damage had been done. Then, my mother killed herself."

I close my eyes as they prick with tears, pulling her tighter. "I'm sorry I wasn't here, Lily. I'm so, so sorry."

"The note said she killed herself because she was under so much pressure. No sorry for everything she did, no sorry for leaving me. Nothing about her grandson. Even in her last moments, she couldn't think about me."

Her tears drop onto my chest. "Max didn't seem too bad when he was a baby. All his problems surfaced as he grew older. It became obvious he had learning difficulties, and that he was smaller than the other children. And it was just me, Adam. No one helped. The only person who ever seemed to care was Mrs Murphy. Remember her from school?"

I nod. It was in Mrs Murphy's class that I'd met Lily. I still remember locking eyes on Lily that first time, trying to take a peek at the face hidden behind the long, blonde hair. I was rewarded with the big blue eyes she now shares with my son. One look had set my fourteen-year-old heart racing.

"This was her place. But that's a whole other story."

I reach for Lily's face, tilting it toward me to look into her eyes. "You don't have to worry about help now. I'll give you all you need. I'll be here for you and Max. Whatever it takes. I came back to town with a plan to start my life again, and you two are going to be a part of that. Hell, you *are* that life."

"There was never really anyone else for me," she whispers.

My lips brush hers. "It wouldn't matter if there was. When I got the call to tell me Mum was sick, you were in my thoughts. I still had hope you would want me."

Her smile lights the dim room. "I do. I tried to move on, but no one else would ever understand. Max and I are so tight. I was always terrified that someone new would try to come between us." Her eyes are so sad. While I'd been happy to discover she was single when I first came back, it was clear there had been no one she thought she could trust enough.

"I'm glad you didn't think I would."

"You're his father. It's different with you. You're not going to want to send him away and in to care. Are you?"

"Never," I whisper and pull her closer. She's safe now, in my embrace and back where she belongs.

I'm home.

19

ADAM

I wake to the sound of her crying.

"Lily," I whisper, reaching for her. In the night I got up to use the bathroom and when I got back, I entangled myself in her. Since then, we've become detached, and I slip my arm under her neck to pull her back toward me.

"No." At first I loosen my grip, but she's panting and shaking, and it's not because of me. She's dreaming. At least, I think that's what's going on.

She makes a sound. It comes out like a word, but nothing I recognise. She's struggling with something, and I'm not going to wake her. I've been here before.

When she lunges for the bedside cabinet and flicks on the light, I let her go. She sits up, still breathing quickly, her expression strained.

"Did you turn out the light?" She gasps as she speaks, struggling to catch a breath.

"I closed the door when I went to the bathroom. Didn't

want Max walking in on anything you didn't want him to see."

"The dark ..."

Those two words tell me everything, and regret fills my soul. Did I really think she'd have walked away from her ordeal unscathed? I have enough scars, mental and physical, to understand the inability to let go. "Shit. Lily. I'm sorry. I didn't know."

She shakes her head. "No. You didn't. It's not your fault."

Her breathing slows, and I place my hand on her thigh, gently stroking her skin. "Leave the lamp on and lie back down with me. I want to show you something."

Lily lies back down, and I fold her in my embrace. She's safe, even if she doesn't feel it. Her eyes are so heavy, and I understand even more the reason for her fatigue. It's not just Max or the farm. It's her.

I palm her cheek, and she closes her eyes at my touch. My body's on fire again with want and need. All for her.

"What did you want to show me?" she asks as she opens her eyes again.

"Just give me a second. I want you to stop shaking first."

"I'm sorry." The words are a whisper, as if she has anything to be sorry for. I'm the one who owes her.

I press my nose to her nose. "There's nothing to be sorry for. We all have fears. Even me."

A smile spreads across her face. "Here I was thinking you were brave and tough."

"Not all the time."

I guide her hand to my right shoulder, and her fingers probe the skin. Never taking my eyes off her face, I watch as her brows knit, and she frowns. "What's that lump?"

"That's where I got shot in the shoulder."

Her eyes widen. "Adam?"

"It's okay. It bled. I survived. But because of it and other things, I freak out at sudden loud noises sometimes."

Her lips twitch.

"Hell of a problem when you're working on old cars. Never know when those things are gonna backfire." I'm semi-joking to try and lighten the mood, but she sucks in her lower lip, her eyes searching mine.

"The point is that we're both a bit broken, and if being together is what helps fix us, I vote we try."

She raises her arms, repositioning herself to wrap them around my neck, her grip tightening as I stroke her back.

"It's okay, Lily. I'm here."

Right where I always should have been.

———

I WAKE AGAIN, this time to the sound of gravel crunching under a car tyre.

Lily stirs. "Crap. What's happened now?"

I prop myself up on one elbow watching as she stumbles out of bed and starts to dress. In the daylight that now fills the room, I can see for the first time how painfully thin she actually is, and as she turns to pick up her pants, I reach out and run a hand over her backside.

"Stop." She laughs, slapping my hand.

"Never."

A loud knock on the door makes her jump, and she drags on her pants, zipping them up and running from the room. The knocking gets louder. "Open up." From the bedroom I can hear an angry male voice, and I slide out of bed, tugging on my jeans and heading downstairs to take a look.

Lily pulls the door open. It's Eric.

"Lily, the damn sheep got through the fence again."

"I'm sorry, Eric. I'll go down and look at the damage."

He sighs loudly. "Yeah, well, if you just let me take over this place, the sheep would be somewhere more secure."

I walk up behind her, eyeballing the guy and sliding an arm around Lily's waist. "There a problem?"

She turns her head. "My sheep keep breaking through the fence."

Eric narrows his eyes. "Adam."

Lily rests her head on my shoulder as if to show our unity.

"Oh. It's you." Max's voice comes from behind us, disappointment in his tone.

I turn my head, but Max looks past me and out the door at Eric.

"Hey, buddy. How's it hanging?" Eric asks.

Max pushes between Lily and I, looping his arms around our waists. He stares at Eric, and my chest bursts with pride at how he's handling the interloper, and that he's seemingly accepting of me being here. *My son.*

"Hey Max. Want to go with Mum to get some breakfast, and I'll take care of whatever Eric wants?"

He grins up at me. "Can we have something yummy?"

"I'm sure I have some Coco Pops in the kitchen if you want," Lily says. I loosen my grip and let go of Max. Lily turns to face me. "Thanks."

I lean over and kiss her with a longing I hope is obvious to Eric. She's mine again.

173

"I'll just grab my shirt and we can head out." I say. Eric nods stiffly.

Lily follows as I climb the stairs, two at a time. "Let me know what needs doing and I'll organise someone to come and fix it."

"I'll sort it out. Don't worry about it." I pull my T-shirt on and peck her on the lips. "You're not getting rid of me any time soon, so you better get used to me pitching in."

"It doesn't mean you take over everything." She pouts, and I press an index finger to her lips.

"No. It doesn't. But it does mean that I'm going to contribute. It's long overdue."

She can't argue with that; she knows I'm right. "Just behave with Eric. He can still make my life difficult. I might have the use of the property and house, but technically it's his."

I waggle my eyebrows. "Not yet anyway. I'll be good." In the rush to get out of bed, her hair's loose, and I push the locks back behind her ears as she shakes her head. "I'm not here to disrupt your life."

"It's a bit late for that." Her lips twitch as she fights a smile. *If I didn't have to get back downstairs ...* damn it. I laugh and grab her arms, twirling her around and pushing her down on the bed. She shrieks as I run my fingers over her waist, right in one of the spots where she's ticklish.

The sound rings out through the open door, and I know Eric must be able to hear her. This is the sound of Lily happy, and it makes me happy. Happier than I've been since I don't know when. I'm a world away from the man who drowned his sorrows in his apartment. I have Lily back and I have a son. That still warms my heart, and I burst with pride at that smart, crazy kid.

"Mum," Max calls.

"I have to go." She giggles.

"So do I." I pull her close and linger on her lips.

"Mum," Max yells louder and reluctantly, I let her go.

"Be back soon," I say.

"You'd better."

————

THE DAMAGE ISN'T TOO bad. Whoever fixed this last didn't do the best job, but most of it held. Eric and I tidy it up as best we can.

"That should do it. I'll head into town and grab some supplies and fix it properly, but that should keep them in while I'm gone."

He nods. "I hope it's fixed properly this time."

"I'll sort it." He always did get up my nose. He never gave Lily the time of day until she became my girl and only then started taking an interest in her.

"How on earth did you persuade Lily to take you back?"

His question catches me by surprise. "There wasn't much persuasion. She loves me."

"You left her." His tone is flat. I assume it's because he never had what I have—Lily's love.

"I didn't know what happened to Lily. Not until last night."

He doesn't believe me. It's written all over his face. "You didn't know."

"I was devastated she didn't turn up to our wedding. I ran

175

as far as I could and stayed away. Now I know I should have come back, but we were so young. And I was stupid."

His shoulders slump. "Yeah, you were. It didn't matter how far away you were, it was always you she wanted. I knew that, and I still thought that maybe one day she'd love me."

"I'm sorry. Lily and I always had that bond—"

Eric looks up at me, his eyes blazing. "That you left behind. I was the one who was here for her."

"I know, and I am so grateful. But that doesn't change Lily's feelings, nor does it mean this is going to be easy for either of us. She's made her choice. We both made that choice a long time ago."

His jaw is set as he fixes his gaze on me. "Don't you ever hurt her. I will be on your arse so fast ..."

"I know. I have a lot to make up for." All I can do is hope he sees my sincerity. I want to give Lily the world, everything she should have always had. At least now I'm in a position to do it and not starting from scratch with nothing.

"Yeah, you do."

20

LILY

Max wolfs down his breakfast, and I smile at him taking the morning in his stride. Finding Adam with me could have gone either way—he's that possessive of me. Maybe Eric being at the door distracted him.

Max has always been a good judge of character. He took a dislike to Eric from an early age, but then, he's seen enough of Eric pressuring me to move in with him. I couldn't be prouder of my boy for taking a stand today.

I lean on my elbows at the kitchen table to watch him. Max finishes the last spoonful, and picks up the bowl, drinking the chocolate milk from it. "Finished."

"Good boy." I reach over and tousle his hair.

"Adam's going to kick Eric's arse," he declares.

I stifle a giggle. "Max. You shouldn't say things like that."

A wide grin spreads across his face. "My daddy could kick anyone's arse."

My stomach falls to the floor, and I open my mouth to say something only to close it again. What on earth?

"I like Adam. Are you getting married?"

With a dry throat, I manage to croak. "I ... I don't know."

He grabs a colouring-in book from the end of the table and a packet of coloured pencils. Opening it to a random page, he starts colouring. I have nothing more to say, so I keep watching. Soon the sky is coloured blue, the grass green, just the way it should be. The house in the middle of the picture becomes fuchsia.

"Is that supposed to be the colour of this house, Max?" It doesn't look like it, our house is more of browny dirt shade. *Is old a colour? The colour of rust?*

He shakes his head. "This is your house, Mum. You like pink."

I laugh. "I guess I do."

"Maybe Daddy can build you a pink house."

I close my eyes, holding back the tears that threaten. Sometimes Max is far smarter than anyone thinks. These little moments always catch my breath as my adored boy comes out with his words of wisdom. Has he worked out that Adam's his father? Or does he simply wish for it? Whatever it is, it's wonderful.

Max goes back to colouring in while I get up and run water for the dishes. Adam will be back soon, and my heart races at the thought of his arms around me again. Every nerve in my body comes alive with him, his touch setting me on fire. All those years ago when Max was conceived, Adam had been so unsure of himself, as had I. Now he's back, knowing how to touch me, how to make my body hum.

When I first saw he'd returned, I tried not to get too

emotional in case it all crumbled in front of me. One night is all it's taken to melt me inside, and if I have any control left, I'll hold onto that as tight as I can.

Lost in thought, I jump when Adam's hand lands on my shoulder.

"It's not too much of an issue to fix. The sheep are fine for now, and I'll go into town shortly and grab some bits to sort out the fence properly."

I sigh. "That should have been done last time. I even paid for it."

"I'll sort it. Don't worry about anything." His eyes are so full of love as he bends to brush his lips against mine.

"Daddy, look what I drew," Max speaks, waving his colouring book around.

Adam's expression makes me catch my breath, the awe written all over it. He smiles at Max. "Great going, champ." He shifts his gaze back to me. "You told? I thought we'd do it together."

I shrug. "He worked it out for himself. He's not as dumb as some people think he is." I shoot a glare at Eric who has walked in behind him. Eric who asked me to spend my life with him. Eric who wanted to send Max away to a home for special kids and then wondered why I wanted nothing to do with him.

"Wow. That's great." There's a hint of disappointment in Adam's voice, and I understand. He wanted to see Max's reaction, and so did I. I twist the ring around on my finger—not that I need to give myself that reassurance anymore. He's here.

"Thanks for sorting it out, Adam. Lily." Eric nods before leaving.

"Ha ha." Max grins at Adam. "He's gone."

Adam roars with laughter and walks around the table to take a closer look at Max's colouring. "Mum wants a pink house, so I made it pink," Max says.

"Oh, does she now?" Adam's gaze penetrates me, and my insides melt at his intensity.

"Max thinks I do. I'm happy with a house that has all of us in it." Have I said too much too soon?

Adam's eyes blaze with desire, and I squeeze my thighs together thinking about what might happen if Max wasn't here.

"I've got an idea about that," he says, never taking his eyes from my face.

If he asked me now, I'd live in a tent with him.

———

MAX HAS days where he fixates on one thing. Today, it's colouring. It started with the pink house; now I lie on my stomach on the floor with him, doing some colouring myself. I love these quiet moments with my boy. He's so full on, having them is a rare and wonderful thing.

I lick my lips. "Can I ask you something?"

"What?" He looks at me with suspicious eyes.

"How did you work out Adam's your father?"

Max grins, chuckling as he picks out another coloured pencil. "It was easy. I thought maybe when I saw him I looked a bit like him, and he knew you. Then he was in your bed last night, and no one's ever been in your bed but me."

I gape, and he selects a different pencil, nothing disturbing him from his task. "How do you know?"

"I heard a noise. Thought it might be a visitor. You told me to check who it was first, but it was night, and I thought it might be the zombies so I went to make sure you were okay."

Breathing suddenly seems difficult as I look at him. I love this kid with every single fibre of my being, and my little detective has hit the nail right on the head. "You're so smart, Max. I'm so proud of you."

He pauses, raising his head to smile at me. "I know, Mum."

I don't know if that's a response to the first sentence or the second, but I do know that I couldn't be more proud in this moment.

And then he tops it all off. "I'm glad he's here, Mum."

"Why's that?"

"You slept. I've never been able to sneak into your room without you waking up. Last night you were asleep, and I don't think anything could wake you."

I can't stop the tears that roll down my cheeks. I've been a light sleeper for as long as we've been in this house. It started when Max was born and never stopped. I'm so used to listening out for him, and the odd night when Eric would hammer on the door. I hadn't even realised I'd slept so well.

"I love you so much, Max," I whisper, wiping the tears away.

"Love you too, Mum. Don't cry. Dad'll make it all better."

As much as I love Adam's return, and now know he never would have stayed away if he'd known about what happened, the thought of him leaving again still terrifies me. He's done without us all these years. What's to say he won't decide to do without us again?

"He makes you smile."

At the sound of footsteps, I look up to see Adam in the doorway. "You two want fish and chips for dinner?"

Like the love-struck teenager I was the last time we were together, I push myself up off the floor and run to him, wrapping my arms around his waist and nestling in against his chest.

"What's all this about?" he asks in an amused tone, kissing the top of my head.

"As much as I like the idea of fish and chips, I don't want to let you out of my sight."

"I've been out fixing the fence. Isn't that out of sight?"

I raise my head to meet his gaze. "Even that's too far."

"You got it bad, Ms Parker." The grin his lips have spread into says it all.

"So do you, Mr Campbell."

"Always," he whispers, sending a shiver down my spine. "I thought we might all go for a drive to get dinner. Especially if you're not going to let go of me."

"A drive?" I turn my head at Max's voice, and his face glows with excitement.

"Just a little one. We can bring dinner back here."

Adam leans his head on mine, running his hand up and down my back. His presence is more calming than I ever thought it would be. He can't undo what happened, but us being together is the best medicine, even after all these years.

Max stands and wiggles his hips. "We get to go in Dad's car."

I shake my head, rolling my eyes. "Maybe we should take mine."

Max's face falls. "It's not fair."

Adam's hand rests on my back, and he squeezes me a little tighter. "If it's okay with your mother, we can take my car. We can fit more food in it. Besides, it's not a death trap."

I narrow my eyes at him and slap his chest. "You'll keep."

"I'm counting on it." In his eyes, the only thing I see is love.

I have got it bad.

———

THE DRIVE DOESN'T TAKE LONG, and we park a little down from the fish and chip shop. It's Sunday, but the store is surprisingly busy. It's usually a lazy day for the town with nearly all the other stores closed. Adam gets out of the car first and walks around my side, opening my door and Max's. He holds my hand as I step out and wraps his free arm around my waist.

"I didn't think. Are you ready for people to see us together?" he asks.

I shrug. "What difference does it make?" They'll talk either way, and that's the least of my worries if he leaves again. I'd had to stop worrying about what people thought a long time ago.

"Let's just get this food and go home." I look toward the store. Max stands with his arms folded, tapping his foot on the pavement.

"Max?"

Max and I both turn toward the voice that approaches. Owen walks toward the fish and chip shop, presumably having come from his flat, behind the bakery.

"Hey, Owen," I say.

He pauses, not even looking at me, his eyes fixed on Adam. "What are you doing here?"

"Getting dinner with Lily and Max."

Owen casts his eyes over us, lingering on Adam's arm around my waist. "You're with him?" Disbelief is all over Owen's face, and my heart sinks. I owe him so much, owe all the brothers. They helped me through so many hard times. But then again, I don't owe anyone any explanation about who shares my bed or holds my heart.

"Owen, I ..."

"After what he did to you."

"I didn't *do* anything," Adam speaks, but all it does is make Owen glower even more.

"Are you kidding?" Owen's loud, louder than he should be around here. He knows how small towns talk.

"Owen. Please. Listen to me." I take a step forward, placing myself between the brothers. There's only one person who can defuse this, and that's me. I know how protective Owen is of me, but now he needs to respect my wishes.

"What are you doing, Lily?" Owen's eyes plead with me for answers.

"Adam didn't know. You have to believe me. He didn't know any of it. Your mother kept it from him for all this time, and now he's back." I speak before Adam can get a further word in and make things worse.

Owen scratches his head, the anguish on his face clear. I know it—I feel it. The complete and utter hopelessness when you know something must be true, but you can't quite believe it. "How is that even possible? She never said anything?"

184

"Not a word. She told me Lily was with Eric after I left. That they were together. Why do you think I stayed away for so long?" Adam says softly. He's handling this far better than I'd thought he would. When they were younger, the boys would often be at each other's throats. Being so close in age, there had been a lot of sibling rivalry.

"Twelve years." Owen chokes as he speaks.

"It broke me."

I get pangs at Adam's words, knowing how much hearing he had moved on had hurt me. Taking a breath, I lick my lips and place one hand on Owen's chest. "We're just going to grab some dinner and take it back to my place. How about you come and join us?" Meeting his gaze, I smile in the hope he'll accept. That would be good for all of us.

His eyebrows twitch, and he glances between Adam and I. He's still unsure, I can see it in his eyes, but he nods. "Sounds good."

"Maybe you can bring over some of those gingerbread men," Adam says.

I turn back toward Adam, my eyebrows raised. What that's about I have no idea, but the chuckle coming from Owen tells me it's some inside joke between them. All I know is that they're Max's favourite treat.

"Sold out today. Maybe I can make some fresh ones tomorrow, if you want to swing by the bakery?

"Can we get dinner now?" Max tugs at my sleeve, and I reach down and stroke his hair.

"Let's get going," Adam says. He steps around me now, and for a moment, he and Owen look one another over before Adam pulls his younger brother into an embrace. It brings a tear to my eye to see them together. Maybe it'll be one more reason for him to stay.

"You're still an asshole," Owen says. Like all the Campbell boys, he still has a small hint of an American accent. Some words just don't sound right to my ear and make me laugh. That's one of them. I giggle.

Adam's eyebrows creep up as he moves his gaze to me.

"What? You guys have always talked funny. You even more so since you've been away."

Adam's large hands land on my waist, and I lean back against him. "I know where you're ticklish, remember?" he mumbles in my ear. Every nerve in my body is alive, and we haven't made it to ordering dinner yet.

"You do talk funny," Max says, and I hold up the palm of my hand so he can high five me.

"Two against one, huh?" Adam says. He rests his head on my shoulder, and I'm surrounded by him.

I close my eyes for a second and take a deep breath. "Not all the time. Just most of it." I lean my head on his.

"What did you want, Owen? We'll grab it and meet you back at Lily's if you're coming," Adam says.

"A piece of fish and some chips. I'll stop by the bakery and grab some drinks from the fridge."

"Sounds good." Adam lets go of my waist and laces his fingers in mine.

"See you soon." Owen smiles and turns back down the road toward the bakery.

I face Adam as he reaches up, stroking my hair. "You defused that pretty quickly."

"I hope he believes me. At least you'll have a chance to talk."

Max tugs at my free arm. "Come on."

———

Owen waits outside the house when we arrive back home, and he's got James with him. The two of them lean against Owen's Toyota. He's got a newer Corolla than me, though only by a few years. So many times I've threatened to switch them while he's not looking.

I unbuckle my seat belt as Adam pulls to a stop, climbing out the car and opening the rear door for Max to get out. This time, my son does what he should without leaving dirty scuff marks everywhere. Adam says it doesn't matter, but it matters to me.

"I tried to get hold of Corey, but he's probably up the mountain shooting possums or something," James says.

"Just as well we got some extra food. I figured Max would eat more than he asked for," Adam says. From the back seat, he picks up the box of paper packages. Max isn't the only one with a big appetite. "I missed these so much. Never managed to find anything quite like it overseas. Nothing like Kiwi fish and chips."

"Shouldn't have stayed away so long." Owen laughs, and my heart aches. Why didn't Adam come back earlier? Twelve years is a long time to have carried this on his shoulders. It bugs me, maybe way more than it should. It's an indication of just how deeply he was hurt thinking I left him.

Lost in thought, I stay standing beside the car.

"Mum, are you going to unlock the door?" Max calls.

I blink slowly, shaking my head awake to the amusement of the boys in front of me.

"Wake up, Lily," Owen says.

"Be quiet, smart arse." I poke my tongue out at him as I walk past them all then slip the key into the front door.

Inside, the boys busy themselves getting plates and unwrapping the food. I feel like a visitor in my own home as they do all the work and I sit back and watch.

"Help yourselves," Adam says, stepping away. He walks to the dining table and grasps my hand, pulling me to my feet. "You first. I'll help Max."

"I can wait."

"I think you've waited long enough." He pushes me toward the bench and the pile of plates. In front of me is a huge feast. The fish and chip shop was busy before we got there. I'm pretty sure the Campbell boys cleaned them out.

One by one everyone fills their plates, and we all file into the living room, the dining table abandoned.

"It's good to see you two," Adam says to his brothers.

"Yeah, well, it seems like I wasn't fair to you when you came into the bakery," Owen says between bites.

Adam shakes his head. "It's understandable. Once James explained it everything made sense."

I'm sat next to Adam on the couch, and he tangles his ankle around mine as I lean against him.

"So you two really are back together?" Owen asks.

"I think so. If she'll have me." Adam shoots me a smile.

"Maybe. If he behaves."

He plants a kiss on my lips, all salty from the fish and chips.

"Eww gross, you two. Do you have to do that in front of me?" Owen raises his eyebrows.

"It is gross," Max says.

I laugh, leaning my head on Adam's shoulder. Maybe we are gross, but we're together.

———

AFTER HALF AN HOUR of eating and laughing, the stories are flowing and I need some quiet.

"I'll do the dishes," I say.

"No, you're not." Adam shakes his head.

"Yeah, I am. I need a little time out from you lot, and you've done enough." I place a kiss on his salty lips and smile.

"You're not going to budge, are you?"

"Nope." I stand and gather the empty plates from the coffee table.

In the kitchen, I run the hot water in the sink, closing my eyes as it fills.

Owen appears in the doorway. "Want some help?"

"I'm fine."

"You're always fine. I'm helping anyway." He laughs.

"I'll wash, you dry." I throw the tea towel at him.

He grins. "So, you and Adam."

"So, you're straight into it."

Owen laughs. "I don't have much time. There are only five plates to wash."

"Yes. Me and Adam."

"How did that happen?"

I raise my brows at him. "A series of events brought him back into my life. Your mother being ill, then Max going missing." I sigh. "I always thought he'd left and stopped caring. That he knew what had happened to me and moved on anyway."

"I guess you didn't go looking for him either ..."

Rolling my eyes, I shake my head. "I shouldn't have had to. Your mother should have told him when she spoke to him. Instead, she lied. I had enough to deal with back here."

The water's hot, and I scrub the first plate before handing it over. "It was just so confusing when he came back. All of a sudden he appears and takes an interest in Max. It scared the hell out of me, Owen. I could have lost him when he was born, then his father just reappears?"

Owen nods, drying the plate. "I can see how that could be confusing."

"I didn't know whether to believe him when he told me he'd just found out. Not at first. But he's done nothing to convince me otherwise, and he and Max already have this bond. It freaks me out a little."

A smile spreads across Owen's face. "You'll always be number one in Max's world. You should know that."

"I do. Max loves all of you too, but there's this connection he has with Adam that took me by surprise. I guess it shouldn't have." I hand him the next plate. "The only thing I'm worried about now is that he'll have to go back to the army. What happens next?"

"Shouldn't you ask him that?"

"I will. I just don't want to ruin this."

Owen's right eyebrow quirks. "Ruin it?"

"Everything's just right."

"Are you going to be okay if he goes back?" Owen asks.

I gulp and lick my lips, trying to find some moisture in my mouth to answer the last question I want to. "Honestly? I don't know. After all this time, I don't want to lose him." I lower my voice to a whisper. "I'm scared every time he leaves the house it'll be the last time I see him."

He nudges my elbow. "Tell him."

"I already told him I'm scared he'll disappear."

"What did he say?"

I raise my eyes to his. "That I had it bad."

"Lily, I barely know my brother anymore, but I can see a man in love. Tell him how you feel—tell him you want him to stay."

I nod, my hands shaking as I squeeze them together. Despite my not wanting Adam to leave town again, how can I stand in his way if the army is what he wants?

"If the reason he stayed away all this time is because his heart was broken over you, shouldn't getting you back be the best reason to stay?"

Owen's always been the most grounded of the Campbell boys. As soon as the bakery came up for sale, he did all he could to get hold of it. He's been as unlucky in love as the rest of us, having sampled several of the local ladies. Sometimes I wonder if any of them will truly settle down. The closest any of them have got is Drew, with his girlfriend, Lucy. Not that I've ever met her. I think she's a city girl through and through.

He's right. Max and I are a good reason for Adam to stay. "I guess."

"There's your answer, then."

21

ADAM

A week later, I'm still at Lily's. I haven't spoken to my parents; I've been too angry. I went into town at the start of the week and bought some new clothes and toiletries to keep me going.

But it's Friday again and while Max is at school today and I'm missing my buddy, I'll bite the bullet and visit. "I'm going to Mum and Dad's place to get my things."

Panic fills Lily's eyes. She doesn't need me, she's spent all this time demonstrating that, but she's nervous about me leaving. I can't blame her; it's not like I haven't done a runner before.

It's going to take some time for us to both settle into this.

"I'll be back as soon as I can. I need to talk to Mum and Dad, too. Find out why things happened the way they did."

Lily nods and slips her arms around my waist. My heart still hurts at the thought of her alone and struggling. I can never make up for it, but I can make sure she gets everything she needs from now on. This is my family.

I press my forehead to hers and close my eyes. "I won't be long." Kissing her nose, I let her go and she's straight-faced as I walk out to the car. As I reach it, I turn and look back at the house. This place has been enough for her, but I want more for us.

Over and over again in my head, I practice what I'm going to say to my parents. Not only did they let me go all this time without the truth, but they neglected Lily and Max. I expected better. At the very least, they could have made sure my son was provided for. It's disappointing.

Dad's by the back door as I pull into the yard. He tries to smile at me as I exit the car, but it's strained. I did walk away from him the last time I was here.

"I'm glad you're back," he says.

"Just to get my things. I'm staying with Lily."

He nods. "I thought you might be. We need to talk."

"Too right we do." It's hard to not be angry. Even when I came home they sat by and said nothing.

He turns to go back into the house and I follow. "Your mother's having a nap."

"Probably just as well."

"I was about to make a coffee. Want one?"

I nod and take a seat at the dining table. "Can I ask you something?"

"Anything."

"You wanted to talk to me about something before James told me about Lily. Was this it?"

He gives a stiff nod as he mixes two cups of coffee and

places them on the table. The sugar bowl is already sitting in front of me and he walks back to the fridge, returning with the milk and a couple of teaspoons from the drawer.

I stir sugar into my coffee. Now I'm here, I don't even know what to say.

Dad takes a sip of his coffee and sighs. "Adam, I'm sorry …"

"How could you not tell me, Dad? I almost understand Mum with her need to control everything, but you?" I want to know what he's thinking. It's always been clear he's under her thumb, but surely this was too big to say nothing about.

"It's complicated. I did my best to make sure Lily was taken care of." His tone is pained, and I can see how much he hates this rift the lies have caused. I haven't seen the man in twelve years, but I love him. He's my dad.

"Then why is she living in the middle of nowhere, struggling, by herself?" Slamming my mug on the table, I look Dad in the eyes. I thought I could do this, stay and have a civil conversation, but the reality hits me that it's too late for that.

Dad's eyes fill with tears, and he looks away. "Adam, there's more at stake than just Lily. I did my best."

"Your best wasn't good enough." I slam my fist on the table. "Max is your grandson. What the hell is wrong with you?" My heart is shattered by my parents' seeming indifference toward their own flesh and blood.

I stand and head straight to my room, throwing my few things in my bag and leaving the house without another word.

I'm done.

———

LILY HAS the patience of a saint.

I've sulked since I've been back at her place, and I know it. The quick conversation with Dad didn't resolve anything as I let my temper take control of me.

Still, she's taken me back when I chose to stay away for so long. She didn't need to, and I'm so aware of that. I left and didn't look back. I betrayed her just as much as anyone else did.

When I returned from Mum and Dad's, she greeted me at the door and wrapped her arms around me, as if she knew that no good had come from my visit. She was always all I needed.

In the evening, she cooks dinner. I stopped along the way to her place and grabbed some meat from the supermarket. I had all the intention of cooking, but Lily took charge, delighting in having some pork chops to do something with.

I'm torn. I still don't have the answers I sought from my parents thanks to my own impatience, and I'm not good company for Lily and Max. Max seems oblivious to my mood. He watches some TV before settling down to read a book. He's so much like Lily in that way—she was one who had a love of reading.

"Max, it's bedtime," Lily speaks, waking me from my stupor. "Get your pyjamas on and brush your teeth."

"Can Adam tuck me into bed?" He's stuck to Adam for the day, not Dad as it was the day before in front of Eric.

I stand and ruffle his hair as he goes past. "Sure can, bud. You get ready for bed and I'll be right up." We still need to sort out this whole parental thing, work out where I fit in. For now, I'll just back Lily up.

Watching my son climb those narrow stairs, I sigh as Lily wraps her arms around my waist.

"Are you okay?" she asks.

"Yes and no. I didn't really get any answers."

"I'm sorry." She leans her head against my chest, and I close my eyes.

"Once Max is asleep, I'd really like to crawl into bed with you. We've got some catching up to do."

She chuckles. "All in one night?"

"Depends. How much energy do you have?"

She raises her face to me and I give her a tender kiss. "You're a good man, Adam. I always knew that, despite feeling as if I'd been deserted."

"Thanks."

"You know what I mean. And I know you felt the same way. I spent so long thinking I'd be alone and that you didn't want us. But I knew you better than that. I just thought..."

"Thought what?"

"What your mother said was right—that you thought you were too young for the extra responsibility. For ages afterward I thought you'd come back, and then you didn't. You being here with us is everything."

I raise my thumb to her right cheek to wipe the tear rolling down it. Lily was always good at looking at the positive. "It's everything to me too. When I think that I missed out on this for all this time ... I'll spend the rest of my life making up for it."

She lets out a sigh. "Finding out that you didn't know and having you here already makes up for so much."

I run my fingers through that long, blonde hair. "I wish it was more."

"Stop it. Go and tuck that son of ours in."

A smile spreads across my face, and I kiss her one more time before letting go. "I will. And I'll make sure he falls asleep so then I get to catch up in other areas with you."

"Other areas?"

I chuckle. "I'm going to assume his mother will be waiting in bed for his father?"

"I'm pretty sure it's safe to assume that."

Max is in the bathroom as I climb the stairs. He's already in his pyjamas, and I stand at the door and smile at him as he scrubs. When he's finished, he rinses and turns back toward me, a big grin on his face. I cock an eyebrow as we stand there, locked in place, him showing off his teeth.

"Well?" he asks through gritted teeth after a moment.

"Well, what?" I'm so confused.

"Do my teeth look okay?"

The penny drops. This must be the routine he has with Lily. I take a couple of steps and bend over to take a look. "They look fine to me."

He shoots past me, running across the hall and leaping on his bed.

I follow, shaking my head as he nestles under the covers.

"Am I allowed to call you Dad?" he asks.

"You were calling me that yesterday."

"I know, but I didn't know if I was supposed to."

I grin. "You're allowed, Max. I am your dad."

He sits up and gives me an intense look. There must be so much going on in that head of his. "Where have you been?"

The question hits me right in the chest. I wasn't where I should have been. "I was in the army and travelled all over the place."

197

"You didn't visit me." His tone is flat.

"Well, I was so far away I didn't know you were here. But now I'm back." His lower lip wobbles, and I reach out, running my knuckles under his chin. "I'm not going anywhere. I'll be right here for you and your mum. No more going away," I whisper. This hurts so much and yet it's what I need to do. To tell my son how I feel. I've had so little time to absorb everything, but being with him feels more right than anything ever has.

I lean over, and he slips his arms around my neck. "It's good you're home, Dad."

Tears roll down my cheeks as I hold my boy tight. I grip his head and kiss his hair, my stomach churning with regret for not being here sooner, for not being here for him. Renewing my relationship with Lily is one thing—developing a relationship with Max is right up there with it.

"Don't cry." Max pulls away.

"I love you and Mum so much." As I let him go, I force a smile through the tears.

"We love you too. Have you seen this?" He points at his bedside cabinet. There's a framed photo of Lily and I on what was the best night of my life. We'd gone to the school ball, danced all evening cheek to cheek, and then driven somewhere secluded where we both lost our virginity.

"Not for a long time."

"It's you and Mum."

I nod, reaching for the photo frame. My overwhelming memory of that night was the love between Lily and I. We were seventeen, and it felt as if we'd waited forever for that night. Within a year our lives were torn apart, and I, being a heartbroken teenager, had run away from it all. Guilt hung over me as I took in every detail of that photo. How had I not stayed? At least until I knew where she was?

"You're still crying, Dad." Max tugs on my sleeve as I put the photo back.

I can't speak, and I wrap my arms around him again. I'll never let either of them down again, never run, never hide from anything. No matter how hard things get. At eighteen I thought I was a man. Now I know for sure what a boy I was.

"Goodnight." Max's voice is muffled, his face pressed into my chest. I release him from my hug, but cup his face.

"Have a good sleep." My heart swells just looking at him. My flesh and blood.

I turn as Lily places her hand on my shoulder and I look up to see her eyes full of tears too.

"Night, Max." She leans over and kisses Max's cheek. He grins as he lies down and pulls the blanket up.

For a moment we watch him, and he closes his eyes.

Our boy.

———

MAX IS ASLEEP, and I take Lily by the hand and lead her to the bedroom, closing the door behind us. We can reopen it when we're done.

"Sorry I'm not waiting for you," she says, swinging her hand in mine.

"I loved it being the three of us in there. Being with you and Max—I can't even begin to tell you how much it means." I smile. "Seeing that old photo was overwhelming."

She grins. "I dug it out the first time you visited. Max caught me sleeping with it."

I catch my breath at the thought of her reminiscing, all the while keeping those walls up. "So I was in your bed almost as soon as I arrived in town?"

She slaps my arm. "I have to admit I was a little overwhelmed with memories. Didn't help you looked so good."

"How good?"

She reaches for my shirt, and I watch her face as she unbuttons it. It's so freeing to be here with her without restriction. Lily focuses on her task and pushes the fabric back, running her hands over my chest. "That good." Her breath hitches as our gazes lock, and I lower my head to kiss her.

"You like, Miss Parker?" My lips seek hers, and she relaxes in my arms as we come together.

"Very much," she says as we pull apart.

I raise my hand to touch her face, anchoring my fingers in her hair. She gives a little sigh when I tighten my grip. "I think you're overdressed."

Her fingers trace lines up from my chest to my shoulders. Every little touch is magical, sending warmth through my body that I haven't experienced for so long. It's like my body knows she's the only one for me.

Running my hands down her back, I drop them to her thighs, pulling her up to hook her legs around my waist. I want her, want inside her, but tonight we take our time—it's not the mad, frantic rush that's ensued every other night.

"I love you," she whispers.

In response, I move us to the bed, turning and gently lowering her onto her back. My mouth is on hers, tasting her tongue as it tangles with mine. I always loved kissing her, and now it's all I want to do.

I raise her T-shirt, pushing it up and over her breasts, cradled in her bra. She lets out a contented sigh as I nuzzle a nipple through the thin fabric.

"Adam." Her fingers claw my scalp as I push her bra up and take that nipple in my mouth. It pebbles under my tongue, and her repeated sigh tells me why.

"I love you too." My fingers work on her jeans, and she helps, pushing them down before I take over. She raises her hand to my face and I kiss her palm, sucking her fingers one by one as I spread her legs. I kiss my way down that flat stomach and bury my face between her legs. Tasting her is almost too good to be true, and I lose myself as she surrenders to me.

"Adam," she cries, raking her fingers through my hair again. The act pulls me in closer, and the taste and scent of her send my senses into overdrive. I can't respond. This is heaven. My heart is whole, and now I get to spend every second I can showing Lily just how full it is.

I back off, planting kisses on her inner thighs, raising my eyes to meet her gaze. Her eyes are wide with anticipation, and she cries my name again and again when I raise a finger, drawing circles around her clit.

"What are you doing?" She gasps.

"Making you wait."

"Why?"

I stop, crawling up her body until I look her in the eyes. "Because I want this to last as long as possible. I want to enjoy you as long as possible."

Her lips twitch. "You can enjoy me as often as you want. I think I've waited long enough."

My mouth claims hers as I taste her tongue.

She's right. I push into her, unable to hold back any longer.

I can't keep my girl waiting.

22

LILY

Twelve years ago

I no longer fear death.

Nothing I say has gotten through to Mum, and I've been here weeks, or is it months?

My once tight clothes now hang off me as the weight continues to drop off. My stomach is rock hard and bulges a little. I wonder if the same thing that happens to starving children I've seen pictures of is happening to me.

Mum remembers to bring me food every two to three days. I'd be dead already if it wasn't for the bathroom with the little hand basin. It takes a lot of effort to get there, but it's the only source of water I have.

When she does bring food, I try to make it last, but it's hard. With every bite I know she's added something to it, something to keep me weak as she "protects" me.

There's no point fighting her. I stopped arguing a long

time ago. She thinks she's doing what's best, and I can't persuade her otherwise.

Pain in my stomach grips me and I cry out to an empty room, maybe even an empty house. Mum won't hear me, and while I might not be scared of dying, what I want is to curl up in a ball in her arms and go to sleep. But there's no chance of that.

I don't know how long I suffer, but there's blood on the mattress, too. It's confusing. My periods have long since stopped, and I assume it's the fact that I'm no doubt suffering from malnutrition.

All because my mother couldn't bear the thought of losing me.

Light floods the stairwell and hope grows that she's come to help me. She appears with a tray of food. I don't know how much time has passed as I float in and out of consciousness.

"Here you go," she says. She's thin, and I don't think she's taking any better care of herself. She's certainly in no kind of mental state to look after me. What if she forgets I'm here?

"Mum, you need to get help," I croak.

"You're safe here."

The pain hits and I cry out, clutching my belly.

Her eyes dart around me, and her gaze lands on the mattress. "What's wrong?" There's panic in her voice.

"I don't know. I'm in agony," I sob, but there's not a lot of moisture in my body. Getting to the basin has been so hard the past two days.

"You're bleeding." Her voice is soft and scared.

"Mum, you need to call an ambulance, get a doctor, something." I'm grasping at straws.

As she places her hand on my stomach, her eyes fill with sadness. "I'll go and do it now."

Hope builds in me alongside the crushing discomfort that builds to pain again. I close my eyes, unsure of what is happening to my body, of what my mother will do, if I'll make it out of here alive.

I was a fool to think I could ever leave this place, get away from her and the town belief I'd end up the same she did. So much of her sewing work came to her because people were sympathetic and wanted to make sure her daughter had enough to eat. Where did they all think I was now?

Adam. I twist the ring around my finger, the one I was supposed to wear on my wedding day. The finger that it once fit snugly on is so much smaller, but the ring holds on and gives me faith that everything will be okay.

At least I hope so.

All I can do is wait.

———

I WAKE SQUINTING in the bright light that floods the room, I look around. I'm not at home anymore. The walls are white, the furniture's white—everything is white.

A hospital.

I'm in a hospital.

My heart soars at the thought of freedom, but the pain grips me again. It's not as severe this time, and I take deep breaths until it passes.

"They managed to stop labour."

Shifting my focus to the voice, I see a man I don't know

in the doorway. He's tall with greying hair and a short, neatly trimmed beard, and he has kind eyes.

"Labour?"

He gives me a small smile and approaches the bed. When he extends his hand toward me, I automatically reach out to shake it.

"Hi, Lily. How are you feeling?" He must be a doctor.

I lick my lips, letting go of his hand. "Umm a bit groggy. I feel like I've slept, but I'm still tired."

He nods, and I return to the unanswered question. "You said they stopped labour?"

In return I receive another nod. "It wasn't easy, but you responded to the medication. The doctor will be through shortly to talk to you."

This isn't the doctor? "I don't understand. Who are you?" He must have me confused with someone else, surely. My head's still fuzzy. He said labour?

There is that smile again, the one that told me he has a great deal of sympathy for me, but doesn't give me anything else to go on. "My name's Joseph Waterson, and I'm the case worker who's been assigned to you. The medical staff managed to stop your labour, but your pregnancy is along enough that the baby's viable." His smile grows. "But it's obviously better for both of you if your baby stays inside. At least for a while longer."

Baby? My heart races now. It's like a lightbulb moment as I realise what that hard lump in my belly is. And if the baby is viable …

"What's the date?" I ask, my mouth dry.

"Sorry?"

"Day, month. What is it?"

He frowns. "October twelve."

My eyes sting with sudden tears. "Six months," I whisper.

"I'm here to talk to you about how you move forward. You'll be in here for some time, and we need to make sure you're taking care of yourself."

"Taking care …" I stumble on the words. "Do you have any idea what I've been through?" The tears roll down my cheeks, and his eyebrows twitch in confusion.

"Lily, I've been brought in because your mother said you haven't been taking care of yourself. Not eating, not sleeping, and we'll need to talk about your toxicology results."

My head spins. "You don't know. How can you not know?" I roll onto my side, burying my face in the pillow.

"Know what? What do you need to tell me?" He's confused, I can hear it in his tone, and it sinks in that Mum's lied to them, spun a story to get herself out of trouble. She's still got enough sense to do that.

"She drugged me to stop me getting married. I've been trapped in that house for six months, and no one came looking. She's sick. She needs looking after."

Through my teary eyes, I look at this man whose expression has switched to one of horror.

"If there are drugs in my blood, they're her prescription meds. All the crap that doctors have given her over the years. Some things helped, some didn't, but she had them all. God knows what she gave me." I swallow. "The only reason I'm here is because my pain and bleeding forced her to do something." I close my eyes. "I didn't even know I was pregnant. I thought I was dying." Opening them again, I look at the only person I've seen other than my mother in six months. "What chance does my baby have now?" *Adam's baby.*

"I ... I see." He's clearly shaken. Who wouldn't be? What a weird tale. Does he even believe me? Would I believe me?

He blinks a few times, as if he's trying to process what I've said.

"Where's my mother?"

"You had to be airlifted. You're in Waikato Hospital," he says quietly. "She said she would follow as soon as she could."

My stomach tightens. "Someone needs to go and check on her. How long have I been here?"

"Two days." His voice drops to a whisper. I'm free and still no one has worked out what happened. She could have done anything by now. I'm angry at her, but scared for her too. I want her to be punished. I want her taken care of.

Mum.

———

BY THE MORNING, she's in custody.

I don't know how to feel. She hurt me and my baby, but she's still my mother, and I love her no matter what.

My baby.

The knowledge I'm pregnant is still sinking in. I need Adam—where the hell is he? Why did he never come for me? So many questions.

To give me some freedom, I've been taken off the IV fluids for a while, and I leave the room, walking down a corridor and surrounding myself in the glorious hum of hospital background noise. It doesn't matter what they're saying or doing, just as long as I'm not alone anymore.

Down the hall, there's a small communal area with a tele-vision on the wall and a phone on the table. I sit on a chair beside the phone and look at it for a moment. As much as I want to speak with Adam, it scares me that he doesn't know where I've been all this time and doesn't seem to have made any effort to find me.

I pick up the phone and dial, closing my eyes as the line rings.

"Hello?"

Damn it. Adam's mother.

"Hi, may I speak to Adam?" I ask.

"He doesn't live here now. Who's calling?"

My stomach sinks. If he isn't there, where is he? Is he as heartbroken as I am?

I have to tell her—it might be the only way to get hold of him. "Mrs Campbell, it's Lily."

Silence greets me.

"Lily Parker?" I try again.

"I know who you are. What I don't know is why you're calling for Adam when I'm sure you know he's not here." Over the years her accent has been softened by living in New Zealand, but when she's irritable, her American heritage is as clear as a bell. It doesn't help that she's always scared the shit out of me.

"I ... I'm sorry, but I didn't know. Do you have a number I can reach him on? I need to speak to him urgently."

"Shame it wasn't so urgent when you hurt him so much six months ago. Goodbye, Lily."

"Please, Mrs Campbell." I look up at the ceiling.

"What could you *possibly* want after all this time?"

"My mother ... my mother has been keeping me prisoner. I just got out." This whole thing must sound like an insane excuse, but what else is there to say?

"How stupid do you think I am?" the other woman hisses.

"Please, Mrs Campbell. I'm pregnant and alone." Tears roll down my cheeks. "I need Adam. They're putting me on a nutrient drip to try to save the baby, get him big enough so he can be born."

"I suggest you get the father of the baby to help then. You've done enough damage to my family."

"How heartless can you be?" I scream into the phone. "This is Adam's baby." I slam the receiver down and look up, spotting Joseph in the doorway.

"Are you okay?" he asks.

"I just tried to call the baby's father."

"Oh? Does he know what happened?"

I shrug. "I don't know. His mother said he doesn't live there anymore. She thinks I'm lying about everything. I missed my wedding day because of this, and Adam must think I'm the most heartless bitch that ever lived."

Joseph places his hand on my shoulder. "I'm sure we can find a way to get through to her, make her understand what happened. Now the arrest has been made, it's likely to make the newspapers."

I grimace. The thought that all of Copper Creek will know just how crazy my mother has acted doesn't sit well with me. As it was, the kids at school had teased me for years, 'Crazy Parker' they called her, not bothering to laugh behind my back.

"Do you have any family to stay with, Lily? I mean, you'll be in hospital for some time to come, but someone who can help you with the baby?"

I shake my head. "No. My dad bailed years ago—I wouldn't have a clue where to find him. It's been me and

Mum for as long as I can remember. I don't really want to go back to the house."

Joseph frowns. "I don't really want to tell you this, but there's no house to go back to."

"What do you mean?"

"Your mother stopped paying the mortgage at some point, possibly even before she did this to you. The bank has control of the property. They're trying to sell it."

The sick feeling in my stomach grows. I might not want to live in the house, but my mother has just lost her only asset. I'm not even sure if there'll be any money left after the sale.

What the hell am I going to do?

23

LILY

Now

I fought to get rid of the dreams.

With Adam back, I sleep a lot better. I've had a month of peaceful nights for the most part. But when the dreams come back, they're more vicious than ever, reminding me of a time I've tried so hard to forget. As my life comes together, my dreams leave me falling apart.

I wake, unable to breathe, and I claw at the air to get release. Panting, I sit up, clutching the sheets to my chest. Beside me, Adam sleeps peacefully, and I envy him the sleep he enjoys.

Gazing at him is calming, knowing he loves me as much as I love him. I spent so long wishing I could stop my feelings, but despite thinking he'd walked away and never looked back, part of me always wanted him to return. For so long I wished he'd come and rescue me. I guess I finally got my wish.

There are nights when he doesn't sleep in peace. When he seems to be disturbed, waking and wanting me with desperate need. I respond as we take what we need from each other.

Afterward he holds me tight, as if terrified to let go, and I cling to him just as fiercely. Part of me believes if I close my eyes, even for a second, he'll turn out to be a dream and disappear into the night, never to be seen again.

He will at some point. The army won't let him stay away forever.

"Lily?" Adam stirs, his eyes opening a notch. He raises his arm, pulling me back into bed. "It gets cold without you," he mumbles.

I smile as he drifts off to sleep and stroke his face before closing my eyes again. He seems reluctant to let go of me even for a moment. Maybe he shares my fear. I think he needs me as much as I need him.

In the morning I wake to gentle kisses, enveloped in his strong arms. This is what I want every day.

"Hmmm," I nuzzle his chest.

"I love waking up with you," he murmurs.

These kisses are sweet; the passionate ones happen in the night. Most of the time our mornings are G-rated, just in case Max walks in. He hasn't jumped into my bed at night since Adam arrived, nor have we had night visits from Eric.

My life, especially during the day is infinitely more peaceful with Adam back in it.

"We should get up. Max will want breakfast, and I could do with something to eat."

Despite my protests, Adam took us to get groceries and filled the freezer. We've never had so much choice. I'm still cautious, still scared that this will all end in an instant and we'll be back to where we were. He tells me off for not eating enough, but it's habit. I still have my son to support.

Our son.

"I might let you get out of bed." He kisses my cheek and I linger a little longer before pulling away and getting out of bed. I open the drawer, pulling on a bra and slipping a T-shirt over my head while he whistles. "If only I could keep you naked all day."

"Unfortunately, there are things to do. The shearing's underway. Eric will take care of it, but I want to check in to make sure everything's okay."

Adam sits up and grabs a shirt from his bag beside the bed, tugging it on as I pull on my jeans. "I hate Eric doing this shit for you."

I shrug. "He gets a better price if we do both flocks at once. He benefits from this too."

Adam stands and walks to the window, pulling the curtains back. Sunlight floods the room.

"It's such a gorgeous day out there. Does Max play sport?" he asks, taking in the view. Not that it's that exciting—the dusty brown yard, with green paddocks behind it.

"A little. He loves anything where he gets to run around."

"I'll have to get Max a baseball mitt."

"He already plays softball at school."

Adam turns and rolls his eyes at me.

"Isn't it basically the same thing?" I ask, walking toward him.

I squeal as Adam leaps at me, pushing me backward and

pinning me to the bed. "Do you really want to discuss all the differences?"

"Not really." I laugh. "I'll bow to your superior knowledge. But just so you know, kids still play rugby here."

Adam drops his head and nips at my neck. I sigh, my body stirring. Hell, all he has to do is look at me for that to happen. All the feelings I've suppressed for so long have been woken. I'd missed the days in my early twenties when other women my age were going out, having fun, and falling in love. Instead, I'd brought up Max, struggling with a special needs child, and all of a sudden I was thirty. Now, I'm enjoying making up for lost time.

"I don't care what Max plays," I whisper, "as long as I get to play with you."

Adam's eyes are full of mischief as he raises his head, and my heart leaps at the love written all over his face. "Always."

———

AFTER BREAKFAST, we all head out toward the sheep. Eric's already there, rounding them up to take them to be sheared. He usually gets mine sorted out before his. He has more sheep than I do, and the quicker mine are done, the quicker I can sell the wool. He's taken care of me in his own way.

"Lily, Adam." He greets us with a nod. Max giggles as his favourite sheep dog, Happy, nearly bowls him over, she's so excited to see him. He sits on the ground as the dog licks his face, wrapping his arms around her neck.

"Have you got a friend, Max?" Adam asks.

"This is Happy." He grins up at Adam.

"Happy? That's a weird name for a dog." Adam squats and pats the Border Collie on her head. "Hi, Happy."

"Max named her when she was a puppy," Eric says.

I don't miss the expression on Adam's face at that news. He knew I'd been here since Max was a baby and had had a lot to do with Eric. The news his son even named Eric's dog doesn't sit well with him, but he'll just have to deal with it.

"It's a great name then." The smile returns.

"How are things going?" I ask Eric.

"Good. We're on track to get your sheep done before lunch."

"Brilliant."

Eric turns to Max. "Sorry, bud. Happy's got to get back to work now."

Max pouts, but stands and lets Happy go.

"I'll bring her to see you again soon." Turning back toward the sheep, Eric whistles for the dog. Happy barks at Max, then runs toward the sheep with her master.

Adam wraps his arms around Max. "That's a pretty cool dog."

"I'm not allowed one." Max's tone tells a story of resentment. Eric had meant for Happy to be Max's dog, but I couldn't take in another mouth to feed. She'd become Eric's best sheep dog, and there wasn't much chance of Happy coming to live with us now.

Adam meets my gaze. "One day, bud."

I stiffen. He can't make Max promises he can't keep. My trust in him is building, but I'm not completely there yet.

"Go home, Lily. We've got this." Eric says.

"Thanks."

Eric shoots me a smile that doesn't get past Adam, and I see the question in his eyes when he looks at me.

"We'll see you later, then." I nod at Eric.

We turn back toward the house. Adam links his fingers in mine and raises my hand to his lips to kiss. That brings a grin to my face. He used to do that back when we were love-struck teenagers.

"What else can we do today?" Max asks.

"We could go for a drive to the cove. I never did quite get there," Adam says.

"It's so awesome there. Maybe we can go for a swim." Max skips as he walks beside us.

"I don't know. It might be sunny, but it's not exactly warm," I say, reaching to run my fingers through Max's hair.

"Maybe we could grab our swimming things just in case. I've got a pair of shorts I can use, so if Max is up for it …" Adam grins.

"Can we take Happy?"

I sigh. Now he's seen him, Max will spend the next few hours talking about it. Maybe swimming would be a distraction.

"Happy has to work. How about you put your swimming togs on under your clothes just in case it's warm enough to swim."

That satisfies him, and he bounces along beside us.

I only hope it's enough to distract Adam from questions about Eric.

———

It's busy at the cove. With the weather warming up, people come down here for a swim all the time. The small shop cashes in when it's busy, and there's a queue for ice cream. It always amazes me the place is still here, but these days must make up for the slower ones.

Adam's car rumbles down the road as we look for a parking spot, and Max spots a gap first, bouncing in the back seat and pointing at it.

Max taps on my window. "Mum, there's Karl."

My heart sinks to see Sasha with her son a short distance from where we're parking. They're walking toward the water. For Max, what happened before is like water off a duck's back. He never holds a grudge against anyone except Eric.

"Adam," I murmur.

"I saw."

His tone is terse, and I look at him to avoid seeing Sasha and Karl as we pull into the park. Adam's hand lands on mine and pulls my fingers to the gear stick. He squeezes them slightly, and I turn my head to see him smile at me.

"Can we get an ice cream?" Max asks.

"Are you kidding? Did you see the size of that queue?" Adam asks.

I laugh. "We have ice cream at home."

"It's not the same." Max pouts.

"Pretty sure it is. We'll have some ice cream when we get back. Let's just go down for a walk and see how cold the water is." I grab my bag and the towels from the back seat of the car. Throwing my bag over my shoulder, I lay the towels over it.

Turning toward the water, Adam loops his arm around my waist, and I lean my head on his shoulder.

"Sorry if I sounded grumpy. I didn't want to have to actually talk to Sasha. That woman gets up my nose."

"She's good at that."

I gaze up at him as he pecks me on the lips.

"Can you two not do that out here?" Max grumbles.

"Sorry." I ruffle his hair, and he laughs. "Let's go check out the water."

The sunshine is warm on my shoulders, and the air is filled with laughter, just as the people fill the water.

"Looks like it might be a go for swimming," Adam says.

"Come on, Dad." Max slips around the other side of us and grabs Adam's hand. Adam turns to check my reaction.

"Go with your son. I'll be right behind you." What I really want is to sit and dig my toes in the sand. Just sitting in the sun for a while seems good to me.

I find an empty spot and sit, watching Adam and Max approach the water. From the way Max jumps around, it seems as if it's a little cold, but having been here so often, it'll just be a case of getting in and getting used to it.

Max strips off his shirt and pulls down his shorts, handing them to Adam. Adam looks around, and jogs back toward me, a grin on his face, dropping Max's clothing on the ground. He reaches for the bottom of his T-shirt and tugs it over his head.

"You know every girl on this beach will be looking at you," I say as he pulls his wallet out of his pocket and hands it to me.

"You know I don't care what every girl looks at. Just you."

He laughs. "Max is really keen for a swim. It's a bit chilly, but we'll be good for a while."

He bends to kiss me, and I raise my face to meet him.

A loud shriek fills the air. *I know that sound.*

I'm on my feet before Adam registers anything's happened. "What's …" he starts before turning around. I'm sprinting, running into the water to my knees, pulling a much larger boy off my screaming son.

"What do you think you're doing?" I yell.

Max gulps for air, but at least he's not screeching. "Karl pushed me."

"I did not." Karl stands beside me, his hands on his hips.

"I saw you with your hands on him. Did you hold him under the water?" I pull Max up. He's okay. I'm the one shaking.

It's clear Max has been under. This is a boy so cautious that he takes forever to adjust to the temperature. He'll go in just a little bit at a time, and on previous visits we've been down here and barely put our knees in.

"No."

There's another shriek, this time behind me. I turn in time to see Sasha entering the water, her eyes full of anger, all directed at me. "Get your hands off my son."

I raise myself to my full height and stand toe to toe with her. For years she got jibes in where she could, little snarky remarks about me, about Mum, about the Campbells, even when I had nothing to do with them. She'd been one of those mean girls at school and never changed. Now I'm determined it will. "I pulled him off Max. Get your son to leave mine alone."

She rolls her eyes. "Everyone knows it's your son who has

the problem. He's mentally deficient, Lily—you can't just leave him by himself."

"I think I know more about what my son is capable of than you. Apparently I know more about what your son is capable of, too."

Adam arrives at my side, and his hand lands on my back. "If you want to have a go at who left Max by himself, have a go at me. But it seems to me that Karl is the one who can't be trusted." He runs his hand up to my shoulder and squeezes.

Sasha's face goes a brilliant shade of red. She's quite happy to run me down, but Adam's another story.

"Come on, Max. Want to go for a swim?" he says.

"Yep, Dad." Max has already bounced back, and as he grabs Adam's hand, Adam leans over and pecks me on the lips.

"Have fun, you two." I wade out of the water and back to where I abandoned my bag on the beach. Thankful for the fact that Copper Creek is a small town without too much in the way of crime and that my things are where I left them, I spread out a towel so I can dry without getting sand on my now wet shorts and watch Adam playing with our son. Sasha stands off to the side while Karl swims by himself.

I might feel sorry for him if he wasn't such a bully. It's clear where that comes from. From what I've heard, his elder brother is the same. I'm grateful that at least he's in high school and not around to pick on other kids. He's nowhere to be seen today, and I assume he's off somewhere wreaking havoc.

Leaning back on my hands, I raise my face to meet the sun and close my eyes. Having Adam around has already been good for me. I'm nowhere near as tired, and I know I can depend on him. For now.

My chest still clenches when I think about him leaving, even for a short time. He hasn't told me much about his deployment yet, where he's been, what he's done. It scares me to think about him at war. Although, it always did. Even when I thought he'd turned his back on me, I still worried about him.

I lose myself in the now as I shift my gaze back to the water. Adam and Max splash each other, and I can hear the laughter from where I sit. Karl still hovers not too far from them, watching Max playing with his father. I wonder if it's envy that drives his behaviour.

It's warm, and I lie down on my back. A slight breeze wafts over me, but the sun is calming, and it'd be so easy to fall asleep.

Max's shriek fills the air, and I'm jolted out of my daze as I sit. Max is fine, I can see him, but Adam's swimming out farther and I stand again, running toward Max as he points into the distance. When I reach the edge of the water Max runs to me, his arms flailing about.

"Dad saw Karl in trouble. He's gone to get him."

I look around for Sasha. She's nowhere to be seen, and I growl in frustration.

There's no sign of Karl, and Adam dives under the water. My heart is in my throat as we watch them, Max wrapping his wet arms around my waist. I don't care. Around us, people run into the water. The water's so calm here, and it's not like a big beach where there are lifeguards.

I can't take my eyes off the spot Adam went under, and I hold my breath waiting.

He pops back out of the water, and tears well. Karl's in his arms. Adam swims, then steps as he draws closer.

"What's going on?" Sasha says behind me. I turn to see her, ice cream in hand.

"Karl disappeared into the water. My dad saved him," Max says proudly.

"What?" Her eyes fill with fear, and she drops the ice cream in the sand, the seagulls swooping in to fight over the cone. She wades into the water to meet Adam. She strokes Karl's head as they walk back to the sand.

"He's okay, just went too deep. He'll be fine." Adam's reassuring her, and when they're clear of the water, he lowers Karl onto the ground. The boy coughs and splutters a bit, and Sasha kneels beside him. There's a cheer from the water as people watch.

I can't find it in myself to get petty payback for the harsh words she used on me earlier. Instead, I say nothing.

"Thank you," she says, taking her son's hand in hers.

"You're welcome," Adam says.

"I hope you're okay, Karl." Max's words touch my heart. It wasn't that long ago Karl was cruel to him, but Max rises above it. My pride in him grows.

We walk away with Sasha berating her boy for going in over his head. Max knows better than that, but then he also knows how to swim. I made sure of that.

When we reach our things, Adam wipes himself down, tugs on his shirt and wraps the towel around his waist. "How about we swing by the store on the way home and pick up ice creams? Screw standing in that queue."

Max follows his father's example, drying off his chest as Adam smiles.

"You're a good man," I say.

"I am now."

I shake my head. "You always were."

Adam takes me in his arms, and I raise my face to look into his dark eyes, the ones filled with love and desire all for me. He says nothing but presses his lips to mine, dragging my bottom lip through his teeth as he lets go. There's no mistaking the message he's sending.

Tonight can't come soon enough.

———

AFTER DINNER, I tuck Max in. Being in the sun and water wore him out, even though we weren't out for long.

"I'm going to get in the shower," Adam says.

"It's a shame I had one before dinner. I'm going to bed."

He chuckles. "Meet you there?"

Pulling a big T-shirt on to sleep, I lie down and close my eyes. After a few minutes, the mattress sinks as Adam joins me. "What's the deal with you and Eric?"

I sit up. "What do you mean?"

"Were you two together?"

I swallow. Adam's so passionate about this new start and us being together. The last thing I need is him going after Eric. "Kind of. I mean, we dated for a while."

"Is that why he thinks you're fair game?"

I sigh. It wouldn't be the first time testosterone's kicked in with those two. This is part of my story we just haven't discussed. "When Max was born, Eric's mother brought me back here and gave me a place to live. We stayed in the main house for a few days before this place was ready for us. I was so focused on Max I barely noticed Eric was around."

Adam smirks.

"Besides, there was only one man I wanted, and I had no idea where he was. "

He reaches up and rubs my shoulder. "I'm sorry."

"You didn't know. This place was used to house farmhands when the property was bigger, but it had been empty for a while. Mrs Murphy had everything moved from Mum's house and brought here. It became our home."

Adam smiles, leaning his hand on my arm. "I'm so grateful for her."

"She was amazing, and Eric was attentive and kind to me. When Max started having issues, Eric's mother would look after him so I could get a break, and I spent some time with Eric." I drop my gaze. "We grew close, but it was never right. I hadn't seen you for maybe four years, and I still felt guilty about letting anyone near me. So I broke it off."

Adam frowns and pulls me back down to the bed. His eyes search my face, and all I feel is pain. I still remember the moment I knew I couldn't move forward with Eric. We were in the car, parked in a remote spot after spending an evening at an outdoor movie in the cove. We'd taken things slowly. He was very sweet and gentle and kissed me with more feeling than I'd had in a long time.

I'd let him kiss me, and the simple act had left me missing what only Adam had ever given me. Needing to feel wanted, I'd ignored my heart and listened instead to the nagging feeling that told me I'd never get Adam back, that this life was it.

"We didn't have sex, but I was intimate with him."

Adam huffs. That's not what he wanted to hear, but it is what it is.

"When I broke things off, he responded by asking me to marry him. But there were ..." I sigh. "Conditions."

Adam's breathing grows heavier. "What kind of conditions?"

"Max had always been small for his age, but then he missed milestones. Even before he started school it was obvious he needed extra help." I lick my lips. "Eric wanted to find a special school for him to go to. One that could cater to his needs. He offered to pay for it all ..."

"But you wouldn't let him," Adam whispers.

Tears prick my eyes. "Max was all I had. It didn't matter what he needed—I had to make sure he had it while he was with me. He was all I had of you."

Adam presses his lips to mine with so much tenderness, it just makes the tears worse. There can be no more words. What else is there to say?

Our little family is whole again. That is all I've ever wished for, even in the times I'd resented Adam for leaving, for not carrying any of the responsibility I'd had to. But I'd do it all over again if it meant Max had the same childhood, full of love and laughter.

What Eric wanted hadn't mattered.

Max and I'd had each other, and that was everything. And now we both have Adam.

24

ADAM

I swear my older brother is seven foot tall.

Corey stands in the doorway of Lily's house, gawping as he runs his gaze up and down me as if he can't quite believe what he's seeing. For his part, he's tanned and bearded, in his Swanndri and gumboots. "Adam?"

He's been off hunting for part of the time I've been back, and completely unable to get hold of. The look on his face is worth it as he cracks a smile.

"The one and only. I've been trying to call you."

"You and everyone else. I'm good at using the 'delete all' function on my answer phone."

I step back to let him in, and we embrace, slapping one another on the back. Corey was the brother I was closest to growing up, the one who always took my side. Our last words to each other were harsh, but I hope that's in the past.

"So, you're back, and with Lily." He pulls away and gives me a huge smile.

I nod. "There's a lot I need to tell you."

"Hold that thought."

He heads back out to the ute, opening the rear door and pulling out a large container.

"I could kill a coffee. There's some meat in the chilly bin for Lily." He passes me as he comes in the front door and places the box in the hallway.

"Awesome. She'll be stoked. I'll go and start the coffee."

He follows as I make my way into the kitchen. "It's so good to see you. Are you back for good?"

"If things work out. Either way, I'm not living without Lily again." I flick the switch on the jug.

Corey grins. "She was never the same without you. I wanted to get on a plane and smack you, but if Lily's taken you back, she must be okay with what happened. We all took care of her."

"So I've learned. Did you really think I'd decided to stay away? Knowing my own kid was back here?" The water boils, and I lean back on the bench.

Guilt sweeps his face. "I didn't think so. It was really confusing. We had that argument and I knew you weren't planning to come back. And then Mum said you were in the army and you had a girlfriend. I guess I thought you were being selfish, but I also got it. You guys were kids. We all were. None of us knew what responsibility really was. Some of us still don't."

"I didn't know about Max. Mum kept it from me."

I wish I could say my big brother's surprised, but all he does is shrug and sit down at the table.

"That doesn't shock you?" I drop teaspoons of coffee and

sugar in our cups and pour the milk with some vague memory of Corey taking his coffee the same as mine.

"Owen caught me up. Do you remember what Mum and Dad were like when we were little? Dad had balls back then —he'd stand up to her. Something happened, Adam. Something killed him inside, and I've been trying to work it out what it is for ages."

Pouring the water into the cups, I carry them to the table. "I have some vague memories."

"She's holding something over him. Has to be. He laughed when I asked him, but he doesn't say boo unless she agrees to it."

I sigh. "Nothing would surprise me. How did things get so screwed up? When I hit him up about it, he said there was more at stake than just Lily."

Corey smiles. "Whatever it is, I'm glad you're back. What do you think of Max? I thought I might offer to take him off Lily's hands for the day."

The back door opens and Max comes bounding in, followed by his mother with a basketful of laundry.

"Corey," he shrieks, and runs around the table to sit beside him.

"Hey, Max. Lily. There's a chilly bin full of meat by the front door."

Lily places the basket of washing on a chair. "Thanks. It's good to see you."

"Great to see you guys. Especially this one." He grips my shoulder. "I wondered if Max wanted to come and hang out with me for the rest of the day. I'm going to Owen's to hang out and watch some movies." He shifts his gaze to me. "I'd ask you too, but I have a feeling a day alone with the lovely Lily is probably more to your taste right now."

Lily leans on my other shoulder. "Do you want to go, Max?"

He nods so hard I think his head might drop off. "I wonder if Owen will have some gingerbread men."

"We'll have to find out. I'll just finish my coffee if you want to grab anything you need." Corey grins.

"I don't need anything. I've already got socks and shoes on from helping Mum."

"Well, there you go." Corey grins at us. "Enjoy your time alone, you two. Don't do anything I wouldn't do. I'll bring him home around five so he's back for dinner?"

Lily nods. "Sounds great. Max, you be good for Corey."

"Yes, Mum."

"Max is always good for me. He's my little buddy, aren't you?"

I smile at the easy relationship Corey and Max have, and yet I get pangs of jealousy. What Max and I have is special, but he's had time to build that ease with Owen, Corey, and James.

It'll take me a while to get over that.

———

LILY WAVES from the door until Corey's car disappears from sight. It's funny how Max wears her out, but the second they're separated, it's as if she's no longer whole.

"As nice as it is to get a break, this place is so quiet without Max." She walks back into the kitchen and toward the table where the coffee cups sit.

"It doesn't have to be quiet. We can make our own noise."

She laughs. "What are you suggesting?"

Picking up the cups, she takes them the short distance to the bench. I'm right behind her as she turns, and I press myself against her as she gasps. "You, me. Here."

"Here?"

"We're alone. I'm not very patient."

Her breath quickens as she gazes at me, and she runs her fingers up my chest. Every touch only makes me want her more, and I can't get enough.

"Now," I growl, and her eyes widen. I spin her around and bend her over the kitchen table.

"Here?" she asks again.

"I'm not waiting."

She lets out a joyful laugh as I reach around her waist and unzip her jeans, pushing them down to her ankles. Her body shakes and she pants staying still as I drop her panties right behind her jeans.

"Adam," she moans. I haven't even touched her yet.

Slipping my hand around her hips, I stroke her thigh before shifting my hand a little and finding her clit. She pushes back against me, another tiny moan escaping her lips. She knows what's coming. She wants it. She wants me.

"You're ready for me?"

She nods, and I slide my fingers back a little to double check. It doesn't take much to prompt a response, her body clearly craving mine as I crave hers.

"Lily," I whisper her name in her ear, and she shivers. Letting go for a moment, I unzip my own jeans and push them down. I vowed we'd never rush sex, that I wanted her naked so I could touch her, take it slow, but that vow is forgotten as I drive into her, and despite her knowing I'm right behind her, she gasps.

"Adam," she cries, and leans over a little more giving me a better angle.

"You're all mine now." I laugh as I slide in and out of her. This—this is all I've ever needed. The greatest love I've ever known, and she belongs to me again.

"I always was." She moans, pushing her hips up to meet me. Being inside her brings back memories, like the scent of leather car seats and sex mingling in the air as we hid from the world and promised to always love one another. At least now I can keep that promise.

"Being like this makes me think of old times. You still feel amazing," I say.

She lets out another moan, and I tense, the build-up taking over my body before I close my eyes and let go. Everything I am and everything I have is hers. It'll never be anyone else's, and it never was. I was a fool to think I could be happy without her.

"Being able to do this is amazing." She stills, and I stay there for a moment, her warmth around me.

"I'm not finished yet."

I love the sound of Lily's laugh, and as I slide out of her, she stands straight and turns. Her eyes are full of love as she places her hands on my chest. "Be that as it may, I'm going to clean up and I'll be back in a second." She raises her face to be kissed and I accept her invitation, the taste of coffee still fresh on her tongue.

"Make it quick."

"It's hard to go anywhere quick with your pants around your ankles." She chuckles as she shuffles out of the room. I can't help but grin at the sight of her bare arse disappearing through the door. Little does she know that when she comes back, there'll be a whole lot more of her exposed.

That's the first room other than the bedroom christened.

———

I'M WAITING when she returns, grabbing her arms and kissing her. I want this for the rest of my life, only I can't scare her just yet with that news.

"You pulled your pants up," I say, raising my eyebrows.

"I'm too scared I'll trip."

"I'll catch you." I slip my arms around her, pulling her in tight.

"That's the corniest thing I think I've ever heard."

My hands are on her jeans again, and as I push the zip down she sighs. "Again?"

"Again. Figure we've got twelve years of sex to catch up on."

Lily snorts, reaching for my shirt. I take a step back, and she follows me into the living room. "That's a lot of sex."

"I couldn't keep my hands off you back then, remember?"

She nods, pulling my shirt over my head as I push her pants back down. I ache to have her again, to touch her, to taste her skin.

"Seems like you can't keep your hands off me now," she whispers.

With her pants around her ankles, I pull her T-shirt over her head and unclip her bra. She's so beautiful naked, her breasts peaking into those dusky nipples.

Laughing, I pull her gently to the floor with me, and we

lie down on the rug. Lily relaxes, closing her eyes and sighing as I cup her neck before running my hand down her shoulder and onto her breast.

Taking her other nipple in my mouth, I run my finger around the first one in circles. Her body shifts as her breathing grows faster. Unlike the fast pace we enjoyed in the kitchen, our living room sex is going to be slow.

"I bet you never thought you'd be naked on your living room floor with me," I murmur, laughing softly.

"The thought never crossed my mind." She runs her hand over my chest before dropping it to my jeans. As she pushes my jeans down and wraps her hand around my cock, her chest rises and falls quickly, and she meets my eyes with that innocent look she does so well. It sends a lightning bolt through my body, giving me the urge to corrupt her— although I think we did that to each other a long time ago.

Her hand drives me crazy, her gentle touch leaving me straining to maintain control. She props herself up on one elbow, and I don't need to ask what she has in mind. So many nights when I was away I'd dream of her, of the times I would sneak into her room and we'd hide under the covers of her bed, touching each other, loving each other.

This is all those dreams coming true. Lily switches from angel to devil in an instant, a glint in her eye leaving me in no doubt as to what she's about to do.

"You're all mine now," she says, mimicking my earlier words.

"I always was," I repeat hers back to her and gasp as she lowers her head and takes me in her mouth. The pain of holding on is unbearable, but I don't want this over quickly. I close my eyes, lost in her touch, moaning at the feel of her taking me deep.

She picks up the pace until I can't control myself and I lose it, crying her name as I spill into her mouth. "Holy shit, Lily."

Lily holds for a moment before lying back down beside me. "Good?"

"Well, that wasn't how I thought this would end." I grin, pulling her into my arms and kissing her on the nose.

"Better, or worse?"

"It doesn't matter what you do, it's all amazing."

She laughs, placing her hand on my chest and pushing herself back to a seated position.

For a woman who wasn't that confident about her body when I first knew her, she now seems content to be sitting in the middle of the living room floor without a single piece of clothing on. I've never seen her look so beautiful.

"Well, maybe what we need now is a shower. If you're lucky I might make you some lunch." She stands, and I prop myself up on one arm, placing a hand on her ankle.

"I thought maybe we could go upstairs and you could *be* lunch."

Lily's mouth twists as she seems to ponder my suggestion. "Race you."

I chuckle. My pants are still around my ankles as I watch her take off up the stairs, and I lie back and smile to myself.

What have I started?

———

"Knock, knock." Corey's deep voice echoes in the entrance-way. I step through from the kitchen, where I've started cooking dinner, to greet him and Max.

Max is exhausted. He walks as if he's asleep on his feet, his shoulders slumped and his head down. My poor boy.

"We watched some movies, then Owen and I took him to the park to throw a ball around. You'll be lucky if he stays awake for dinner," Corey says. "So, you're welcome."

Max heads straight for the living room and the couch, where he flops down.

I grin. "Here I was being all organised so he had some-thing to eat. I'm cooking one of your roasts. Lily's having a sleep."

"You wore her out that much?"

"No comment."

Corey slaps me on the back as we walk through to the living room. Max's eyes already heavy.

"Want some dinner, bud? It's just about ready."

While he nods, it's clear his heart isn't in it.

"How about I make you a sandwich instead? Then you can go straight up to bed."

He gives me a tired smile and nods. I turn back toward the kitchen.

"It is okay for him to be sitting on that couch, isn't it?" Corey asks.

"What are you talking about?"

He shrugs as I pick up the loaf of bread and pull out a couple of slices.

"I don't know. Leftover bodily fluids. It's been a long day." Corey guffaws as I throw a slice of bread at him.

"The couch is clean. I don't know if I'd sit on the rug though." I turn back and take out another slice of bread, opening the cupboard to get the peanut butter. Max loves that.

Arms slip around my waist, and I turn my head to receive a kiss from my girl. "I heard that."

"It's only Corey."

"No one important, then." She slips past me and onto Corey, wrapping her arms around him and kissing him on the cheek.

"I feel honoured. What did I do?"

"Gave us some time. Took good care of Max."

"He's on the couch, nearly asleep."

She lets go and heads toward the living room. I lather the bread with peanut butter and pull a plate out of the cupboard.

"Can you have sex with your girlfriend more often? I get all of the love." He laughs that throaty laugh of his that's only become deeper since I've been gone.

"Just as well I'm not the jealous type." That's a lie and he knows it, but from behind his bearded face, he smiles, showing off his teeth.

"Whatever, Bro."

I carry the sandwich out to Max. He's resting against his mother, who strokes his hair and kisses his temple. The love between them warms the whole room.

"Look what I've got." I hand the sandwich to him.

"Thanks, Dad."

I squat in front of him. "Did you have fun with your uncles?"

For someone so tired, he becomes incredibly animated

when I ask that, his whole face lighting up. "They're my uncles?"

"They are. Corey and Owen are my brothers. Drew and James, too."

Max grins, then takes a bite of his sandwich.

"We never really called them that. They were just friends." Lily smoothes his hair.

The sandwich disappears, and I make Max another one before he admits defeat. I hug him, kissing him on the head before he makes his way up the stairs with his mother.

"Goodnight, Max." I say.

He turns and gives Corey and I a little wave.

"He's such a good kid. Just needs to be stimulated and entertained," Corey says. "I was like that."

I nod. "Finding out about him has been mind-blowing. From the moment we met I felt this connection with him, and I thought it was just because he was Lily's."

"There's a whole lot of you in there." Corey claps me on the back.

"Want to stay for dinner?" I walk back to the kitchen to check on the roasting meat. The meat's cooked, as are the potatoes and vegetables. He's timed this just right.

"Smells great. I'd love to." Corey sits at the table. "You can cook?"

"Enough to survive."

"Hey, Lil," Corey says. I turn to see Lily in the doorway. "I was just voicing my amazement that Adam can cook."

"He's actually got pretty good." Lily sits opposite Corey. "I've been surprised."

"Don't you start. Max asleep already?"

"As soon as his head hit the pillow. He'll be full of energy in the morning for school."

I grab a tea towel and pull the roasting dish forward, sticking a fork in the small venison roast and lifting it onto the chopping board.

"That smells amazing." Lily smiles.

"You'll eat well out of that lot. There's wild pork and quite a bit of venison. The old guy who hired me had a real issue with the deer killing native trees on his land," Corey says.

"I appreciate it, but I still wish you didn't have to kill them." She frowns.

"We have this conversation every single time." Corey rolls his eyes. "They're a pest."

"Doesn't make me feel any better."

"What are you going to do when you leave here? I assume that's what's going to happen now Adam's back. What about your sheep? Will your freezer be full of mutton?"

Lily narrows her eyes at him. I love my brother, but I need to talk to Lily about what I want from the future before I announce anything to anyone else.

"You should really quit with the foreplay in front of my brother." Corey grins, but it only lasts a few seconds. "Ouch. Don't kick me under the table."

I laugh. "Stop antagonising her, Corey."

Slicing through the roast, I dish it up on plates with roast potatoes.

"You did well. Adam's doing a great job there," Corey teases. I'm a little envious of the ease between them, the affection. I need to stop it. It's my own fault they've developed a family-like relationship without me.

I spoon peas onto the plates and retrieve a couple of knives and forks from the drawer.

"Ladies first," I say as I place Lily's plate in front of her.

I make my way around the table, and slip Corey's plate down. "Like I said, ladies first."

"You haven't stopped being a smartarse," he says.

"Not where you're concerned."

"Guess I have to stop flirting with your girl, then."

I grab my plate and cutlery and turn back to the table. "It'd be a good idea."

He grins as I sit down. "It's good to have you back home. We've got a lot of catching up to do."

I nod. "I know. I got vague directions to your place, but wasn't quite sure where it was."

He grins. "Up McKenzie's Mountain. Just past that cult place."

"Is that still there?"

"Yep. Somehow they haven't run out of virgins to sacrifice or whatever it is they do."

Lily snorts with laughter. "Mum used to do some sewing work for them. They didn't seem that bad."

Corey shrugs. "I dunno. They seem harmless, but you gotta wonder what's going on behind those gates. All of the farmers up that way need pest control, but not them. They're really cautious about who they let on their property."

"So, not going to see them to pick a wife?" I laugh as he taps my forehead with the back of his fork.

"You know me, Bro. I'm too much of a player to settle down."

Lily meets my gaze with an amused expression on her face, and the pair of us burst out laughing. Corey was always the one who might move from girl to girl, but he was the kind of guy who when he finally fell, he'd fall hard. At least he had been at the age of nineteen, the last time I saw him.

"Sure. You and the possums. I bet you have a lot of girl-friends." I smile innocently at him.

He rolls his eyes. "I mean it. I'll never have anything as perfect as you and Lily do. All those years apart and here you are having sex on the rug in the middle of the day?"

We both look at Lily. Her skin slowly goes a shade of dark pink, but all she does is shake her head and laugh.

Corey shoots glances between us. "Nothing's changed, has it? Not really. It's like you two have never been separated."

Lily reaches for my hand and squeezes.

Life is so good.

When dinner's over and the dishes have been done, we walk Corey out. He kisses Lily on the cheek and winks at her. "Look after my brother for me. He looks like he's been neglected. He's such a small man." Anyone would be in comparison to Corey.

She laughs. "I'll look after him if he looks after me."

He nods. "That sounds fair."

We step out the front door and into the chill of the early evening.

"Drive safe. I'll bring Max up to visit sometime if we can work out when you're home," I say.

He grins. "Sounds good." Gripping my hand, he shakes it. "I'm happy for you, and even happier for Lily. She toughed it out for so long, but she looks so relaxed now. Maybe having her family together was all she needed."

I nod. "For me too. This wasn't at all what I expected, coming back here."

He smiles. "I'm glad you're home, little brother." Letting go of my hand, he slaps me on the shoulder.

I watch as he drives off in his mud-covered ute, and I smile. He's not the boy who moved here either. But he's his own person, and I couldn't be prouder of the man he's become.

The mixed emotions I feel are confusing.

I'm glad to be home and for the way things have turned out, but the missing years still leave me aching.

25

LILY

Twelve years ago

I cry as my baby comes eight weeks early, and has just a few seconds on my chest before they whisk him away. At thirty-two weeks, he's so small and he'll need help. As if that wasn't enough, the cord had wrapped around his neck during delivery. It's like nature is doing its best to rob me of Adam's and my child, but my baby's much too big a fighter for that.

We fight together.

As I sit in the NICU with him, he kicks his legs and opens his eyes to look at me. His little face screws up as he adjusts to his new environment, and my heart already belongs to him. Adam will love him, too. I waver between being angry at him for not coming back and wanting him so badly it makes me cry. The pregnancy hormones don't help.

I fill the syringe with the milk I've expressed and place it in the feeding tube. The tube goes up his nose and down into his stomach, and it breaks me to have to feed him this way. I want to snuggle him against me and give him what he needs directly. In four short weeks, I've had to adapt not only to being pregnant, but to giving birth and being alone through the whole process. I haven't bothered calling Adam's house again. I can't even begin to deal with that.

Now all my focus is on this little guy. He's the love of my life. I have to work out what's best for him.

"Lily?"

I turn to see Joanna Campbell in the doorway—the last person I thought I'd ever see. We haven't spoken since the day I called to look for Adam. Since then, my story was in the newspaper, albeit with our names suppressed.

"Mrs Campbell."

For the first time I can remember, she smiles at me. From around the corner, James appears. Maybe Adam's not here, but for two of his family to be here fills me with more hope than I can bear.

"I thought it was time I came to see this baby."

"Where's Adam?"

Her dark eyebrows knit as she lets out a humph sound. Like she's annoyed at me for asking. "He's in the US. He went to stay with some friends, and now he's enlisted in the army."

"The army?" That isn't the Adam I knew. That Adam doesn't share Corey's love of guns. This is weird. "Really?"

"He's planning on making a career out of it. He'll be training as an army mechanic."

Those few words crush whatever hope I had. She doesn't have to spell out that Adam's in it for the long haul.

She crosses the room, peeking into the plastic hospital crib. "Boy or girl?"

"Boy. His name is Max."

Her face cracks into a small smile. "How sick is he?"

My boy is a sight with monitoring probes attached to him. I don't know how long we'll be in the hospital, but everyone's taken such good care of us. He's doing so well I think they'll send us home soon, not that I have a home to go to.

"He's okay. Underweight, but that was to be expected. He'll be smaller than other kids for some time, but eventually he'll catch up. That's what they told me, anyway."

I study her face. She's always been so stiff with me, but as she looks down at the baby, her expression softens and she reaches out to stroke his cheek with her index finger. "He's got Adam's dark hair," I say.

"They all have dark hair when they're born. It'll fall out and maybe he'll be fair like you. Who knows?"

She almost smiles at me, and my head swims at the thought that maybe I'm winning her over. Maybe she'll help me connect Max with his father.

"I'm sorry Adam's moved on. I'm sure if he didn't have a job and a girlfriend he'd come back to visit."

The news Adam has a girlfriend hits me like a bowling ball to the head. "Girlfriend?"

She nods. "He met someone when he got to the US. She sounds nice."

In that moment, my heart shatters into a million pieces. I thought if he found out what happened, if he knew about Max, he'd do whatever it took to be with us.

Tears roll down my cheeks, and a small hand slips into

245

mine as I look down at James. I don't know how much of this he understands. He's six. I give him a small smile. This is my son's uncle.

"Adam's young. He's not mature enough to accept responsibility for you *and* a baby." Mrs Campbell shoots me a look full of sympathy.

"I thought he'd come back," I whisper.

She takes a deep breath, and that holier-than-thou expression I'm so used to returns. "He's left this life behind, Lily. I'm sorry if you're disappointed, but he has a new life to live, and he won't return."

I rub my forehead with my fingertips, trying to gather my thoughts. If I don't change the subject, I'll go mad. "Did you want to hold the baby?"

"He's so small. I'd be too afraid to hurt him."

I nod. "I understand." But I don't. If I was in her shoes, I'm sure I'd want to hold my first grandchild.

In all of this, Max is the one who misses out. With his father turning his back on us, I'm all Max has.

My life is his.

———

It's not enough.

The body blow I was dealt at finding out Adam had moved on with someone else was just the start.

Two days after Joanna's visit, Joseph appears at the door to my room. With Max in NICU, I've got a room to myself which I've been grateful for.

"How's it going?" he asks. I've known this guy a few weeks, and every day he's been calm and smiling. It's been reassuring. Now, he frowns, worry lines crossing his forehead.

"Good. Max is doing well. What's going on?"

He licks his lips, a nervous expression on his face. Whatever it is, I'm not going to want to hear it. "I've got some bad news. I'm so sorry, Lily."

Behind him, two policemen enter the room, and I'm bewildered, my heart in panic over what's to come. *Is it Mum?*

"Your mother committed suicide in remand. She ... well, I don't want to get into any detail if it's too much. There's a note."

Tears flood out of me, and I bury my head in my hands.

The woman who brought me into the world is gone, without even seeing her grandson. Before Adam came to town, I'd been so alone and for such a short time I'd had companionship with him. Love. Her illness wasn't Mum's fault, she couldn't help the issues she had, and now my heart's filled with regret for what could have been. Not just for me, but for her.

"Can I see it?" I ask.

Joseph nods. His face is so full of sympathy. He knows how hard it's been. His job has been to come here and take my baby away when my toxicology results came up showing what drugs I'd been on. Instead, he's become my biggest supporter.

One of the policemen steps forward. "Hi, Lily. I'm Constable Dave Rigby. I'm so sorry for your loss."

I blink back tears. "Thank you."

From a folio in his hands, he produces a plastic bag. "I'm

sorry, but it's in an evidence bag. While we investigate what happened, we'll need to hold onto it."

"What happened?"

He frowns and looks down at his feet. "She hung herself with her bed sheet. They had additional guard checks for her, but she must have worked out how long until the next one. Earlier in the day she'd been allowed a pen and paper to write you a letter. She said it was an apology. She misled the guards to write this instead."

Oh, Mum.

He hands the bag to me, and I take it with shaky hands. The letter only has two lines.

I can't do this anymore.

I'm under too much stress.

"That's it?" My head spins at there being no mention of me, no goodbye for me. Nothing.

I hand the note back to Constable Rigby, not wanting to touch it even through the plastic. For the first time in years I'm angry with my father for leaving us. For so long I understood. He couldn't handle her the way I thought I could. But he left me to the mercy of a woman who in the end couldn't even take care of herself, let alone me.

They leave me alone with my thoughts, and I curl up in the hospital bed barely wanting to go on. Everyone's left me, but I have to be strong for Max. Max Adam Parker.

I hurt for everything I've lost, everything Max has lost. But I have to pull myself together. I just have to.

When there's a knock on the door, I bury my head under the pillow, unable to take any more. I have nothing left.

"Lily?"

A voice I think I recognise comes from the door, and I lift my head. The biggest lump forms in my throat when I finally see someone from my past who might just care. "Mrs Murphy?"

My favourite teacher at primary school, the one who had nurtured my love of reading. She's the first person who ever saw beyond me being just Mum's daughter. The first person who truly saw *me*.

Tears roll down my cheeks as she approaches. This has to be one of the worst days of my life and she's appeared like my guardian angel.

"I came as soon as I heard."

"Do you know about Mum?"

She frowns. "I know what she did. It didn't take much to put it all together."

"Mum's dead." I let out a sob as I say the words. I'm in a state of disbelief, unable to get my head around everything.

"Oh, sweetheart." From her reaction, Mrs Murphy didn't know that bit. She reaches the end of my bed as I sit up and she reaches for me, wrapping me in her arms like a mother should.

Mum.

I weep for the woman who gave birth to me, the woman who raised me, the woman who struggled to keep her head above water each and every day. She loved me. I do know that much.

"What happened?"

"She committed suicide. There's a note, but the police have it until they've finished with it. They have to investigate a death for prisoners in remand." I sigh. "They showed me. It said she couldn't cope anymore. Being arrested had caused her too much stress." I look up in to Mrs Murphy's eyes. "What am I going to do? Where am I going to go?"

"You don't have to worry about anything. I'm here, and there's always room at my place."

"I can't ask …"

"Lily, you don't have to ask. My home is open to you and your baby. Tell me about him."

The tears won't let up. I am so full of love for Max despite every other thing in my life sucking. "He's amazing. I was so scared I'd lose him, and he's still in the NICU for observation, but he's doing so well." I sniff. "He looks so much like Adam."

"Can I see him?"

My chest bursts with pride as I think of my little fighter. "Of course."

26

LILY

Now

When I was a child, I had dreams. When I met Adam, I thought maybe they'd finally all come true. We had plans to go with the dreams. They weren't much but they were ours.

For six months, I thought I'd lost everything and couldn't dream of anything but getting out of the hell my mother had created. Even in my darkest hours, I had to believe the bad times would end. It was one of the things that helped keep me alive.

When I found out about Max, I had love again.

Now, for the first time in years, I have hope.

Hope is wonderful.

The nights are still dark, but the days are so much brighter. The longer Max, Adam, and I are a family, the more that brightness spills into the dark, eating away at it little by little. Maybe one day it'll all be gone.

All I know is that after those first weeks, I haven't slept so well in years.

I lie in bed, my limbs entangled with Adam's. Life has gone on as normal since his return, but my heart is so much lighter.

"What do you dream of?" he asks. I didn't think he'd noticed me waking in the night past that first time, but clearly he has. There's only one thing I can do. Be honest.

"Mum. The house. Max."

His eyes are so sad. I know he wants to take all the bad dreams away, but I don't know if anything will ever do that completely.

Adam nuzzles my cheek. He brings me more comfort than I can say.

"I dream about when I got out, when I was in hospital. There was a case worker assigned to me, you know, because they got my toxicology results and thought I was taking drugs. It wasn't until I woke up that I told them what happened. My case worker was ready to take Max." Even now the thought that anyone would think I'd do anything to hurt my baby stings. From the moment I knew about Max, he was my focus, no matter what else was going on in my life. Twelve years on, nothing has changed in that regard.

"Take Max? Into care?"

I nod and understand the pain that sweeps his face, the hurt in his eyes.

"When he realised the truth, he helped me instead. I don't know what I would have done without Mrs Murphy, though. She was like my guardian angel."

He smiles. "She always did have a soft spot for you."

"She used to pack some extra lunch so she could help me out when Mum forgot mine." I snuggle in to his chest. "Before you arrived."

His arms are so warm and comforting around me. I never want to leave them. I never want him to leave.

These past weeks have meant so much, but I retain the feeling of being on a precipice, so close to falling if he goes. He has a life far away from here.

"Lily?"

My eyes meet his. "Sorry?"

"Where were you? There are times when I know I lose you."

I shake my head. "Nowhere important." Stroking his chest, I sigh. "Do you ever think about your home?"

"What are you talking about?"

"Where you lived before you came back."

He sighs. "I lived in an apartment when I wasn't deployed or travelling."

"Do you miss it?"

The corners of his mouth curl a little. "I'd much rather be here with you."

Whenever he says things like that my stomach flips like a gymnast at the Olympics. He says all the right things, does all the right things, but after all I've been through, I'm still terrified.

I'm more in love with him than I've ever been.

It'll be harder to break my fall next time.

———

MAX DRIVES me nuts on Monday morning. He might have had lots of sleep after his day out with Corey, but Adam returning and moving in is an adjustment. It doesn't show at first, but little by little Max's routines are out of whack, and with it his behaviour at times.

"I don't want to go to school." He throws his clothes across the room.

"Well, you have to go. You know you do."

He pouts. "I want to stay home with Dad. He's going to teach me how to fix a car."

"Not today he's not. It's a school day."

"I don't want to go."

There have been days when he's been difficult, but I know where his limit is and when he really is too out of sorts to leave the house. This is just him being stubborn.

"Too bad. Get your clothes on." I pick up his shirt and walk toward him. These are the days I am getting afraid of. When he gets to the point where he's physically bigger than me, this will get a lot tougher. At least now Adam's here that aspect of the future should be easier.

"Mum." He whines, but I'm not letting him win this one.

"Come on, Max. Get dressed and we'll go get you some Coco Pops."

He rolls his eyes but obeys, unbuttoning his pyjama shirt at sloth speed.

"You guys okay?"

Max's eyes light up at the sight of Adam. "Dad. I told Mum I can't go to school 'cause you're gonna teach me about cars."

He shakes his head. "Not today, bud. We can take a look after school. Maybe I can pick you up?"

Max nods like crazy. "Cool. Where's my T-shirt, Mum?"

I raise my eyebrows at Adam, and he smiles and shrugs before disappearing out the door presumably to go downstairs. I've been Max's sole caregiver for so long. Adam being around is wonderful and hard all at the same time. I'm so used to doing everything alone—this is going to take some getting used to. It's hard not to be resentful when my son dresses with enthusiasm after speaking with his father.

It's as if Adam senses it when I come down the stairs. Max is right behind me, full of energy and enthusiasm to get to school, no doubt so he can finish for the day and come home to Dad.

"You okay?" Adam says quietly.

I nod. "I'm fine. I'll have to add you to the school's list of carers who can pick Max up so if someone sees you with him they'll know not to call the police. Although given he was left to his own devices that day I was late, I don't know how useful their list is."

"I didn't think of that."

Slipping my arms around his waist, I press my head against his chest. "All your brothers are already on that list."

He chuckles, his chest shaking as he smooths my hair with the palm of his hand. "I'm glad you had them here for you."

"Mum. Where are the Coco Pops?"

I let out a sigh.

"I'll get them," says Adam. "Go get some time with Max before school, and I'll make you a coffee."

This—this is what makes adjusting to him being around worthwhile.

———

THE IRRITATIONS of the morning are gone by lunchtime. Adam gets out and into the garden with me, and helps clear a new patch for planting. I grow a lot of my own vegetables, both to eat and to sell at the local farmers' market once a week, and I'm rewarded with fresh carrots, lettuce and onions among other things.

"This is so much easier with you helping."

He grins. "I do wonder if it's a waste of time."

"Why?" I stand up, wiping my forehead with my sleeve. It's hard work turning over the soil.

"Are we going to stay here, or go somewhere else?"

"Where would we go?" This place isn't perfect, but it's home, and I know at the very least that Max and I will always have a roof over our heads.

Adam shrugs. "I dunno. We could find another place closer to town and school. We could move to the city. The world's out there for us to explore."

"Max's needs have to come first. I don't know if he'll cope in the city. This is his home." I go back to digging.

"I know it's his home, but it doesn't have to be. Lil, you've done the best job you can, but I'm here now. I can—"

"If we're going somewhere else, we have to decide as a family. You don't just get to waltz in, turn our lives upside down, and move us around." The truth is the thought of living anywhere else scares me. What am I going to do being with a man who could be called overseas to fight? What if next time he goes he doesn't come back?

Adam sighs and walks towards me. He wipes his hands on his jeans and places them on my arms.

"Of course we'll decide as a family. I want to give you everything, no matter how hard I have to work." He presses his forehead to mine. "We all missed out on so much. I think we're entitled to making a life together, and a good one."

I sniff. "I love having you here, but this is such a big adjustment before we consider moving anywhere else."

He lingers on my lips as he kisses them. "Can we take a break?"

"Not yet. I need to get more carrots planted."

"If you come with me I'll show you all the carrot you'll ever need." He gives me a slick smile as he pulls away, and all I do is roll my eyes.

"You'll have to come up with a better line if you want to persuade me to stop working." I pull away, digging and turning over more soil. "Besides, you haven't seen the size of my carrots. I bet they put yours in the shade."

I squeal as Adam grabs me around the waist, dropping the spade and surrendering as he takes my breath away with his kiss.

"Are you sure I can't distract you for a little while before Max comes home? I'll finish the garden."

There's a moment when I want to push him away, make him wait until I'm finished. I can't neglect real life for this fairy tale he's offering. But then again, he's been trying so hard to help.

"Fine. For just a little while." His lips trail down my neck and I lose all concentration. "I think I should warn you of something," I whisper.

"What is it?" He's pressed against my body, and I know how much he wants me.

"I'm not a fan of carrots." Laughing, I give him a little

257

push, separating myself from him and running back toward the house.

If I could just stop worrying for just a little while, life would be perfect.

———

"Adam?"

"Hmmm?"

We've been lying in the afterglow for I don't know how long. Now, I know it's time to get back to reality. "Your parents don't want us to be together. How are you going to deal with that?"

He shrugs. "I'm a grown-up. I've lived my life away from them for twelve years. I don't need their approval. You and Max are family enough for me. We'll work out what we're going to do with our future together."

"Is that what you really want?" I tilt my head to get a better look at him.

"I want *us*. It's what I've always wanted. Mum stood in our way for so long, and I don't care anymore. Not when she withheld so much that I would have wanted to know. If I'd had any inkling of what you'd gone through, I would have been by your side in an instant."

Stroking his bicep, I run my finger down his bare arms. When he grasps my arm in return, his touch is gentle, loving —everything I missed. I'll never get enough of this.

Even the small amount of time we've had together has changed my life. I'm no longer as stressed and tired. Having Adam's support has given me time to take a breath while someone else takes the reins. Someone I can trust.

"I love you more than anything, Lily. I can't even begin to tell you how much my heart missed you."

There are tears in my eyes as I meet his gaze, and I run my thumb down his cheek. "I think I know," I whisper. "It's like the other half of my heart is home."

He curls around me as we snuggle under the sheets. I feel safe, protected from all the bad things in the world.

I need to get back to planting, but I treasure these moments we have. They've been a long time coming.

He's what I've always needed.

27

ADAM

Some nights Lily has dreams—dreams that leave her struggling to breathe, dreams that leave her clutching the sheets and crying out.

It breaks my heart. I've had times in my life when I've felt helpless, unable to stop what's happening before me. Those situations happen all the time in a war zone. None of it compares to this.

I think of that day—the day I went to her house looking for her. I can't help but feel I didn't try hard enough, that I needed to look harder. She was right under my nose the whole time, and if I'd found her then the months of being under her mother's control wouldn't have needed to happen. Guilt sits as a weight on my chest that just won't go away.

Meanwhile, Lily is everything. She's my morning, she's my night, and she's every single moment in between.

It's clear that she's struggling with my arrival. We both want this to work so much, but she's so used to doing everything alone and it causes unnecessary tension between us. We'll get there.

We lost each other once. It won't happen again.

I head over to Mum and Dad's. I lost it last time and left, but Mum still needs to explain to me why she did what she did. She owes me that much. She owes Lily and Max so much more.

To my surprise, the rest of my brothers are there, all four of them.

"Adam." Drew stands from his seat on the deck and walks toward me. We shake hands before I pull him into my arms and embrace him.

"It's good to see you. Were you planning to drop in on me and Lily?"

He nods. "On the way back tomorrow. I'm here overnight."

"What are you all doing here?"

Drew speaks up first. "We all came over for lunch to try and talk out what happened to you. I think I speak for all of us when I say we're pissed. Corey tried to speak with Mum about it, but she's not saying a word."

"She will when I speak to her."

"Dude, she's not well," Drew says.

I look my brother in the eyes. I know she's ill, it's why I came home, but before anything further happens I need to know the truth. "I need her to talk to me, to explain why."

He nods. "I can't pretend to understand. I'm sorry we didn't do better. We should have chased you down regardless."

I know he's genuine, that they all feel that way. They're as torn about it as I am. "Well, I'm going in to talk to her."

"Beer's here when you're finished." He grins. "We have lots to catch up on."

"We do."

I push open the door and step into the kitchen. There's no sign of Mum or Dad, but the TV's on in the living room.

She sits on the couch, watching *Family Feud* and drinking a cup of coffee.

"Mum."

She looks up. Her skin is pale, and I'm not sure if it's at the thought of facing me or if she's just having a bad day.

"Do you want a coffee?" she asks, standing.

"I'm just here for some answers."

She swallows. It's now I see how much she's aged. I hadn't noticed it that much at first, but her hair, slightly silvery when I left, is now almost completely that colour.

"You kept everything from me. What happened to Lily. That I had a son. I'm *your* son, Mum. What about me?"

Her nose twitches, but her expression remains calm. "I was protecting you. You had a new life, and you didn't need to be dragged down by being a young father."

"Shouldn't I have made that decision? What did you ever do to help her? Max is your grandson."

"I know," she snaps, and for the first time I see tears in her eyes. "Who do you think told Ada Murphy where to find her?"

I catch a breath and stare. She set this whole thing up? Then told me all about how Lily had moved in with Eric?

"She understood, and she always had a soft spot for the girl." Mum sits down, folding her shaking hands in her lap. "I saw that baby, Adam. All tubes and wires. I didn't know if he'd survive, and I didn't want to put you through finding out only to lose him."

I run my fingers through my hair. "You still should have told me. If he'd died, I'd have never been able to hold my own son, my flesh and blood."

She stares at me, tears rolling down her cheeks. All this time she's acted as if she didn't have a heart. "Lily couldn't be a part of this family. You two would have ended up back here while you worked out your life, and I didn't want her in my house."

Anger takes hold of me, and I shake as I narrow my eyes. "I asked you this before, Mum—what did Lily ever do to you?"

"Nothing. It was her mother," she yells, and I take a step back. "Her mother nearly broke this family apart, and I did not want a repeat of that with her daughter."

"What are you talking about?"

She closes her eyes. "We came here because Corey was acting up, and because we were in trouble. Your father and I had been through some rough stuff, and I thought this place would be better for all of us. I made him apply for the transfer." Opening her eyes again, she reaches out and touches my arm. It tears me up as I'm so angry and yet I can see how hard this is for her to talk about. "When we got here, your father had an affair with Lily's mother. When you took up with Lily, it broke my heart. I couldn't lose both of you to her."

My mind reels at the revelation. How on earth was this possible? We never got a whiff of anything being wrong between Mum and Dad.

"Mum, I love Lily. I'm sorry for what Dad did, but she did nothing, and she's the one who's suffered for it."

"I know." She looks down.

"I don't know what hurts more—the fact that you kept this from me, or that you deliberately let Lily and Max struggle. Don't you see? Even if Max had died as a baby, Lily would have had me, and we would have had a chance. You left us with no hope."

She swallows. "I had to protect my family."

"You sacrificed my family to save yours."

I leave her there. She's crying, but I can't comfort her. I'm so angry I can't stay—I'll just end up saying more things that maybe I'll regret one day.

But there's one thing I'll never regret.

Coming home.

———

I MIGHT HAVE my answers from Mum, but there's one more thing I need to do before I leave.

Drew greets me with a beer when I come out.

"What happened? That was quick," Corey says.

"I need to process it." I crack open the beer and smile. "Did you guys want to come over for dinner? Lily's cooking one of Corey's pork roasts."

"That's a great idea," Owen says. "I was about to leave anyway. We've just had lunch."

I pinch my forehead. "So they invited all of you over, but not Lily, Max, and I?"

Owen looks at his feet. Corey just rolls his eyes. "I

thought this would be the last place you'd want to be. Especially with Lily and Max."

I shrug. "I thought maybe now it's all out in the open, they might make an effort. Then again, after the conversation I just had with Mum ..."

"How did *that* go?" James asks.

"Like I said, I need to process it. I'll tell you later." I let out a breath. There's so much I need to think about from the conversation I just had with Mum before I can tell anyone else. "I do have one more mystery to solve. Which one of you has been dropping off supplies at Lily's place?"

The brothers exchange glances.

Owen shrugs. "I drop off bread and cookies from time to time."

I shake my head. "No. Clothes for Max. Lily says she gets up some mornings and finds boxes on the doorstep."

"No idea, little brother," Corey speaks up. "I've dropped meat off for her before when I've been hunting, as you know. I'm pretty sure she knows about anything we've delivered. Maybe she has a secret admirer?"

"Or Max has a grandfather who couldn't be part of his life, but didn't want him to go without." From behind me, the soft voice of Dad comes, and I turn to face him.

"You?"

"I made sure Lily didn't have to spend money buying him new clothes. It wasn't always easy to get to the city to find things, but when we made the odd trip I'd leave your mother shopping and sneak pieces of clothing into the car. Max's mother had other things to worry about."

I look around. "Why don't any of you ever stand up to her?"

"She's dying, Adam. Has been for some time. She hasn't been easy to live with for so long, and once we knew about her health issues, it made it that much harder. How could I upset her?" Dad says.

"We all had Lily's back," Drew says.

"That's not the point. Why did none of you try to contact me?" Every single face is guilty, Owen avoiding my eyes completely. It is such a simple question with a simple answer.

"Mum said she did. That you'd moved on and weren't interested in coming home." Corey gulps. "We decided that if you weren't prepared to take care of Lily, we would help where we could. We're her family."

If my heart had been broken before, it shatters now. That my mother had been the source of all of this, had kept me from knowing about Lily and Max, had turned her back on them ...

"You're the worst." I shift my focus back to Dad "I'm your son. Did you know she lied about me knowing?"

Dad drops his gaze. "You were young and impulsive. I thought ..."

"You didn't even know me," I growl. "How could you if you thought I'd stay away from my family for a second?"

"Adam—"

"Screw you, Dad. I know why she rejected Lily now. You always fall into line with her, even when she's wrong. Grow some balls."

I turn and walk toward the gate.

"Where are you going?" Corey asked.

"Where else? Home. You guys coming?"

Home is anywhere Lily and Max are waiting.

28

LILY

I check the oven again, breathing in the smell of roasting meat. Wild pork has such a strong taste, and it's a rare treat. Even Max enjoys it, and he drives me nuts he's so particular when it comes to food. I've never had all the Campbell brothers over for dinner at once, but then life has been filled with a lot of new things lately.

I've got Adam back, and he loves me just as much as he did all those years ago. He's squashed my fears of being abandoned again, but him returning to the army still haunts my thoughts.

"When's dinner?" Max mopes around the house, waiting for his father to come home. He only called me five minutes ago to tell me we were going to have a full house.

"I just have to put the potatoes in and sort out the vegetables."

He frowns. "I don't want vegetables."

"Not even carrots?" They're his favourite, closely followed by peas, despite his protest.

Max rolls his eyes. "Carrots are okay."

"Good."

"Where's Dad?" He's asked that question a million times since Adam left for his parents' place.

"He's gone to see his mum and dad."

Max looks up at me from under his fringe. He needs a haircut, but that'll be a drama in itself. Maybe Adam can get him to sit still long enough to get it done. "Is that Grandma and Grandad?"

The question breaks my heart. While Adam's dad is pretty harmless, his mother is a cranky old bitch.

Now I know the years apart were unnecessary. Nothing can make up for the heartache and tears I dealt with on top of what happened with Mum and then Max. I don't even know if I would accept an apology from Adam's mother.

Now Max has Adam in his life, I guess he should know he has grandparents. "I guess so, honey."

"That'll be why Grandad dropped off the boxes in the mornings."

I study him closer as he returns to his book. *The boxes of clothes?* "What do you mean?"

"I saw him a couple of times. He was here really early. I thought it was zombies at first."

"You didn't open the door."

He grins. "I did once. He said 'Max, I am your grandfather.'"

It's my turn to roll my eyes. "Are you sure that wasn't you watching *Star Wars*?"

Max shrugs. "It was still him."

Could that be true? All the while Adam's mother was cutting ties, pushing me away, her own husband had been working to help support their grandson. Sometimes I'd wished the packages had contained money—that would have really helped. But in the absence of that, I've not had to buy new clothes for Max since he was little. Something always appears.

"Are you sure?"

"I'm never wrong, Mum."

I smirk at my son's confidence. He's rarely wrong, he doesn't speak up until he's sure. If what he said is true, we've received more support from the Campbell family than I ever realised.

Part of me wonders what Adam will think about that.

———

I HEAR them all before I see them—the rolling laughter, Corey's booming voice. Max's head shoots up, and he races from the table to the door.

"Dad," he shrieks.

Adam crosses the room, Max hanging off his arm, and pecks me on the lips. The others might be having fun, but I can tell from his eyes that he's troubled.

"Are you okay?"

He nods. "We'll talk later. Right now, I want to spend time with my two favourite people in the world. And these other hobos I brought home for dinner. Need any help?"

I shake my head. "Nope. Everything's under control. I don't know if I have enough drinks …"

"We stopped and got some beer." Corey opens the fridge and starts piling the bottles in.

"Just as well the living room is a decent size. Plenty of floor to sleep on," I tease.

"I wouldn't sleep on that floor. Never know what's on it." Corey winks.

Drew makes a beeline for me as soon as Adam sits down. Wrapping his arms around me, he squeezes my arse and buries his nose in my neck. "How's it going, Lily-bell?"

Adam's growl can probably be heard from the city, and I chuckle as Drew gives me another squeeze.

"You took way too long to come back. I tried to talk her into hooking up with me, but for some reason she wasn't keen on marrying a doctor." Drew beams.

I shove his shoulder as he lets go and heads toward the table, sitting next to Adam.

Adam looks between us, an expression that's way too serious for this situation all over his face. "Really?"

"No, he's talking crap." I laugh.

"I always knew my love would never be requited."

Rolling my eyes, I take a step and hook my arms around Adam's neck. "Meet your brother, the big tease."

Drew pokes Adam's shoulder. "It's okay. I always knew Lily-bell only had eyes for you."

Adam meets my gaze, and I smile back, my heart filled with so much love for all of them. In my lonely years, they'd become my brothers. He slips his arms around my waist and leans his head on my chest. Closing my eyes, I stroke his hair. I don't know what happened with his mother, but whatever it is, it isn't good. His disappointment seeps from his every pore.

"I'll turn the potatoes over," Owen says, and instead of insisting I'll do it, as I'm apt to do, I just hold Adam. When I open my eyes, Drew gives me a little smile.

"It'll be okay," he mouths. I nod, and bend to kiss the top of Adam's head. It's been a rough day for him.

Whatever happened.

―――――

AFTER DINNER OWEN and Corey pick up all the plates from the table and start the dishes before I have a chance to protest. Instead, I sit at the table, Adam and Max disappearing into the living room with Drew and James.

"Earth to Lily." Owen waves his hand in front of my face.

"What?"

"You're miles away. Corey and I were just speculating on what Mum told Adam that has him so rattled."

I shrug. "I'm sure he'll tell us all when he's ready."

When I sigh, Corey walks around the table, squatting in front of me. "You okay?"

"Do you think Adam's going to stay? He's in the army, Corey. What if he leaves again?" Saying it out loud helps me let go of so much tension.

"He loves you. Have you asked him about it?"

I shake my head. "I'm almost afraid to. I don't want to know if he's just going to leave again."

Corey places his hand over mine. "Do it, Lily. After what's happened, I'd be surprised if he leaves again. Hell, I'm surprised he's left you in another room."

I reach over and put my hand to his beard.

"Careful, he'll growl at me next."

Laughing, I wrap my arms around his neck. "You guys are all like brothers to me. I don't know how I could have got through the last twelve years without you."

"We all love you. It's been easy. Max is pretty epic, too. That's one good kid you've got there."

I lean over, hugging him tight.

"You better let him go before Adam throws us all out," Owen says.

I chuckle, releasing Corey.

"Go talk to Adam," he says.

Nodding, I stand and walk to the doorway. Max sits on the couch, Drew and James on either side. The three of them are engrossed in cartoons and I smile, shaking my head at the sight. "Do you guys know where Adam went?"

Drew shakes his head. "He headed that way." He points out the door and into the hallway.

"Thanks."

As I walk out and into the entranceway of the house, I turn my head and find him on the deck, sitting on the steps and looking out at the yard. The sun's low in the sky, almost ready to give way to the night. "You okay?"

He turns his head and smiles at me, raising his hand to take mine. "Just thinking."

"About your mum?" I sit on the step beside him and rest my head on his shoulder.

"She told me why she doesn't like you."

It should come as no surprise, but the words still make my stomach clench. I always knew it, but could never work out what I'd done to cause it.

"It's not you, Lil. It's not your fault." He swallows. "She's been keeping more than one secret."

I lift my head. He has worry etched across his face, and my stomach sinks.

"Do you ever remember my dad visiting your mother?"

I nod. "She did some repairs for him. He said he couldn't work out the machine, and your mother's sewing wasn't that great."

He snorts. "Yeah, she had a few failures, but that's not why he saw her."

"What?"

"Mum says after they got here, my dad had an affair with your mum. She held it against you. It was never about anything you did—it all came down to her own hurt feelings."

My mind reels. There were a couple of times I'd been sick and stayed home from school when Adam's father turned up. It hadn't seemed out of the ordinary, Mum had people drop off little repair jobs all the time. "How could we not know?"

"I think we had other distractions, and I don't know how long it lasted."

Adam was right. We were so preoccupied with each other, the world could have ended and we would have barely noticed. We loved so much in those four short years we had, and if anyone ever asked me about anything else that had happened during that time, I'd barely have had a clue. "There's something else."

What else could there possibly be?

"Those parcels you were getting, the ones with clothing? It was my dad."

"I know."

His eyebrows shoot up at my casual response.

"Max told me today. He saw him delivering one once, but

I don't think he said anything because he knew he'd be in trouble for opening the door without checking who it was first."

Adam's lips curl into a lopsided smile. "Max knew? That kid of ours."

"So now what?" I ask.

Adam takes my hand in his, threading his fingers through mine, and raises it to his lips. "We make our own future. You, me, and Max. We're enough. He'll have his uncles. That's all the family we need."

I sigh. "I guess it's more than we had before."

"Plus, one day we'll grow our family. At least I hope we will."

I raise my head. "Do you want to know what I want?"

"Of course."

"This is probably gonna sound a little silly, since you basically just moved in, but I want to date. I want us to really get to know each other again. It still feels like we're scratching the surface at times."

Adam presses his nose against mine. "Anything you want."

"What I want is for you to stay."

He pulls away, his eyebrows knitted as he frowns. "Why wouldn't I?"

"Your job. What happens if they send you away again? I lost you once—I don't want to lose you again."

A smile creeps across his face, and in an instant his lips are on mine, his tongue pressing into my mouth with urgency. This is comforting and scary. Is he trying to distract me or reassure me?

"You'll never lose me. I'm not going back. Ever."

Tears roll down my cheeks. My biggest fear finally evaporates as he holds me tight, lodging his fingers in my hair and pulling me close.

"I love you. I'll spend the rest of my life trying to make up for the years we were apart. If you'll have me."

I sniff. "Did you just propose?"

He laughs into my hair. "I promise I'll do it properly after we've spent more time. Once we've broken through that surface."

"Mum?" Max is right behind us.

"Hey, baby," I say.

Adam lets go of me, and I reach up to grab Max's hand. He steps down and sits between Adam and I. "Are you crying?"

I nod, wiping my eyes with my fingers. "Because I'm so happy. I have you and Dad. We're a family, Max."

He rolls his eyes. "You cry when you're happy, too? I'll never understand girls."

Despite myself, I laugh, and Adam does too. Max squawks as we both hug him tight.

My whole world on this doorstep.

29

ADAM

From the outside, the old garage has seen better days. A big, old concrete building, the windows are boarded up with odd-sized blocks of wood, and it looks as if it's been untouched in years. In truth, it's been less than a year, but in this town, it fades into the background. To me, it represents the future.

I learned so much in the army, and my mechanical skills will come in handy in this rural community. There have been so many times I've had to improvise to repair vehicles, which fit so well with the ol' Kiwi number eight wire mentality. I might not be MacGyver, but I have a knack for pulling things together when I need to.

Here, I'll have a proper garage and be able to buy real parts for vehicles. When this workshop closed, the nearest place to get any mechanical repairs done was more than fifty kilometres away. I want to reverse that.

I haven't told Lily about my plans yet, I want it to be a

surprise. She's been through enough pain for a lifetime, and all I want is to give her the future she doesn't dare to dream of. The best part of the whole deal is the house.

Behind the garage is a three-bedroom home, complete with a separate sleep-out. The backyard opens up into bush-land, and I'll have to fence it to stop Max from wandering in after any animals. There are plenty of those about. He'll love it.

"What on earth are we doing here?" Lily asks as we pull up outside.

"This is our new home. If you want it to be," I say as I take her hand. Her brow wrinkles in confusion, but she smiles as I squeeze her fingers, giving me a little bit of sorely needed sunshine. I'm prepared to do whatever it takes to make her happy.

"Yay!" Max yells from the back seat, I grin at his enthusi-asm. *My son.* The house they're in has been their home for so long, but it doesn't belong to them. This will.

Lily shoots me a sideways glance, and no wonder. All she sees is the garage, the house behind still hidden from our sight. A million thoughts must be running through her head. This has to be one of the greatest gifts I could ever give her.

I tousle Max's hair as he unlatches his seat belt and sticks his head between the two front seats. "You like it, buddy?"

Max is happy, nodding with so much enthusiasm I think his head might just fall off. Lily's more reserved.

"Come and have a look. I promise you'll love it."

She lets out a sigh. I grasp her hand tight.

"Come on, Mum," Max moans. His constant thirst to keep moving isn't quenched by sitting in the car.

Lily laughs. "Fine."

She's still scared. I see it in her eyes, and I understand it. This is so new yet familiar, and I sense her fear whenever I leave.

"Trust me?" I murmur.

Lily licks her lips and slowly nods.

I let go of her hand and open the car door, Max leaping over into the front seat and following behind me. He's so excited. It's like bringing a puppy to a new home, and I already love how happy it'll make him to see what I have in store.

Lily's opened the car door, and I hold it for her while she steps out.

"This is the garage. James will help me sort it out, take the boards off the windows. We'll tidy it up," I say as I close the car door.

She nods.

"But this is what I need to show you." I take her by the hand, and lead her and Max through a side gate and down a driveway leading behind the building.

Her gasp is audible as we turn the corner and she lays eyes on a house that's been maintained despite the state of the garage.

"Mum, look." Max squeals as he sees it, and I wrap my other arm around his shoulders and pull him toward me. "Get off, Dad."

It's beautiful, the verandah running around the outside, the wooden steps leading up to the decking edged by intricately carved hand railings. I let Max go and turn my focus to Lily. Her face is full of awe and longing.

"Like I said. This is our new home," I whisper. "If it's okay with you. It comes with the garage, so we don't *have* to live here."

Her smile spreads into a grin. "Are you kidding me? If the inside is as beautiful as the outside ..."

"It is."

Max tugs at my shirt. "Can I look around?"

I grin at my overexcited son. "Of course you can. I even have the keys so you can pick which room you want."

His eyes widen. "Really?"

"There are three bedrooms. Mum and I get one, and you can choose out of the other two."

He jumps up and down, grabbing Lily's other hand. "Come on, Mum. Let's check it out."

Lily laughs, and turns her head to peck me on the lips before she lets go of my hand and runs toward the house hand in hand with Max.

"Come on, Dad."

My heart swells when he calls me that. All the years I never knew he existed evaporate at the sound of those words. We're close despite the previous distance. When Max loves, he loves big.

"On my way." I breathe deep. This is perfect.

I follow them up the verandah and unlock the door, pushing it open. Max runs past, but I scoop Lily into my arms and carry her over the threshold. Peals of laughter echo through the empty house, and she has so much love in her eyes as she presses her nose to mine before I set her down on the floor. "What do you think?"

"I love it," she whispers, clinging to my arm. "I had no idea this place was here."

"Jack Kirby built it, but he prefers living at the cove. I

asked him about the garage and when we came to take a look, I realised there was so much more. As soon as I saw it, I knew this place was you."

Max screams past, sliding in his socks on the polished wooden floor. "Zoom, zoom."

"Max, be careful." Lily's laughter captivates me. I never thought it would be possible to be so in love again, but here I am, a little battered, but back with the love of my life. I slide my arms around her waist.

"It's all ours, Lily. All ours. We can move in straight away."

Her smile grows, and I let go of her waist, grasping one of her hands. "Want to explore?"

Max has already checked out every room, and by the time we get down the hallway he runs along behind us, panting, explaining what each room is.

"We'll need furniture. Our house is a mix of the old stuff from Mum's place and what was already there. Some of it doesn't belong to me."

"I already thought about that. We'll go for a drive to the city and shop." I lower my voice. "Just imagine. A new bed for a new start."

She flings her arms around my neck.

"We're finally going to get our happy ending, sweetheart."

Her eyes shine. "This is exciting. More than I ever thought possible. It's beautiful, Adam."

I drop my head to kiss her, and Max runs circles around us as we embrace.

Lily laughs. "This is perfect."

―――――

AFTER AN AFTERNOON of checking out the new property, I drop Lily and Max at home with a promise of a takeaway dinner, but I've got unfinished business elsewhere.

As I head down the long and twisted driveway toward Eric's place, all I can think about is Lily, and how she told me of the nights when she hid in her bed while he hammered on the door, trying to get her to let him in. Of his hounding her to marry him. Of his harsh words where Max was concerned.

He answers the front door, beer in hand, sighing at the sight of me.

"Eric."

"Adam. To what do I owe the pleasure?" He takes a sip of his beer, narrowing his eyes.

"I'm just here to let you know that Lily and Max will be moving out in a couple of weeks. You can have your land back."

One of his eyebrows creeps up. "She's leaving?"

"I just bought a house. She'll be moving in with me."

He smirks, and for the first time it registers just how glazed over his eyes are. That's not his first beer. Is this one of those nights when he'd likely end up at her place, begging to be let in? "How long is *that* gonna last?"

I bite down my temper. Before I came, I knew I might have trouble keeping my cool. But he's not worth it. Being with my family is. "I'm going to marry her, Eric."

He sneers. "You'll play happy families for a while, then disappear and leave her struggling again. I'm the one who's been there for her, the one who wanted her when you didn't."

"You wanted her but without any strings attached. I want her, strings and all. Because her strings *are* my strings."

Eric takes a step forward, but I stand my ground as we eye each other, Eric taking a swig from his beer.

"She's mine. Always has been. Now she always will be."

He shakes his head and takes a step back. "Whatever. You're welcome to her. Her and that idiot kid of yours."

I grit my teeth, fisting my hands, and it takes all my willpower to resist punching him. Instead, I turn and walk back toward the car.

Opening the door, I lean on it. "You know, Eric, the way I see it, Max is a hell of a lot smarter than you are."

He rolls his eyes. "Why's that?"

"He knew his mother wasn't interested in you. It's a shame you still don't get it."

At that, I get into the car, start it, and back down the driveway. Eric stands motionless. I smile at getting that last jibe in. Once we sort out the furniture, I'll get Lily and Max out of that damn house and away from him.

———

IN THE MORNING, I go out to get supplies and return to find Lily on the deck with her arms crossed. She's stone-faced as I exit the car and walk toward her.

"You okay?" I ask.

"What did you say to Eric?"

Damn. Caught.

"I told him you were coming with me. That's all. Why?"

"He's offered to buy the sheep." The look in her eyes softens. I know how much all of this means to her, and I don't want her to have to give up everything she's worked for. Whatever it took, I'd have found some way for her to keep the flock if she wanted it.

"We'll find somewhere else for them if that's what you want. Maybe clear some of that bush behind the house."

"Don't you dare."

I drop the grocery bags on the deck and hold my hands out, grasping her arms. "Then tell me what you want."

"He offered me a really good price for them. More than I ever thought I'd get." She's torn. It's written all over her face.

"Lily, you've worked so hard for everything. I'll do whatever it takes to make you happy. If you want to sell the sheep, do it. If you want to keep them, we'll find a way. All I want is to give our family a home. You, me, and Max."

Lily sighs and wraps her arms around my waist. "I sold them."

"You mean you made me go through that for nothing?"

She shrugs. "It was worth seeing you wriggle." The smile on her lips as she raises her head is worth my previous discomfort.

"I'm sure it was. I'll get you back tonight."

"What's that supposed to mean?"

I run my hands down her back until I reach her waist, and I grip her as she holds me. "It means I'll make you wriggle in return."

The flush that hits her cheeks is sweet and sexy. She has no idea what she does to me, never did.

"Where's Max?"

"In the kitchen having a snack. Why?"

I lower my head to brush my lips down her neck.

"Because the thought of going all day without touching you is driving me crazy."

"You'll just have to wait." She laughs softly, but not for long as my mouth seeks hers, the first lips I ever kissed and now the only ones I ever will.

"Adam," she whispers as we break apart.

"Every second that goes by, I only want you more."

She reaches up, gripping my shoulders. "I know the feeling. What are you doing to me, Adam Campbell?" Her eyes are filled with love, so much love.

"Not what I'd like to do. Let's get this food inside and plan our day. When does Eric take the sheep?"

"As soon as he transfers the money. Once we're gone from here, he'll move the fencing around and reclaim this part of the property, just as his mother intended."

She lets go and I bend to pick up the bags. "She did such an amazing thing for you two. I wish she was around for me to thank."

Lily opens the door, ushering me through. "I wish she was around to see us back together. She loved Max so much."

I hate that I'll never be able to thank Eric's mother for what she did.

Almost as much as I hate what my own mother did.

30

ADAM

Our journey to the city is Max's first, and we borrow Corey's canopied ute so we can load it up with things for the new house. The settlement on the apartment left me with a decent profit, and I have enough to get what we need and live for a while.

We all have plans. The sooner I can replace that old TV of Lily's the better. I haven't told Max yet, but I'm getting a gaming console, too. There are so many things I want to do with my son.

It doesn't take long for Max to get bored, and he fidgets in the back seat of the double cab. "How far away is it?"

"About an hour or so."

"Can we stop and take a break?"

"If we stop it'll take longer to get there, sweetheart," Lily says.

He crosses his arms and pouts. "Fine."

We get past the winding roads and onto the straight. In

the wing mirror I see him leaning against the door, boredom written all over his face.

"What do you think we need for the house, Max?" I ask.

"I dunno."

"What about a new TV?"

His eyes widen and he sits up, a bit more interested. "A big one?"

"Bigger than the one at home."

"How big?"

"How big is the back of the ute?"

Lily nudges me. "You're not filling the living room with a giant TV."

I laugh. "The living room is huge. There's heaps of space." I glance at her. "I'm good for it. I won't neglect other parts of the house for a big television. It'll all come in under budget."

She sighs. "It's hard to break the habit of a lifetime. I'm so used to watching my spending."

"We'll still have to, but you'll have your house, just the way you want it."

"My house." I shoot her another glance, and she's looking straight at me with a satisfied smile on her face.

"Yes, your house. It's all for you." I grab her hand and raise it to my lips, grateful that my brother bought an automatic vehicle and that I don't have to worry about changing gear. I flick a glance at the rear-view mirror.

Maybe I'll get Max an iPad too, or something to keep him pre-occupied on the drive back. Lily couldn't get internet to the old place unless she stumped up for satellite, but it's being installed at the new house during the week. Max uses the internet at school, but to have it at his fingertips will grow his world by so much.

"Want to play with my phone? There are some games on it."

Max leans forward as far as his seat belt will allow. "Can I?"

Lily lets go of my hand and plucks the phone out of the centre console, passing it to him.

"If you can work it out."

Max laughs. "It's an iPhone. We use iPads at school."

"There you go, then."

No more bored boy in the back seat, and no more fidgeting. Lily smiles at me, and I take her hand in mine again. Nearly there.

———

LILY WAS nervous about bringing Max to the city, with all the noise and the people, but he handles it like a pro. We go bed hunting first to get the things we'll need to have delivered out of the way.

Max just about blows a gasket at the sight of the bunks, and I ruffle his hair as he fixes his gaze on the beds.

"What do you think?"

He nods. "Maybe I can have a sleepover with Karl?"

I frown. "I don't know about that, bud."

"He's soooo nice to me since you saved him. We're friends now."

Lily's eyebrows creep up at that news. "You didn't tell me that."

"He told me he's sad he doesn't have a dad. But I've got one now, and he's the best." Max wraps his arms around my waist, and I hold him tight, painfully aware of his reluctance to be given affection in public. Although, since I met him, that seems to have improved.

"If you want the bunks, they're yours. Now to find Mum and me a new bed."

Max lets go and walks down the aisle, looking at each bed carefully. As if he's taking his time to pick us out a good one.

"So …"

"So what?" Lily asks.

"Is it just his room we're sorting out? Do you think they sell cots here?"

Her jaw drops, but I'm only half teasing. The thought of us having a baby together swells my heart more than I can say.

"I want the whole thing with you, Lily. To experience everything I missed out on with Max. If you want to."

She blinks away tears. "We haven't been back together long. Besides, I don't even know if I can," she whispers.

"What do you mean?"

"I told you I'm on the pill because my body's a bit haywire. Those months messed with me in so many ways."

I shrug. "Then we wait and see what happens. I'm not going to pressure you into something you don't want. I just wanted to make sure I told you how I feel as I think we've both had enough of being in the dark."

She gives me a smile and wraps her arms around me, snuggling into my chest. "I hate the dark."

"I know."

"Mum, Dad, check this one out."

Lily gazes up at me. "What do you reckon, Dad?"

"I think we need to go and find out what our son wants, Mum."

She chuckles. "Once we get the internet we can always order a cot online if or when we *actually* need it."

As she lets go of my waist, I lace my fingers with hers. "I like the way you think."

"I like you."

I bend my neck a little and brush her lips with mine. "Let's go find the most comfortable bed ever."

"Mum, Dad." Max calls again.

"Come on."

———

TWO BEDS and one lounge suite later, we make our way over to look at televisions. Lily rolls her eyes as Max and I zoom in on the sixty-five-inch one with the curved screen, complete with a sound system and Xbox. We've already picked up an iPad which caused Max to get over-excited.

"We don't need this," she says.

"I need it." I grin.

"Yeah, Dad needs it," says Max, eying up that console.

"I notice he's always taking your side now." She doesn't sound annoyed, more amused.

"He's my boy, that's why." I hold out my hand, and Max high fives it. "What do you think, Max? Can we fit this in the back of the ute?"

He nods.

"Yeah, I do too. Let's get this one. We can even install it at Mum's place until we move into the new house."

"Can't we move into the new house now?" Max asks.

I laugh. "Next weekend. They should deliver the beds

then, but we'll move everything else and sort out what we need and what to get rid of once we get there."

"If we take this home, I won't see either of you for the rest of the weekend." Lily sighs.

I can't help but smile. "Well, I was thinking that after I pay for this, we'd grab some lunch, and I'll give you my credit card and PIN to go buy some clothes."

She shakes her head. "You can't do that."

"Sure I can. There's that little lingerie shop by the food court. And when I say little lingerie …" I chuckle to myself as she goes a deep shade of pink.

"Fine. If you insist."

"Make the most of it before I run out of money."

The colour drains from her face. "Adam?"

I place my hands on her arms. "We're good, Lily. Buying property in Copper Creek is ridiculously cheap. We've got enough to splurge now and to live on for at least six months. By then we should have the garage up and running. Jack's already started contacting his old customers for me. They're over the moon there'll be a local mechanic."

She nods. "I guess we'll have the money from the sheep, too."

"There you go. You can get what you need. Don't hold back," I say. The worried look in her eyes gives way to a smile as her lips curl. "You deserve it."

Lily leans over and pecks me on the cheek. "Love you."

"I love you too. I'll spend forever showing it."

As we keep walking, the food court comes into view.

I turn to look at my family. "What do you two want?"

Max tugs on my hand. "Can we have McDonald's? I've never had that."

"Seriously?" I look down at him. If they've barely left town, I guess that'd be right.

"We don't usually go further than Callahans and the surrounding shops. It's too far," Lily says.

"If it's okay with your mother, sure." I shift my gaze to her and she nods.

"We just eat Mum's cooking. She makes burgers, but I bet these ones are better."

Lily fights a laugh as she clamps her lips together. If nothing else, Max speaks his mind. Diplomatic or not.

We walk up to the counter, and I cast my eyes over the menu. "What sort of burger do you want, Max?"

In the end, he decides on a Big Mac, just like Dad is having. We also end up with what I can only describe as a metric shit-ton of McNuggets. Either his eyes are bigger than his belly, or he'll hoover them up.

If it bothers Lily, she doesn't let on. Me? I love spoiling my kid.

Lily gets through her burger and fries, but I know where her mind is already. She keeps looking at the lingerie shop near the food court, and casting her eye across to a couple of clothing stores farther down.

"Go." I nudge her arm and pull my wallet out, handing my credit card to her.

"This still makes me feel awkward."

"PIN is 1907."

Her lips twitch as she takes the card.

"Yes, it's your birthday. That's always been my PIN. Nineteenth of July."

From the look on her face, she'd jump me then and there if there weren't people around. What I'd said was the truth.

I'd kept that as my PIN for years. It had become habit, evidence of my lingering reluctance to let her go. Thank God I hadn't.

"Told you. Never stopped." I don't even have to finish the sentence. She knows what I mean.

"Be good for Adam," she says to Max.

"His name's Dad." Max pokes his tongue out, and Lily raises her eyebrows.

"Fine. Do you want to get some clothes too, while we're shopping on *Dad's* credit card?" She looks at me with her eyebrows still raised, and I grin in response.

"Yep," he mumbles, eating his way through what I think is his twentieth chicken nugget.

"We'll stay here and open up your iPad. Let's download some games to keep you occupied on the way home."

Lily's appreciation is clear in her eyes, and she stands, bending to kiss Max on the head. He doesn't protest, he's so pre-occupied with his acquisition.

"I've got this, Lily. Enjoy." I keep my eyes on her as she heads straight for one of the stores she had her eyes on.

"Dad?" Max places his hand on my arm.

"Max?"

"Can you help me?"

With a song in my heart and a smile on my face, I connect Max's iPad to the free Wi-Fi and start setting it up. "Just you wait until we have internet at home."

"I like our new house."

"So do I. I think we're going to be really happy there."

He links his arm in mine. "Mum'll be happy. I like Mum being happy."

I smile down at him. "You and me both, Max. You and me both."

———

WE SPEND the next half hour finding games and downloading them. Seeing the excitement in his eyes is worth all of this. I think back to when I'd first left the army. I'd been a mess, and no way would I have been any type of decent father to Max.

He deserved better than that. He needed me, and I had the ability and means to make his life better. Already, he's made my life better. Made me better.

"Is that it?" I ask.

Max nods. "I think that's enough."

"Wanna go find Mum?"

His face lights up.

"We'll find Mum, get home and hook up all this stuff. Maybe we can find a good movie to watch tonight."

"Or play games?"

"We'll see. Depends on how late we get home. I think we might have to stop and get fish and chips on the way."

He grins, and my heart stops. Max looks so much like Lily, but there are times when I can see me in him. There's no doubting who his parents are. How did I miss this the first few weeks?

I tidy the empty boxes and packaging from the table as Max gathers his things. I'm not sure what store Lily's in, but I know which direction she went.

We get about three doors down when she nearly bumps into me as she exits the store, bags hanging off her arms.

After her initial reluctance, it looks as if she's been on a spree.

"Are you sure you have enough?" I look at her with bemusement.

"You told me to spend it."

I laugh. "I'm just teasing. There had better be something in there for me."

She nods. "I bought Max some new underwear, pants, and T-shirts, and I got a couple of shirts for you too."

Shaking my head, I pass a bag to Max to carry and taking the rest in my arms.

"I was meaning more something skimpy from the other shop."

"You have a one-track mind." She rolls her eyes.

"You love me anyway."

Lily's cheeks flush pink, and I reach out to push a stray lock of hair behind her ear, just from the need to touch her. "I do. God knows why."

"Shall we go home, Max?" I ask.

He nods.

"Ready to play on your iPad on the way?" It's clutched in his hand tightly.

"Yep. Can we get in the car now?"

Laughing, I nod. "Let's go get our TV and get home."

Lily holds out my credit card. "You can take this back too."

I take it, but I squeeze her hand as I do. "Only until I get you one of your own."

There's no way to miss another eye roll as she steps past me, and I grin to myself because she loves me.

And I love her.

———

MAX FALLS asleep on the way home. The long drive is one thing—the winding roads at the end of the journey finish him off. Lily and I pull over in town, and I grab fish and chips for dinner.

Max's so tired, he can barely stand up as we get in the door. At the realisation that I'm bringing in the television, he finds his second wind.

"Dad," he says it over and over again as I carry in the boxes.

"What's up?"

"When's it going to be plugged in? I want to play."

"It won't take long. I don't know if we're going to play anything much tonight. You look like you need to eat and get some sleep."

He screws up his face. "Can we watch a movie, then?"

"I'm sure we can. What do you want to watch?"

"Wait for it," Lily mutters.

"*Finding Nemo!*" Max jumps up and down, and all I can do is shake my head. Chances are he'll be asleep five minutes into it.

"So, how about we eat some dinner first and then we'll watch *Nemo*?"

I've never seen a kid shovel food as fast as Max does. His eyes are on the box containing the TV the whole time as we sit in the middle of the living room floor and eat our dinner straight out of the paper.

"I don't think we've ever eaten so many takeaway foods." Lily laughs.

"I'm looking forward to the new house and that kitchen. We can take turns cooking meals."

"Do we have to have vegetables?" Max asks.

"Yes, Max. We do have to have vegetables."

Once the fish and chips are gone, we unpack everything. The TV and surround sound system all comes out of the boxes, ready to be plugged in and connected.

I pick up a bag, beckoning Lily. "I bought you a present, too."

"What?"

"This." From the bag I produce two night lights.

"Adam." Her tone tells me she's touched, but she frowns. "I tried one of those. It wasn't enough."

"That's why I bought more than one. One for each side of the room. We'll give it a go. I just want to be able to close our bedroom door so we get our privacy."

Tears appear in her eyes and roll down her cheeks. "What if it's not enough?"

"Want to know what I think?" I ask as I drop the night lights on the couch and raise my thumb to her cheeks to wipe the evidence of her sadness.

"What?"

"I think you need to get out of your own head and not overthink it. We'll try it together and if it doesn't work well, we'll come up with another solution." Raising her hand to my face, I brush her fingers with my lips. "I told you. Maybe we can help fix each other."

"You seem way more together than me."

I chuckle. "Sometimes. Being back with you I feel more settled than I have been in a long time. I think you and Max have been the best medicine."

"Speaking of Max, I think we need to get this movie underway. Once it starts, I don't think it'll be long until he crashes." She runs a finger down my chest.

"What are you up to?"

"I bought you a present too." A smirk crosses her face. Clearly, she's pleased with herself. I love seeing the light in her eyes, the sparkle that's returned.

"Can't wait for that."

"Dad got me a present too, Mum. My iPad." Max clings to his device, and I have to smile at our little family.

Nearly settled.

31

ADAM

It's late by the time everything is set up, and Max, lying on the floor with me, tries his best to keep his eyes open as we watch our first movie on our new TV. I catch Lily's gaze during the part of *Finding Nemo* she always cries at. Sure enough tears are welling, and Max climbs up on the couch and rests his head on his mother's lap.

"Tired, bud?" I ask.

"It's been a long day for all of us," Lily says, stroking Max's hair.

"Bet you're looking forward to the new house," I say, sitting up.

She shrugs. "It'll be amazing, but this place has been our home for so long. Moving out is going to be weird."

"It's gonna be cool," Max murmurs. He's so close to sleep and fighting it.

Lily smiles at me, her contentment clear in her eyes. Coming home has been a whirlwind. In a matter of weeks,

I've reunited with Lily, and we're planning our future. It's almost like the time in between never happened, and while I know the changes scare her, I've never been more confident of anything in my life. We've slipped into what our life would have been like had we been married all those years ago.

"He's asleep," she whispers.

I crawl across the floor until I reach him. He's snoring softly against his mother's thigh, and I raise my finger to stroke his cheek.

"He had so much fun today. You spoiled him." There's so much affection in her voice, and it warms me.

"I hope I spoiled both of you."

She reaches over and strokes my hair. "You did. It's so much, Adam—it's overwhelming."

"Consider it an attempt to make up for everything. I know there are some things that can never truly be made up for, but I'll do my best." I stand, reaching down to scoop Max into my arms. "Must be bedtime."

"For him or us?" A devilish smile plays on her lips, matching the glint in her eyes.

"It's still early. Are you that tired?"

She stands. "No."

"I have no idea why you'd want to go to bed so soon, then."

Turning toward the door, I take a step, and she slaps me on the arse and laughs. "I'm sure there are plenty of reasons."

"Are any of them in that little bag from the lingerie shop?"

"Maybe."

I carry Max upstairs and tuck him into his bed. He's dressed in clothes his mother bought him today, and I'm not about to wake a sleeping boy and make him change into pyjamas. He mumbles as I pull the blanket over him and pause for a minute to stroke his hair.

My mind wanders back to the day James called. I'd been so lost, finished with the army, finished with Jenna. Drinking had become a habit, and yet I've barely had a drop since being back here.

Now, I'm found, and this boy has been such a big piece of that.

I bend and kiss his temple. We have so much to catch up on, so many days of hanging out. It's funny when I consider my reason for coming back. That's been pushed to the side for this life-changing discovery.

I only wish I'd done it sooner.

———

LOST IN THOSE THOUGHTS, I traipse to the bedroom. All the things Max and I can do together roll through my head. I may have missed out on a lot, but there are still so many years together. How did I get to be so lucky?

Max not only fills my life now, he helps give that life meaning, gives me a reason to go on when there have been times when everything felt too hard.

When I push open the bedroom door, I widen my eyes at the sight of Lily on the bed. She's taken my words to heart and wears a barely there, white translucent nightgown. One she won't be wearing in about thirty seconds.

She's way out of her comfort zone. Her fingers grip the edge of the blanket as if she's fighting pulling it up and covering herself, defeating the purpose of wearing it.

"Wow."

"I feel like a dick."

"You're gorgeous." I pause as I take a micro-second to consider the wisdom of my next words. "If you feel like a dick, I'll give you dick."

She picks up a pillow and throws it. It hits the door behind me, falling to the ground with a soft thud. "You *are* a dick. Stop making fun of me."

Turning, I make sure the door is closed and pick up the pillow. Flicking the light switch fills the room with the soft glow of the night-lights. It's romantic and warm, and hopefully enough to stop her freaking out.

Lily's breath hitches, and I make my way to the bed, sitting down and grasping her hand.

"You okay?"

She nods. "It's beautiful."

"So are you."

Even in the dim light I can see her cheeks flush. She hates attention on herself, always has, but I'm going to lavish it on her. I don't ever want her doubting how I feel.

"I just feel so awkward." She slams her head against her pillow.

Standing, I tug my shirt over my head and unzip my jeans. Lily relaxes a little and lets go of the sheet. My eyes drink her in, the light highlighting the curve of her breasts.

I'm overwhelmed by that familiar feeling of wanting to possess her, all of her. I want her underneath me, crying my name as I bury myself inside her.

My heart is filled to the brim, and as I lose the remainder of my clothes, I pull back the blankets and take a look at all of her. I've claimed her, she's mine, but I need her more than ever. She was always my common sense, my centre of being. Losing her was always about more than simply a broken heart.

"I love your awkwardness. I love your heart." Slipping between the sheets, I slide her shoulder strap down, exposing her left breast. "I love these too."

She giggles as I take her nipple into my mouth and her shoulder slumps as her body releases the tension.

"Come here." I roll to my back and pull her with me, and she laughs, straddling my hips. Running my eyes down her body, I let out a low whistle. "You're not wearing any underwear."

Lily licks her lips. She's sweet and sexy all at once. It doesn't take much to get me going when she's concerned. "I couldn't see the point."

"True."

Slowly, she peels off the nightgown and throws it to the floor.

"That was such a waste of time," I say, running my hands up her body and cupping her breasts.

"You wanted me to buy it." Lily leans over, her face inches from mine, and she pokes her tongue out at me.

"I'm glad you did. You are breath-taking in it. Even if you only wore it for five minutes."

She cocks her head. "More like three and a half."

I chuckle, pulling her the rest of the way in for a kiss. Her confidence boosted, she grinds against me, and I'm lost in her warmth, her soft skin, the scent of her arousal.

"You have no idea just how beautiful you are, do you?" I whisper.

The pink in her cheeks slides down to the tops of her breasts. "Adam," she says affectionately.

"My sweet Lily." All the years fall away as I brush my fingers down her arms.

She sighs a contented sigh, and I slip my thumb between us, stroking her clit.

"I love that I get to do this whenever I want." I chuckle.

"Well, after Max is asleep."

"I'll concede that point."

Her breath hitches and she leans back a little, giving me better access.

"I still love that I get to share a bed with you every night."

Lily closes her eyes, rocking her hips against my hand. Her lips part, and her breath grows heavier with every stroke. She's lovely, her smooth skin, those puffy lips that beg to be kissed. She bucks against my hardened cock before pushing up a little and sliding onto me.

Being inside her is like heaven, and her silky softness wraps around me. I take a deep breath and close my eyes. I'm lost again. Lily surrounds me and I'm more at ease than I have been in months. She's all I need, and the only one I'll ever love. She's my true safe harbour.

When I open my eyes, the brilliant blue looks back. There's radiance to her that tells me she knows the effect she has on me.

She keeps me under her spell as she quickens the rhythm, and I lose all control. Pressure builds inside me, and I pull her down to run my tongue along the seam of her lips before parting my own to kiss her. I shatter into a million pieces, falling apart right underneath her.

All I see is her.

All I am is her.

"Adam," she whispers my name this time, and warmth travels the length of my body.

I have no words, and I respond by kissing her again. She giggles as I roll, pulling her with me. I bury my face in her neck and she's left gasping as I suck gently on her ear lobe.

Spent, I lift off her to lie flat on my back and take a deep breath.

"I think you've worn me out." I laugh.

"I think I did all of the work." She runs her fingers through her long, blonde hair.

Grinning, I roll to my side again. "Do you know why I think this is going to work out for us?"

She runs a finger down my arm, setting my heart alight. "Why?"

"You. You've spent so long being practical and doing what you had to do. You're my rock, Lily. Yeah we spent some money today, but we'll settle in to get this business up and running, and you'll control the spending and make sure we have enough."

"That's a pretty big ask when there's currently a finite amount."

"You and Max are motivation enough to get the work done and bring in the money."

She smiles. "After everything we've been through, this is probably one of the scariest things I've ever done."

"Me too. But I could live in a caravan at the cove with you and be happy. I think that's the advantage we have."

Her smile lights up the whole room, and she giggles as I kiss her tenderly.

This is contentment.

This is love.

———

I WAKE to Lily wrapped around me. If she was disturbed during the night, she didn't wake me. I watch her sleep, her arm draped over my chest, her right leg hooked around my left. She's so peaceful, and I don't want to move for fear of waking her.

When she stirs, I brush my fingers down her arm and back up again.

One deep breath and her eyes flicker open. That lazy smile returns to her lips, the one that shows how happy she truly is.

"Morning," I murmur.

She lets out a contented sigh. "Good morning."

"Sleep well?"

Lily nods. "The light worked well, and being with you helps."

"You are rather entangled." I shake my leg and Lily laughs, tightening her lock on me. "I'm not complaining."

Her smile grows. "Good. I rather like sleeping like this."

I nuzzle her cheek, my lips finding hers in a tender kiss.

Slam.

The door bursts open, hitting the wall behind it. Lily jumps, and I sit up, grinning at Max standing in the doorway, his eyes as big as saucers.

"Dad! Can we play a game now?"

I chuckle. "Give me a minute to get dressed, and I'll be with you."

He shifts his gaze to Lily. "Mum, are you naked?"

Only her shoulders show, but I guess he's not used to seeing her like this.

"I..." she starts.

He rolls his eyes. "I'm *so* glad I didn't hop into bed with you last night, then."

Turning, he disappears, presumably heading to the living room. Lily's a brilliant shade of red and I can't help myself, laughing as she slams her head back onto the pillow.

"Stay here. I'll bring breakfast in after I've got him sorted out."

She reaches up, dragging her fingers through my beard. "You're good to me."

"You deserve it." I shuffle off the bed, dragging on my clothing before I can get distracted by her again. "Besides, if I can keep him busy, I might just be able to get a quickie out of it."

Lily laughs. "I don't know if there's such a thing as a quickie with you."

I waggle my eyebrows at her. "Try me and find out."

Fifteen minutes later with Max playing *Lego Batman* downstairs, I show her exactly what I mean.

———

IN THE AFTERNOON, I set off for Corey's place. In exchange for using his ute, he borrowed my car, which I'm anxious to get back. I'm guessing he gave it a good thrashing.

With Lily's directions, I set off up McKenzie's Mountain. It was named for the first settler family to the area. They sat on the hill and watched as the township sprung up beneath them. There's no hope of watching from above now—the bush has grown dense and it's beautiful in its own way.

The road is sealed, but bumpy. I doubt it's had any maintenance in years. With no other traffic, I slow as I pass the commune or cult, or whatever it is. When I was a kid, the people from the group used to come down into town often. The only thing different about them was that they all dressed the same and that their kids didn't go to school with us. From what I hear, they've become more secluded, cutting themselves off from the outside world as much as possible.

I shiver and push on. Corey's place is supposed to be just over the ridge. It turns out to be easier to find than I thought it would be as I spot my car just off the road and the small house behind it.

It's beautiful in its solitude, but still not too remote. It's not far to town, but the house is surrounded by trees, visible only when you get out the front of it.

Corey steps out onto his deck as I pull up his driveway, waving as I get out of the ute. "Hey. Everything go okay?"

I nod as I step toward the house, gravel crunching under my shoes. "Sure did. We've got furniture ordered, and I bought a TV and a few other things ready to go. We'll need your help next weekend though."

"You got it." He nods back toward the house. "Want a coffee?"

"Sure." I trail into the house behind him. It's pretty bare. In the corner of a living room is a television, and opposite that an old couch. In the kitchen is a small round wooden table with four chairs. Corey indicates for me to sit at the table and I do so, looking around the room. "So, this is your place."

He flicks on the kettle and grabs some cups out of the cupboard.

"Yep. It's cosy and does the job. I'm not home a huge amount. Sometimes pest eradication means days away from here."

While Corey spoons out the coffee and sugar, I lean back in my chair. This is such a cosy place, and so Corey. The walls are devoid of decoration, the table's basic with no cloth. I guess it makes sense if he's barely around.

He carries the cups to the table and sets one down in front of me before sitting.

"So, you move into the new house next weekend."

I nod. "Yep. James is helping me with the garage during the week. Jack still has a whole heap of gear he hadn't managed to sell—it's just in storage. I'm grabbing that, too. It's enough to get us open and working. I can't wait to get into the house and online so I can sort out whatever else we need."

Corey chuckles and takes a sip of his coffee. "Max won't know himself. Maybe Lily will take better care of herself, too."

"What do you mean?"

"Come on, little brother. You know more than anyone. She cuts back on looking after herself so that Max has enough. Drives me a little crazy. I'd give her a month's worth of meat at a time, but I knew damn well that she'd stretch it to make it last longer and give him bigger meals." He shrugs. "I mean, fair enough, but she was just wasting away in that place."

Nodding, I sigh, wrapping my hands around my mug. "I thought as much. She's so thin. But I've made sure there's been enough food in the house these past few weeks, and she seems to eat more with each meal."

"That's some white knight shit you've got going on. Think you can keep it up?"

I laugh. "We'll be fine. I lucked out with the apartment in the States, and bought it a few years ago when property prices were lower. They took off and I cashed up. In US dollars, too. I suspect if I was still over there I wouldn't be quite so flush." Sipping the last of my coffee, I put the cup back down. "Between the garage being cheap and Eric paying Lily a decent amount for the sheep, we've got enough to last a few months."

"We'll all help out if we have to as well. Owen will no doubt still deliver bread, plus you'll be closer to him now. I'll still bring you meat when I go hunting."

"It's all appreciated."

"You know …" He studies me closely. "When I heard you were back, I thought there might be trouble and then you'd bugger off again. I'm glad you're here and that you've made amends."

I let out a sigh. "I don't know if I can ever fully make amends for everything, but I can do whatever it takes to support my family."

A smile crosses his face. "Well, if you ever get stuck, you're always welcome here. I reckon I could squeeze you all in."

"Thanks."

He frowns. "What we did was just as bad. I think we were all a bit young and stupid to think you wanted to stay away. But at the same time, it made sense. It was a lot to be lumped with at that age."

"I guess, but then Lily had the whole lot on her shoulders. That wasn't fair either."

Corey shakes his head and sits back in his chair. "What happened to her was so bad. Of everyone, I knew how much you loved her. I told her I'd take care of her in the early days, but she wasn't interested."

I narrow my eyes at him. "You propositioned her?"

"Not like that." He screws up his face. "I told her if she needed someone I'd be happy to take on her and Max. I didn't expect any great romance or anything. Even when you were apart, she was yours. But that lady of yours is way too independent."

I chuckle. "That she is. Though I've worn her down. Even convinced her to spend a little money on herself yesterday."

Corey nods thoughtfully. "That's good. It's Drew you have to watch out for—he's the one who flirts."

Although I've seen it with my own eyes, I know enough to know that Corey is screwing with me. The twinkle in his eyes gives him away.

I look forward to spending more time getting to know all my brothers again.

3 2

LILY

Our first night in our new home.

It took most of the day to get in here. I don't have a lot, but using Corey's ute and a trailer we borrowed from Jack Kirby, we got everything moved.

When I say we, it was mostly Adam and his brothers doing all the lifting. Empty boxes sourced from the local supermarket were scattered around the house, and Max and I started packing. Our whole life together went in those boxes.

We never had a lot of material things, but Max and I had each other. That got me through the hard times, and now hopefully there will only be good.

Box after box goes in the car and the ute.

With the house empty, I stand in the entranceway looking up the stairs. The memories are overwhelming. Max learning to crawl, his first steps, all the times I'd hear him running down the stairs despite me telling him not to. This has been our home.

"You alright?" Adam places his hands on my shoulders and kisses my hair.

"Just remembering. Max and I have done so much in this house."

Adam's warm arms slide around my waist, and I tilt my head as he rests his head on my shoulder. "We'll make new memories now. The three of us."

"I know, it's just …" Tears well up that I can't explain. I had been made welcome to this house, made it my own, and never felt obligated when Mrs Murphy was alive. Part of me looks forward to handing it back to Eric, his mother's will fulfilled, but the rest of me will miss the old place.

"It's okay. I'm pretty sure it's normal to miss somewhere you've lived in for so long. Do you want to take the keys to Eric, or do you want me to?"

I lean back. Adam's arms around me don't just signal his love. They're my support when I'm adrift. The new house is everything I want, but it's hard not to waver when I'm fire-walling my solidity for the past twelve years.

His lips brush my neck, and I close my eyes.

"I'll do it. It's only right, given the way I moved in here."

He squeezes me around the waist before letting go, and I turn to smile at him. Adam nods as he scans my face. I think he's just checking that my expression matches my words. I'm calmer than I thought I'd be now.

"Well, I'll take Max and the last load over to the house and meet you there. Owen was in the kitchen when I left, unpacking your things and putting them away. I think he was planning on making pizza for dinner."

I nod. "That sounds amazing."

Adam pecks me on the cheek and leaves me in the entranceway, closing the front door behind him. I take a further moment to look around and as I hear him drive away, I open the door, looking out into the yard. I'll miss my garden, but there's plenty of room at the new place for one.

Time to move on.

———

I'VE TRAVELLED the road and turned up Eric's driveway more times than I can count over the years, but this is the last time. I can't see us having any reason to visit him again.

He's sat out on his deck when I get there, and he stands as I get out of the car and toward the house.

"Sit for a minute?" he asks as I mount the steps.

I nod. "I can't be too long." Licking my lips I say the words that mean so much. "My family's waiting for me."

He's always been one for trying to analyse situations, and he stares at me for what feels like the longest time but in reality is probably about thirty seconds. "I won't keep you. Just wanted to tell you how much I'll miss you."

I can't return what he's just said. We have been friends, off and on, but it was hard to stay friendly with someone who didn't respect boundaries. Eventually, I settle on the truth. "It's going to be weird. For a while at least."

"If you ever need the house again, it's yours."

I meet his gaze. He's giving me a backup plan in case things don't work out with Adam. I'm grateful, but nothing is going to keep us apart again. "Thanks. I do appreciate it."

Eric lets out a sigh. "I thought for the longest time that we might just end up together. I'll always be sorry it didn't happen."

"Can I be honest?"

His lips curl. "I've never stopped you before."

"Nothing was ever going to separate me from Max. That's all it boiled down to. I wanted someone who would put us first."

He swallows hard. "I understand."

"Do you? You deserve happiness as much as I do. Find someone special and stop being a zombie." I can't help the smile on my face.

He frowns, his pale eyebrows knitting together. "A zombie?" Snorting, he shakes his head and laughs. "Let me guess. It's a Maxism."

"Yeah, it is. No matter what, he's the most important guy in my life. I think sometimes you men forget that."

His eyebrows shoot up. "Us men? Are you talking about …"

"Yes, I'm talking about Adam. He has to understand that, too. He's the love of my life, but what I have with Max is a bond no one will ever break. Even unintentionally."

Eric nods, and I bend to kiss him on the cheek. He turns his head at the last moment, planting a kiss on my lips.

"Gotcha." He gives me a crooked smile, and I roll my eyes in return.

"Nope."

"Don't you dare tell Adam I did that."

I laugh as I turn away. "I'm not keeping anything from him. Just be aware of that."

"Are you sure he's not keeping anything from you?"

I stop and turn back. "What do you mean?"

"He was gone a long time. Man has to have his secrets." Eric's gaze penetrates me as I stand there. I can't let him see that his suggestion has knocked me.

Listening to Eric only creates doubt and doubt kills love. "If there was anything bad in his past, he'd have told me."

Eric nods, scrutinising my reaction closely. "Okay. I'm always here if you need anything."

"I'll keep that in mind."

Hell will freeze over before I ask Eric Murphy for a single thing. Ever.

———

LATER THAT NIGHT, with Max settled and asleep, Adam and I christen our new bed. We've had nights in my bed, but this is different. It's brand new and ours.

"Happy?" Adam holds me in his arms, his right hand stroking my left breast as we lay curled up together under the crisp lemon sheets. He's with me and all is right with the world.

I sigh with contentment, smiling with what must be a hazy look in my eyes. Nothing compares to the freedom of being with Adam in this way, knowing nothing else can rip us apart. We're together and solid.

"I'll take that as a yes?" He grins.

"I don't even know where to begin."

He traces his finger down between my breasts and over my stomach. The past few weeks I've been healthier than I have been in years, and I've even filled out a little. We don't have a huge budget, and things will be tight for a while, but being here and having a view to the future makes it a million times better than it was in the old house. Once Adam gets the business going, things will be even better.

"Do you miss the army?" I whisper, a little afraid of his response.

His fingers stop, and he taps my skin as he smiles, spreading his palm on my belly.

"I miss my friends. Some of us were together for a while. We were brothers." He slides his hand down my thigh. "I wouldn't be anywhere else but here now, though."

"I'm so glad you came back."

He grins and leans over to press his lips to mine, his love radiating through his kiss. His unending affection makes me melt. It's been so long since I've been so loved, and now I'm enveloped in it all of the time.

"So am I. Maybe we can't get back the time we missed out on, but we can sure as hell make new memories."

We lie in silence for a few moments, comfortable in one another's company.

"Eric tried to stir one last time today," I say. I want my earlier words to mean something. There's nothing I want to keep from Adam.

"He's just pissed I got the girl." Adam laughs, nuzzling my temple.

"He wanted me to doubt you. But I can't do that. I need to be able to trust you, and you to trust me."

Adam raises his head. "Lily, if you have any doubts …"

The expression on his face tells me everything. Maybe there are things he's done while he was away, but that was in the past. This is our new start.

"No doubts."

His eyes light up.

"Unless you have a wife and other family tucked away somewhere."

He chuckles. "No wife." When he licks his lips slowly, fear sets in. He looks as if he's about to tell me something big. "There was someone. She put up with me, helped me through the hard shit when I first got out of the army. But you were always it for me. Didn't matter what had happened, how long I'd been gone. It wasn't fair on her. So when it got really serious, I broke up with her."

My heart thuds. I can't help the jealousy that swells inside, but he chose me. Even when he hadn't seen me in so long, even when he didn't know if I'd moved on.

I fling my arms around his neck and hold on tight.

He chose me.

33

ADAM

The garage is close to opening. James has done a hell of a lot of work to help me out tidying the building up and making it my own. I don't think I've ever been so excited in my life.

Word is already spreading. I got a call this morning from a farmer needing help with a tractor. It's in the middle of nowhere, but I'm itching to get my hands on anything mechanical. It's been far too long.

It doesn't take much to get it running again.

"Coffee?" he asks.

"Sounds good."

We walk toward the big farmhouse. As we approach, a litter of puppies come tumbling out from where they've been eating. I laugh as we're surrounded.

"Look at you lot." I grin.

"They're ready to go to new homes. Interested?"

I think of Max and the way he'd acted around Eric's dog. The one he'd named. "Sure am. How much are they?"

"About the same as the repairs you're doing for me."

I chuckle. "What a coincidence. I've got a boy who would love me forever if I got one. Not sure about his mother."

"Pick which one you want. They'll end up on farms around here otherwise. I'm sure one of them will be well loved with you."

I grin and look them over. They're full of life and excited, panting and seeking attention. Except for one of them. He stands a little off to the side.

"That one's a bit more reserved. I think it'll take a special kinda owner for him."

There's only one puppy I can choose.

I head back to the house with the puppy in the back seat of the car. He lies down like he's told.

"If you're going to be this good, we're gonna get along fine. Although we might both have to sleep in the car for a while."

Lily is going to kill me. Without discussion, I just did something that will bring a smile to her face. Eventually.

Max is going to go nuts.

I slow down along the driveway beside the garage. The section is fully fenced now, the result of a weekend of my brothers and I working together. The gate's open though, and I pull up into the backyard before getting out to make sure it's closed.

Flying out the door is Max. Nothing gets past him, and he never fails to greet me when I come home.

"Dad," he calls, flinging his arms around my waist.

"Hey, bud. I've got a surprise. Where's your mother?"

Max turns back toward the house. "Mum," he yells for all he's worth.

Lily appears in the doorway. She looks so full of life now, healthy. Better than she's probably done in a long time.

"What's going on?" she asks.

"Dad's got a surprise," Max shrieks.

"Is that right?" Her eyebrows raise in suspicion.

"That's right. You have to promise not to kill me."

She walks across the deck and down the steps toward the car. "What have you done?"

I take a step back to the rear door of the car and open it up. When I click my fingers, the puppy looks up and trots across the back seat, jumping out the door and onto the concrete pad.

Max's eyes widen. "What's that?"

"An elephant." I deadpan.

He grins. "Don't be silly. It's a puppy."

I shift my gaze to Lily. She's shaking her head, but at least she's smiling. It's better than I hoped for. "It is. What do you think his name is?"

"What?" Max asks.

"Whatever you want it to be."

He laughs. "Can we name him Happy?"

"Another one?" I close the car door and kneel beside the dog. It's like it's meant to be as he licks my hand and jumps up, his front paws resting on my chest. "Hey, boy." I pat him on the back.

"How about Lucky?" Max asks.

"I think that's a much better name. Because we're lucky to have him?"

He nods. "And I'm lucky. I have my dad now."

I look up, and Lily looks away. These moments still hit her right in the heart. I see it. "You do. And you have a puppy."

Max gets down on his knees, and the puppy drops and turns toward him. These two are meant to be and Max giggles, the puppy licking his face.

"He needs to learn to behave, and we all need to teach him. But I think you two are a pretty good team." I stand and Lily strides toward us, taking my hand in hers.

"Thank you," she says quietly, pecking me on the cheek and resting her head on my shoulder.

"I thought you'd be mad."

"Max was so angry with me when I told him we couldn't keep Happy. Now at least we can afford to have a pet."

"As soon as I saw him, I just knew."

Our boy laughs as he hugs the dog, and I wrap my arms around my girl as we watch them bond. She sighs a contented sigh and buries her face in my chest.

I kiss the top of her head. "You okay?"

"I just love watching him. This could be the best thing for Max."

"Until he has siblings."

She raises her face to look at me. "Is that still part of your plan?"

I shrug. "Maybe. If that's what you want too."

A smile lights up her face, and I think I have my answer.

Lily's not going to kill me.

———

IN THE EVENING, our new family member is settled in. Lily went down the road and got a bowl and food for him. Sure it's another mouth for us to feed, and while we grow our business things might be a bit tight, but Max and Lucky are already the best of friends.

It's dark early, and I stand on the back deck looking at our little empire. It feels as if I've been back such a short time, but I have everything I've ever needed.

"What are you doing out here, Dad?" Max comes through the door and stands beside me. When I'm home he's my shadow, and I love spending time with him, making up for the years when I wasn't here. I wish I'd had the chance to hold him as a baby, to clean up his scraped knees, to carry him around on my shoulders. But I didn't, so now I've become friends with my son.

I gaze down at the face looking up at me, eager for answers. "Looking at the stars. The night seems even darker in the country."

"The trees are scary."

I look down at him. "Why's that?"

"They're so big and dark."

Turning my head toward the house, I can see through the kitchen and into the living room. The dog sits at Lily's feet. He's already worked out who sorts his food.

"How about we go and take a look? I'll show you there's nothing to be afraid of."

Max shakes his head.

"Come on, Max." I hold out my hand, and though I can see his reluctance, he takes it, and we make tentative steps toward the bush.

The moon hangs big in the sky, illuminating where we're

going, but Max clings tight to me. It's so gorgeous out here, and we brush against the ferns as we walk. There's no path, but there are small gaps between the plants. Enough for us to make our way through.

We come to a small clearing. It's so quiet and peaceful. The cry of an owl breaks through the near silence and I smile.

"Do you hear the owl, Max?" I ask, resting my hand on Max's shoulders, crouching beside him.

My boy nods with eyes as big as saucers, staring up at the trees.

"I bet he's hunting. They like little animals like bugs and mice."

"Mum doesn't like bugs and mice," Max whispers.

"I bet that Morepork does. Do you know why he's called that?"

Max shakes his head, inching closer to me as the owl calls again.

"Listen to his call. That's what he's asking for. Or at least that's what it sounds like."

Over and over again the bird calls, and Max slowly snakes his arm around my neck. He stares hard at the trees, clinging to me.

"Love you, Max," I whisper.

"Love you too, Dad."

My heart feels as if it's about to explode, love overwhelming me. All the years I was away, I felt empty, like something was missing. Now I've found that something, and I bury my head in Max's chest, holding him close.

"Let go. I can't breathe." Max laughs loudly. A flurry of wings above makes us both look up as the owl flies from one tree to another, dipping before rising up to land on a branch.

"I think he got some food," I say softly. "Let's go and tell Mum about it." I stand, and Max reaches for my hand. "Come on."

As we approach the house, Max waves at Lily through the kitchen window. She's at the bench and smiling at us as he gets her attention. Catching my eye, she sends me a look that tells me exactly how she's feeling. She's happy.

"Want a hot chocolate when we get inside?" I ask Max.

He nods.

"Me too. Let's go get one and settle in for the night."

"Dad?"

I look down at those blue eyes, so dark in the moonlight. "Yes, Max?"

"Can we come out again tomorrow? Maybe the owl will be there again."

I grin, tousling his hair. "You bet."

34

LILY

It's been six months since the day I chased my son down the road as he ran from the bullies, only to come face to face with my past and my future.

I write off the nausea to something I ate, but when it lasts a week, I know there's something else going on.

My periods have been regulated by the pill for so long that they're almost non-existent. I'm left pondering the seemingly impossible.

The only way to know for sure is to get a test and see what happens. I drop off Max at school and head toward the small pharmacy that sits next to the doctor's surgery. The pharmacist has two assistants, neither of whom I can trust to keep their mouths shut, but I just have to know.

I grimace as I spot Sasha behind the counter. Of the two of them, it had to be her this morning. I bite back my urge to run and walk along the aisles.

"Lily." She smiles at me, and I give her a quick smile back before looking away. "Can I help you?"

My mouth goes dry and I nod. "I'm looking for … paracetamol."

One of her eyebrows does this weird quirk, and I can see in her face my hesitation has probably given me away. "I wouldn't buy that here. It's cheaper at the supermarket. Are you okay? You look a bit green around the gills."

"I'm just getting over a bit of a stomach bug." What am I doing? I'm a grown woman. Thirty years old and I can't just buy a pregnancy test and leave.

"Ahh." She smiles widely. "Am I correct in thinking this is what you're looking for?" From behind the counter, she produces just what I'm seeking, and I freeze.

"Uhhh, I …."

"Adam saved my boy. I won't tell anyone."

I'm torn between crying and puking as my stomach roils.

She laughs. "I think I'd better ring this up for you right now before I'm cleaning up after you."

I swipe my card through the machine when it's time and take the package as the little screen comes up 'accepted.'

"Good luck, Lily. I hope you get the result you want."

"I really appreciate your help, Sasha."

She gives me a wistful smile. "I'll be forever in Adam's debt for what he did."

"I understand. Thanks."

When I walk away, it's with a lighter heart. I thought that what happened that day at the cove would have had a passing effect on Sasha. Clearly, it's something that's stuck with her.

It makes me happy, until the nausea hits me again.

Time to see what's going on.

————

"Yuck."

I step inside via the back door, and take a deep breath in relief that the entranceway and hall have wooden floors. There's water everywhere.

It doesn't take long to find the source.

One of the few things we haven't yet replaced had been my washing machine. I'd picked up a decent second-hand one a couple of years before and hadn't felt the need to spend money on a new one until we needed to.

Water flows from along the hallway. The laundry sits up it to the left.

I moan at the sight of the tube that leads from the washing machine to the water dripping. There's a leak near the tap end, and as the machine refilled the water must have come flooding out. I twist the taps to make sure nothing more will come through and turn everything off.

Following the water, I discover it's also entered the kitchen where it comes off the hall and I drop my bag on the bench, retrieving the mop from a cupboard and starting my clean up. The water's everywhere. I'll have to cut off the end of the tube and re-clamp it. It's not the first time it's happened, but in the old house the laundry was separate and there wasn't so much of a mess.

Bit by bit the water's emptied into a bucket, and before I know it, it's nearly eleven and I'm starving.

Owen brought some pies last time he visited, and I grab

one out of the freezer and throw it in the microwave. The warm scent of pastry and steak fills the air.

"Can you chuck one in there for me too, babe?" Adam stands in the doorway. He's in his work clothes, and I grimace as he sits at the dining table all greased up.

"Are your hands clean?"

"I washed them before I came in." He pokes his tongue out. "I just felt crazy hungry. How's your morning going?"

Sighing, I pluck another pie from the freezer and place it on a plate. "Had to clean up after a washing machine leak. You're lucky I didn't float away."

He frowns. "That bad? Maybe we need to replace it after all."

I shake my head. "It wasn't the machine. Just where it connects to the tap. I'll sort it out."

The microwave beeps and I pull out one pie, sliding the other one in. Opening the cutlery drawer, I place a knife and fork on the plate and drop it on the table in front of Adam.

"You're amazing. Have I said that to you today?" He beckons me with his index finger, and I get a tender kiss in return for the pie.

"Not yet." He smells of oil, and the scent is enough to turn my stomach again.

"If I wasn't so busy, I'd stay for a little lunchtime fun." Adam waggles his eyebrows.

I empty the microwave of the second pie, and grabbing a knife and fork I sit at the table with him. "While I love that idea, I've got to get this sorted and put the washing back through the cycle."

He reaches across the table, taking one of my hands in

his. "I know it's still tough and we have to watch our money, but I hope I'm giving you a better life."

Tears prick my eyes. "I wouldn't give this up for anything."

"I'm glad." A smile crosses his face, and with a final squeeze he lets go. "Let's have something to eat before my stomach eats itself."

"Good idea."

The test can wait a while longer.

———

AMONG MY DREAMS are the ones about Max's birth.

The fear that hit me when I realised there was no going back, the waves of agony as each contraction hit. I cried for Adam, I cried for myself, and I cried for my baby.

When they found the cord around his neck.

In that moment, I thought I'd lost everything I'd fought so hard to save. I'd only known about him a few short weeks, but already Max was the most important person in my life. Nothing and no one else mattered but him.

His birth caused me the most pain I'd ever had, and yet I'd happily go through it all again to end up with the child I now have.

With his Apgar score at birth being five, this tiny grey baby was briefly placed on my chest, and I cried all over again after he was whisked off to NICU. At least in the moments in between being born and going to intensive care, his score had changed to a much more respectable seven. Even then I knew Max wouldn't be like other kids, but he was alive and he was mine.

With each successive day I swore that he would have my full attention, that I'd do whatever I could to give him the most normal childhood he could have, one light years from the childhood I'd had. Though what was normal?

As I sit in the bathroom today, staring at a positive pregnancy test, my stomach clenches at the thought of going through all that again.

Tears stream down my face, and I scrub my cheeks with my palms before burying my face in my hands.

Maybe if it wasn't for what I went through with Max, I'd be over the moon. Adam and I have been back together for mere months, but he's made his feelings clear. He wants to pick up where we left off and start a family together, or rather, extend our family. Looks like he's getting his wish.

The garage is still in its infancy, but Adam's busier than he dreamed. For the moment, James helps him, but when he leaves for university, Adam will have to find someone else to assist. Looks like Copper Creek missed having a local mechanic.

I check my watch. It's nearly time to pick up Max from school, so I pat my cheeks clean with a washcloth and look at myself in the mirror. My face has filled out a little, and my eyes, though rimmed with red, look more alive than I've seen them in a while. Blonde hair sits piled on top of my head in a messy bun. Maybe it's time for a change.

There's a fancy hair salon not far from Callahans, and in my new car I'm not worried about the journey. Adam upgraded me to a little Suzuki Swift. It's basic but it's only had one owner, and I don't need to worry about it breaking down. Max loves the crap out of it. Maybe I'll go tomorrow.

Giving my face one last wipe, I head out to the backyard

toward the car. It purrs as it starts, and I set off slowly down the driveway. Adam stands out the front of the garage, waving me down, and I pull up to a stop.

He bends and gives me a kiss when I open the window. "You off to get Max?"

"I sure am."

His eyebrows twitch. "Are you okay?"

He knows. He sees the pinkness of my eyes, understands there's something wrong.

"I'm fine. Just a bit tired."

"Lie down when you come home. I'll sort out dinner." He reaches in the window and palms my cheek. "Just chuck *Lego Batman* on for Max. He'll be fine until I pack up."

Max is close to finishing that game; there's just one bit he's struggling to complete. He'll spend hours playing it if we let him.

"See you soon," I say. Adam waves in response.

School is a lot closer than it was from the old house, and I could have walked if I'd felt up to it. But I love my new car, and any chance to drive it brings a smile to my face.

Sasha waves as I pull up in front of the school. Max and Karl have settled into an easy friendship. I never thought that boy would ever sit at my dining table eating ice cream with Max, and yet it's happened more than once.

When the bell rings, Max is first out the gate, and straight to my car. He loves it as much as I do.

"Did you have a good day?" I ask as I pull onto the road.

"I went up a reading level and I got one hundred per cent in my maths test."

"Again?"

He rolls his eyes. "Every single time, Mum."

I chuckle. "You're right, Max. Every single time."

"I'm always right."

———

I LEAVE Adam and Max playing some car racing game to go to bed a little before seven thirty p.m. My eyes refuse to stay open, and all I want is to curl up and go to sleep.

They're so engrossed they barely notice me go, which is good, because Adam knows me well enough to know this isn't my usual behaviour.

Yet, when I get to bed, all I do is toss and turn. These past months, I've shared a bed with Adam. Being alone isn't what I'm used to.

Just after nine the bedroom door opens, and I smile at the sight of Adam.

When we moved in here, he made improvements on his night-light set up. Wall lamps give off a soft golden glow, which keeps the room dark enough to sleep, and yet it's enough for me to not freak out in the night.

Adam strips off his shirt. The hard work he does every day has kept him in shape, and my heart beats faster at the sight of his solid, sculpted chest. Maybe it's my raging hormones. Maybe it's because he's perfect.

And he's all mine.

I reach out to rub Adam's back as he climbs into bed.

"That boy is amazing. He's so eager to learn," he says.

"He loves learning from you. You're everything he ever needed."

Adam grins, turning his head to kiss my temple. "Don't

sell yourself short. The odds were stacked against you, but you did such an incredible job with him.

I suck my bottom lip through my teeth and lean against his arm. "Let's hope next time it's less of a challenge."

He pushes me down onto my back against the bed, and I squeal with laughter. I melt as his lips linger on mine, as always.

"Next time?" he asks, his breath hot on my neck. "We haven't talked seriously about this yet. Do you want there to be a next time?"

As he raises his head, I gaze into those dark eyes of his. "It's not a matter of want. It's a bit late for that."

Adam's eyebrows rise. "Late?"

"We'll get a chance to see how it goes in maybe eight months?" I can't help the grin spreading across my face. This time he'll be by my side from start to finish. No misunderstandings, nothing to come between us.

His eyes are so full of love and excitement. We have our family, the business, and now this.

It's scary, but I've never been happier.

Nothing and no one will ever keep us apart.

We're all home.

———

WANT MORE? Drew's story starts in Doctor's Orders, and Adam's story continues. Chapter One of Doctor's Orders can be found at the end of this book.

DOCTOR'S ORDERS TEASER

Chapter One
Drew

Today has disaster written all over it. I should have seen it coming.

"Drew, hurry up in the shower."

"Nearly done." I don't even know why she's yelling. It's not like she'll be out of bed anytime soon. I shut off the mixer and dry off before wrapping a towel around my waist, heading back to the bedroom.

She glares at me as I step out of the bathroom and into the bedroom. Still sitting in bed, her arms are crossed, and I continue to get the evil look as I cross the room. "Do you have to use all the hot water?"

"Yep." I haven't, but I enjoy teasing her. It's too easy.

"Maybe I'll call Ray today. We pay enough in rent and surely he can install a larger hot water cylinder."

We.

Rolling my eyes, I open the wardrobe, pulling out a clean shirt and slipping my arms into it before retrieving a tie. Chances are by the end of the day, it'll be a mess, but it's the look that matters. I have outpatient appointments this morning, and I like to come across as professional.

Things aren't good with Lucy. After going out a few times, she moved herself in. I didn't mind. I hadn't lived with a girlfriend before, and we were getting on great.

It was when she quit her job without talking to me that I had a problem.

I always thought I'd have a family one day to support. That my wife could choose whether to work or not. But when your girlfriend quits her job a month into living with you, and you suddenly realise you don't actually know her that well? Yeah, not so great.

Especially when she's so good at spending my money.

I get out the door with her still ranting from the bed about the hot water, even though I guarantee the minute I'm gone she'll go back to sleep for another couple of hours. A real lady of leisure.

Reaching for the door handle of the car, my iPhone slips from my grip and lands with a crack on the concrete driveway.

I sigh, bending to pick it up. The screen's splintered, but not shattered, held in place by a protective cover. I can read the screen at least.

Kind of.

If this is the start of the day, I'm not looking forward to the rest.

The drive to work isn't long, but it's slow in the traffic,

and it's hard not to be annoyed with myself for how my day's started.

There have been too many of those lately.

As I stride into work twenty-five minutes later, I smile at everyone I pass in the corridors. I love my job. Every day brings me into contact with parents and children, and I can't help but smile.

I'm just about to grab some lunch when I get a page to go to one of the delivery suites.

"Doctor Campbell." I'm met at the door by Caitlyn, one of the hospital midwives. Her eyebrows knit in concern.

"What's going on?"

"Clare Peters. The baby's starting to show signs of distress. It's been a long labour, and I'd like your opinion."

"Sure. I met Clare a couple of weeks ago. She has high blood pressure, right? Let's get her through this."

She gives me a thin smile. Of all the doctors here, I think I have a better relationship with other staff than most. Midwives often call me in preference to the others.

I beam at the patient as I walk into the suite. She's clearly exhausted, sweat dripping from her brow, and I note she has no support person with her. That always bugs me. Everyone needs someone.

"Hi Clare, I'm here to check on you and your baby. How's it going?"

She glares at me. "How do you think it's going?"

"I know you just want this over with, so I'm here to help." I flash her a reassuring smile.

Even in her angry state, Clare gives me a faint smile. "Please."

I check her chart. She's not long been given a dose of

pethidine.

"Right. I think I need to take a look, if that's okay with you."

She nods. With a loud retching noise, she projectile vomits. Over the floor, and all over me.

I grimace as I reach for a towel to wipe down. It's not her fault. Pethidine's given with an anti-nausea med. One that's clearly failed to work.

"I'm so sorry." She sniffs, gripping the edge of the bed as another contraction hits her.

"It's no problem. Let's get that baby out and you can have a rest." I grab another towel and wipe down the side of the bed.

As I turn, the midwife shoves the latest readings of the baby's heartbeat in front of me. It's enough to concern me, and I finish cleaning myself as best I can with the towel. I smile as a set of clean scrubs are brought in.

Sliding off my shirt and the T-shirt underneath that's got vomit on it, I decide I can live with the pants. I need to get that baby out, and smelly pants are the least of my problems right now.

I look up, and Caitlyn's eyes are fixed on my chest. I'm pretty proud of my physique—lord knows I've paid enough to maintain it. Smirking, I pull the clean shirt over my head and raise my eyebrows, knowing her gaze will shift. As she meets my eyes, her mouth drops open, and bemused, I turn back to my patient.

"Okay, Clare. Next contraction I need you to push hard."

"Yes, Doctor," she huffs.

I meet Caitlyn's gaze again, and she nods. If this baby isn't born soon, Clare will be in the theatre having a caesarean.

They're not my favourite way to deliver a baby, but in cases like this it sometimes becomes impossible to avoid.

The last thing I want is to freak Clare out. So, right now, my focus is on trying to get this baby out before I make that final decision.

Clare tenses, and the pain is on her face before she groans.

"Here we go," I say softly.

She nods.

"Push. Let's see that baby." *Come on Clare, you can do it. We're in this together.*

She's so close, and from the pained look on her face, she knows what's coming out of my mouth next.

"The baby's crowning. You got this, Clare. Just a few more." I position my hands and nod. She cries out, and I see a little more of the baby's head. "That's it. Keep going."

"I can't," she whimpers.

"Make this next one a big one."

Clare grits her teeth, and closes her eyes. And then it's done, the baby slides out and Clare cries again, but her tone is relief.

The baby's in my hands, and I grin as I take a quick look. Good colour—good movement. He might have been reluctant to come out, but this little boy looks perfect.

"Your son is beautiful." I say.

She lets out a sob. "We didn't know what we were having. He kept closing his legs."

"I'll finish his APGAR check and then you can have a cuddle."

Her chest rises and falls quickly as she succumbs to the emotion. It's common enough, but it hits me square in the heart every time. One day I'll go through this with someone special, hold my own child in my arms. I can't wait for that day, but something tells me it won't be with Lucy.

The baby looks at me with big, dark eyes, and I grin before laying him on his mother's waiting chest. Caitlyn covers him with warm towels, and I pause for a moment to watch the beauty that is mother and baby bonding.

"Typical. You turn up and the baby comes out. Maybe I should just page you at the start."

I grin. It's not the first time it's happened.

"Her blood pressure's down a little," Caitlyn says, handing me the chart.

I nod. "That needs to be monitored, and if it doesn't come back down further by tomorrow morning, we'll look at our options."

"Thanks, Drew," she says quietly.

"You're welcome."

The door flies open, and a dark-haired, stressed-looking man comes running in, his face red and sweaty as if he's just run a marathon. Clare lights up the room with her smile.

"Did I miss it?" He puffs.

"Only just." She laughs, all the stress she suffered minutes ago completely gone with the arrival of her baby boy. Shifting her gaze to me, she still has that hazy, just-having-given-birth blissful look in her eyes. "We thought we had time for Dennis to make one last business trip before the baby arrived. This little one was just too impatient."

"I'm sorry. I'm so sorry." He covers her in kisses, and it makes me smile. His eyelids droop as he looks at me, he's tired too. "I had to fly back from Sydney, and it took forever."

"You're here now, and that's all that matters," Clare said.

"I'm so pleased for the two of you. Congratulations." My phone buzzes, and before I leave, I pluck my phone out of my pocket. I can't help the grin spreading across my face. "My sister-in-law is in labour."

Caitlyn's eyes widen. "Here?"

"No, back home. She's got a midwife, and I'm sure she's good, but Adam wants me to be there. Although, by the time I drive there, there's a good chance she'll have had the baby."

I shift my gaze to the patient. "I've got to go, but congratulations again, Clare, Dennis."

Clare beams at me. "Thank you, Doctor."

"You did all the hard work. He's a beautiful baby."

Caitlyn nudges my arm. "Get going. I'll finish up in here."

"Thanks."

I head out the door and toward the locker room to get in the shower. I need to get clean again before finishing up and getting in the car to see Adam and Lily.

It's not often I shower here. The water pressure is awful, but the heat is relaxing. I lather up the hospital anti-bacterial body wash, and rub it over my chest. My mind wanders to Lucy again. I need to do something about us. We haven't had sex in weeks, and I've become accustomed to spending more time with my right hand than touching her, despite us sleeping in the same bed.

I close my eyes. When we met, she was everything. She had a blossoming career as a buyer for an upmarket women's clothing store. She was so much fun, and whenever I wasn't at work, we fucked like bunnies.

But once we moved in together, she discovered life with a doctor wasn't that much fun for her. I'd given her all my free time, but it was all I had to give.

My eyes spring open as the water runs cold. After five minutes, the staff showers stop giving you hot water. I frown, but I'm rinsed off, and it'll do until I get home.

Towelling off, I pull on my spare shirt from my locker. Despite the water, I still have the scent of vomit in my nostrils. After all that, it might just be easier to shower again at home.

Knowing she was due to give birth any day now, I've already asked a couple of friends to be on standby, ready to cover my shifts, and I text them to call in the favour. In a year, I'll be going into private practice, and my boss doesn't want to lose me so he's being as accommodating as he can. I dial his number.

"Hey, John. My sister-in-law's in labour, so I'm heading off."

"Let me know how it goes." During the years I've been working with him, I've established a friendship with John that continues beyond my work at the hospital. It'll help when I leave and have patients who deliver here.

"Will do. Thanks."

I head out to my car, and look at my phone again. A replacement will have to wait. Lily's more important.

It's a short drive to my apartment. I'll shower again, throw some things in a bag and get out of here. I already know Lucy will have zero interest in going with me. She's never come home to meet my family as she loves the city. The thought of being somewhere remote for even a couple of days doesn't do anything for her.

I open the door.

They don't hear me, so busy focusing on themselves, and I have to admit, the thing that bothers me the most is Ray

Steele's bare white arse on my leather sofa. The leather sofa I've sat on so many times watching sport, beer in hand, my feet on the coffee table, tainted by him sitting naked on it.

Lucy's blonde head bobs up and down so fast, she could take off at any moment. Ray's feeling it, his hips thrusting toward her.

I'm still pissed his naked flesh is all over my damn couch.

I push the door, and it closes with a resounding slam. Lucy, her eyes as wide as saucers, looks up and sees me. The fear in her face has to be caused by the gravy train derailing. I'm the engineer, calmly waiting for the crash, and it's too late to stop as Ray cries out again.

All I can do is laugh as cum spurts from his erect cock, landing in Lucy's hair, covering the side of her head as she squeals in horror. I did love her once, or I thought I did, but finding her like this is the final straw.

She hits rock bottom as he blows his load all over her.

Gaping at him, she turns, rising her hand to her face as one last blob hits her in the eye. He reaches for the closest piece of fabric to him—God only knows where his clothes are—and it's her dress. That very expensive designer dress she raved about for ages before she finally convinced me to buy it.

"You know, people usually have to pay to watch the money shot." I laugh as she glares at me.

"It's not what it looks like." She stands, her hair sadly not resembling Cameron Diaz's in *There's Something About Mary*. It's disappointing. Does cum not work the same way as hair gel? Can't say I've ever tried it.

"What's it supposed to be? It's not every day I come home to find my girlfriend blowing the landlord." I turn to Ray, who's desperately trying to cover his cock and reaching blindly for his clothing. "Are we at least getting a rent reduction for this?"

"You're a pig," Lucy screams.

"You're covered in someone else's cum."

Her chest rises and falls rapidly. It might be distracting if I was the least bit interested in her, but after that performance, I no longer care what or who she does.

"Anyway, I'm going to go and take a shower because I just had a woman vomit all over me, and the showers at work suck."

"Don't use all the hot water."

It's the line she uses every time I say I'm having a shower, but under current circumstances, it's comical. "Are you serious? You're worried about the hot water?"

I laugh all the way to the bathroom.

When I'm finally feeling clean, I go through my drawers and throw some things in a bag. Enough to keep me going a couple of days before I come back and sort out this clusterfuck.

"You can't go." She tries the puppy eyes, the ones I fell for way too many times. My brother, Owen, says I'm gullible, but I think I'm just soft-hearted. It's not working this time.

"Yeah, I can, and so are you. Pack your shit and leave."

Her lower lip wobbles. "You can't be serious, Drew. How will I survive?"

"Maybe you can go and live with Ray."

I slam the door, and a feeling of peace comes over me. I'm angry that she's treated me this way, but not heartbroken.

It's over.

Stand alones

For the Love of Chloe

Coming 2022 Lost and Found

The Friends Duet

Loving Rowan

Three Days

The Forever Series

Something Real

The Right One

Unexpected

Chances Series

Another Chance

Taking Chances

Lifetime Series

In a Lifetime

In an Instant

In a Heartbeat

In the End

At the Start

ABOUT THE AUTHOR

Wendy Smith published as Ariadne Wayne for three years before deciding she didn't want to be someone else all the time. She's an Apple Books and Nook bestselling author, whose book In the End, written as Ariadne Wayne, was named one of Apple's best books of 2017. All her stories come with a quirky sense of humour , and she cries over everything.

Find me online
www.wendysmith.co.nz
wendy@wendysmith.co.nz

Printed in Great Britain
by Amazon

19858672R00205